"[Pete Haut ...]

"Wickedly inventive."   —*Los Angeles Times*

"Among the writers whose name alone promises a great read."
                                        —*The Denver Post*

Also by Pete Hautman

Also by Pete Hautman

Doohickey
Rag Man
Hole in the Sky
Mrs. Million
Stone Cold
Ring Game
The Mortal Nuts
Mr. Was
Short Money
Drawing Dead

THE PROP

A NOVEL

Pete Hautman

SIMON & SCHUSTER PAPERBACKS
New York London Toronto Sydney

SIMON & SCHUSTER PAPERBACKS
Rockefeller Center
1230 Avenue of the Americas
New York, NY 10020

First Simon & Schuster paperback edition 2006

SIMON & SCHUSTER PAPERBACKS and colophon are registered trademarks of
Simon & Schuster, Inc.

For information about special discounts for bulk purchases,
please contact Simon & Schuster Special Sales at
1-800-456-6798 or business@simonandschuster.com.

Designed by Davina Mock

Manufactured in the United States of America

1   3   5   7   9   10   8   6   4   2

Library of Congress Cataloging-in-Publication Data
Hautman, Pete, date.
The prop : a novel / Pete Hautman.— 1st Simon & Schuster pbk. ed.
p. cm.
1. Women poker players—Fiction. 2. Tucson (Ariz.)—Fiction. I. Title.
PS3558.A766P76 2006
813'.54—dc22   2005056324

ISBN-13: 978-0-7432-8465-3
ISBN-10:   0-7432-8465-8

For Elizabeth

THE PROP

J ACKPOT WENT OFF AGAIN LAST NIGHT, Peeky. Seventeen grand."

I hear this from Donny Keyes as I am climbing out of my little ragtop and he is unlocking his sun-bleached blue Cadillac.

"Three o'clock in the morning," Donny says. "Guess who dealt it."

Donny is a big guy with a long face. He makes his Cadillac look small and perky.

"Who?" I ask.

"Tran."

"Again?"

Donny shakes his head slowly, looking at me through basset hound eyes. "The man deals three jackpots in five days. What're the odds on that?"

It's about a hundred five degrees in the parking lot on this Tucson summer afternoon. My lipstick is melting, my blouse is stuck to my back, and my heels are sinking slowly into the sun-softened asphalt.

"I'll have to get back to you on that." I close the door of my Miata.

"It don't smell right, Peeky."

"Later, Donny." I head for the air-conditioning.

The canopied entrance to Casino Santa Cruz is flanked by two stout Santa Cruz security guards. I pass between them and turn right, away from the Card Club, toward the Slot Palace. I need to freshen up, dab the sweat from my forehead, and take a good look in a mirror before I walk into the poker room.

I thread the maze of slot machines and walk past the big acrylic "safe" in the center of the room. The clear-sided cube contains a million dollars in ten-, twenty-, and hundred-dollar bills—part of the Slot Palace May Madness promotion. Two sleepy-looking guards stand on either side of the safe. The promotion has been going on for nearly a month. The million in cash represents all the prizes, cash awards, and jackpot bonuses the regular slot players will earn during May. Right now, the piles of money look as tired as the guards.

The restroom in the Slot Palace is a mess, as usual. Paper towels all over the floor. Slot players are not known for their tidiness. I find a clean patch of mirror and give myself the once-over: low-cut silk blouse, bright green to match my eyes, auburn hair piled up top, red lips and nails, lots of Zuni gold and turquoise around my neck, wrists, and fingers. The hair is mine, if not the coloring. I still look like I got it, and I do. Maybe twenty pounds too much of it, but it's in the right places. Makeup and the right lighting, a few drinks in you, you might mistake me for twenty-nine. At least, if I claimed to be, you wouldn't laugh.

A short, chunky woman comes out of a stall: curly, graying head down, polyester dress, lumpy sneakers, vinyl purse big enough to hide a small dog. She might've graduated high school with me; now look at her. She gives me a sideways, haunted look and bustles through the door into the Slot Palace. Not much hand-washing in this restroom.

I wash mine, mostly to make myself feel special. It's two minutes to five. I give myself a smile and a wink.

Time to go to work.

It's relatively quiet when I enter the Card Club. The Casino Santa Cruz card room has thirty-six poker tables, but this afternoon only a third of them are seeing any action, typical for a weekday afternoon. Darrin McConnell is working the floor, stalking the aisles like a towering bipedal ferret, his head swinging back and forth on his long neck. I do not care much for Darrin. He is suspicious, overconfident, and a rule-monger. And there is something about his voice—a nasal snarl—that makes my ears itch.

Manuel Roca is manning the board at the front of the room. He's a good kid, always has a smile for me. He grins and gives me a salute with his felt-tip marker. I nod back as I check out the games listed on the big white board.

There are eleven tables going—one seven stud game, one Omaha high-low, and nine Texas holdem games. All but one are limit poker, from $3–6 up to $15–30. The game on table 19 is $5–10 pot-limit holdem.

"That pot-limit game still going?" I ask, though I can see that it is.

"Coming up on seventy-two hours," Manuel says.

"Amazing." Big-bet poker games—pot-limit and no-limit—usually don't last more than a few hours. In pot-limit poker, the size of a bet is limited only by the size of the pot. With bets that quickly escalate to the thousands of dollars, players usually bust out quickly. "How's Buddy doing?"

"He's hanging in there."

All the smaller games on the board have lists of players waiting for a seat. Manuel's job is to spread as many games as possible while keeping all the games full. Most poker players like a full table—they do not like to play shorthanded.

"Doesn't look like you need me anywhere," I say.

"I'll be opening a new holdem table pretty quick, Peeky. I might need you in a few minutes."

"I hear Tran dealt another jackpot last night."

"The stud jackpot, yeah." Manuel shakes his head. "To Beatrice and Deng. Unbelievable."

"I'll say." Maybe we are talking about two different things, but I don't think so. Beatrice won the big half of Tran's first jackpot, and Deng was in on the second one.

Manuel sees one of the dealers raise a hand. He checks the board, lifts his microphone, and calls out the next player on the list: "T.J., fifteen-thirty holdem." He scans the room, spots Tom Johnson waving at him from the lounge. "Table seven, T.J." He lowers the mike. "You punched in, Peeky?"

"It's after five, isn't it?"

Manuel grins, showing off his perfect white teeth. He knows I'm there to work, but he also knows I don't punch in. I show up for work on time and I put in my forty hours, but I don't wear blue jeans, I don't pump my own gas, and I don't punch clocks. Vergie Drucker gives me grief about it every Friday. I just ignore her. She still okays my paycheck every two weeks.

I wander over to check out the pot-limit game. Buddy Balcomb is sitting two seats to the right of the dealer, his favorite perch. He's wearing the same shirt he had on last night. The man doesn't know how to take care of himself. He's only got about six hundred dollars on the table. Last night he was sitting on six thousand. Yassir the Greek is hunched over his modest stack of chips looking angry. That's normal for Yassir, who is actually Syrian. Mutter Blodgett, looking ten years older than he is, which is *old*, seems to be on a heater—he's got six towers of green $25 chips, about $1,500 per stack. Al Rafowitz, hiding his bug-eyes behind a pair of oversize Ray-Bans, is also doing well. Next to Al sits a tall kid we call Lemon because of his yellow hair and the fact that he is as tall as Mount Lemmon. He looks sixteen but his I.D. says he's twenty-two. I feel sorry for the kid. Wherever he gets his money it is not at the card table. I hear he has a rich daddy.

The other two players I don't know, but I've seen them around.

Buddy sees me and says, "Open seat, Peek."

I smile and shake my head regretfully. It looks like a good game, but I don't usually play that high. In pot-limit poker you can drop ten grand a night, easy.

The other reason I don't sit down is because I don't like to play against Buddy. Not because he's good, which he is, but because I've got feelings for him. We've been seeing each other a year and three months now, longer than some people stay married. I still go soft in the head when he smiles at me. That doesn't make for good poker. It's one thing to enjoy the people you play cards with. It's something altogether different to play poker against someone you love.

I HEAD OVER TO THE PLAYERS' LOUNGE. I have one of those British mysteries in my purse. I sit down and start reading, and I'm twenty pages in before I realize that I'm not absorbing a word.

I'm thinking about Tran Lui dealing those jackpots.

At Casino Santa Cruz, if you're dealt an aces-over-jacks full house or better, and your hand is beat by someone holding four of a kind or better, you win half of the Bad Beat Jackpot. A quarter of the jackpot goes to the player who beat you, and the other quarter—what they call the "players' share"—gets whacked up for the rest of the table.

The jackpots bring in a lot of players, mostly small-stakes players attracted by the chance to win ten or twenty grand on a single poker hand. The odds are slim—a jackpot hand only shows up about once in every twenty or thirty thousand deals—but it's better odds than the lottery.

The money, of course, all comes out of the players' pockets. The dealers pull an extra one-dollar chip out of every pot to fund the jackpot. All those white chips add up quickly, building the jackpots at the rate of a couple thousand bucks a day. The amount is posted on the wall and updated once a shift. Each game—holdem, seven stud, Omaha—builds its own jackpot. Right now the Omaha jackpot is at $4,600. Seven stud, which just got hit, has dropped down to $2,500. The holdem jackpot has climbed to $29,000. I've seen it go as high as sixty. The woman who hit that one, a tourist from Detroit, got her four jacks beat by a straight flush to the ace. She thought it was the end of the world—she loses the hand and everybody at the table jumps up and starts screaming—until it was explained to her that her losing hand had earned her thirty grand. I thought she was going to have a heart attack and die, but if she did she waited till she got home because I never saw her again.

Anyway, a jackpot usually gets hit once or twice a month, and I wouldn't have thought anything about this latest one except that it was Tran dealing, again, with Beatrice and Deng taking down the big money. The odds against one dealer spreading three jackpots in five days are staggering.

I believe in luck, but the more I think about Tran dealing Beatrice that third jackpot, the more I think that luck had nothing to do with it. Like Donny says, "It don't smell right."

I finally get focused on my book, starting over on page one, when Manuel calls down the list of players waiting for a $3–6 holdem seat. Since there are only seven players on the list, he calls my name, too. Most holdem players like a full table of nine or ten. It's what they're used to.

I buy a rack of chips from the cashier cage and take the eight seat—eight seats to the left of the dealer.

Martha Green, the dealer, spreads a new deck across the green baize, checking for blemishes, crimps, dupes, and missing cards. Martha has a beautiful touch—the cards fan out regular as sprocket teeth.

"I hear Tran dealt another jackpot last night," I say.

"The man is an absolute phenomenon."

"How's Reginald?" I ask after her recently acquired ten-week-old German shepherd.

Martha smiles, picturing her puppy. "Full of P and V and pooping everywhere," she says happily in her Irish accent. "Last night he *devoured* one of my bras."

"The whole thing?"

"It was wireless. Perfectly digestible."

"What a clever pooch."

"He's brilliant. And how is Jaymie doing? Has she left the Black Prince yet?"

"She leaves him repeatedly." Jaymie is my daughter, married six months to Eduardo Montana, a black-haired, black-eyed macho man out of Nogales. "But only for a few days at a time. I tell her she could come live with me but she says she loves him. It doesn't make sense."

"It never does," Martha agrees. "I had a husband who got a bit rough from time to time."

"And you left him, right?"

"Eventually. But only after he accidentally caught his hands in the door of his Jaguar."

"Both hands?"

"Yes. My brothers helped him to accomplish that. It gave me the opportunity to visit sunny Tucson. I rather like it here."

"I see." This is rather shocking coming from Martha, the soul of civility. I guess everybody has a story.

"How long were you married?" she asks.

"Seven years. He died suddenly."

"I'm sorry."

"He was a policeman," I say. I don't know why I mention that. I just feel Robert would want me to say what he did.

"Was he killed in the line of duty?"

"His appendix burst."

"Oh, dear."

"He was my firearms instructor. That's how I met him."

"You married your teacher." This makes her smile. "Were you partners, then? Riding about in your police car, solving all sorts of crimes together?"

"Not really. I was a cop all of nine months, mostly office work. Then I got pregnant and quit. It was not a lengthy career."

"At least it netted you a husband."

"That it did."

Three other players have taken their seats: Suzy Lee, Cisco, and Victor. Cisco is watching me through glasses thick as a pair of votive candles. I nod to him, and he smiles. We are soon joined by Lester, Gene the Machine, and two players whose faces are familiar but whose names I don't recall.

I have in my head a three-dimensional chart of the various types of poker players I have met. In one sector there are the stones, the rocks, the leatherasses—players who sit and wait for the good hands with such stolid patience you would swear they are petrified. In the far sector I put the maniacs, the machines, the steamers. Scattered between and on the fringes are the calling stations, ducks, rabbits, fish, sharks, gamblers, sharps, jackasses, solids, sprouts, and maybe ten, twenty other types that don't have names. When a newbie comes in I watch him until I see where he lands. Mostly I can put a player on a style of play after a few hands, but sometimes it's harder. Some players sit down in a new game and play like maniacs for a few rounds, then they settle down and it turns out they are stones at heart. Or it's the other way around— they play their cards so tight you can hear them creak, and then something clicks and they turn into betting machines. But I've got a good eye and I don't get fooled that often.

Of course, I'm a type, too. I am the chameleon type. Sometimes, when the game is right, I pump money into the pot like a certified maniac. Other times I am granite, just sitting on my money waiting for the nuts and folding just about everything else. In my business you have to adapt.

I have to be good. I'm a prop.

THIS PARTICULAR $3–6 HOLDEM GAME is what I call a low-brainer. Because the players are all regulars and all fairly experienced, I'm not likely to win much unless I catch some exceptional cards. Even if I do get hit by the deck, the limits are too low to make any serious cash. My strategy, therefore, is to tighten up my play and try to avoid losing. This is what props do, mostly. I get my salary—$110 per eight-hour shift—and the health insurance package. In exchange, I put in my time, playing with my own bankroll, trying to win more than I lose.

A prop's job is to keep shorthanded games going—we "prop them up." Most props don't last long. They develop leaks in their game—playing too tight, or too loose, or too passive, or too any number of other things. Even the ones who keep it together at the poker table often go off on the ponies, or at the craps table, or on drugs. Eventually they lose their paycheck too many times and have to go find a real job.

Casino Santa Cruz employs three props: Me, Donny Keyes, and Bert Lyman. I'm pretty sure I'm the only one who turns a profit most weeks. Like I say, I'm good at what I do.

I fold the first few hands, hardly looking at my cards. I am thinking about those jackpots and not concentrating on the game, a good way to lose a lot of money fast. I force myself to focus.

Texas holdem is a simple game on the surface. You get two

cards, you bet. The dealer then turns three cards faceup—what's called the *flop*—and you bet again. A fourth card, the *turn,* is turned faceup. You bet again. The fifth and final card, the *river,* is turned up and there is a final round of betting. Whoever can show the best five-card poker hand out of the cards on the board and the cards in his hand wins. Simple, right?

Not hardly. Even at the low limits I usually play, holdem can be as complicated and confusing as a road map of Mexico City. It takes the right combination of smarts, discipline, knowledge, and heart to beat the game at every level. Few players have what it takes.

Cisco, sitting to my right, is one of the few. I watch him win a sixty-two-dollar pot with three tens. As he stacks his chips he half-turns his head and peers at me through his thick glasses. He says, "Ayyy . . . how you doing, Pee Key?"

"I'm doing just fine," I tell him.

Cisco smiles and nods. When he smiles I think of the Mona Lisa. Cisco is a Santa Cruz Indian, a member of the small tribe that owns the casino. He is somewhere between sixty and one hundred twenty years old, barrel-shaped, gray hair going to white, dark face peppered with moles. How he can see the cards through those glasses I do not know, but Cisco doesn't miss a bet. It's guys like him who make my job tough.

"You look like you thinking," he says.

I give him my biggest, ditziest grin and say, "Me? Think?"

"Like maybe you gonna arrest somebody."

"I'm not a cop anymore, Cisco. It's been twenty-some years."

"Maybe you make a citizen arrest. Somebody try to steal a pot, you cuff 'em."

"We're on the rez, Cisco. I'm not a citizen."

He laughs. "You come see my cactus garden sometime, Pee Key."

"I'll do that, Cisco." Cisco has been inviting me to look at his cactus garden ever since I remarked one day that I'd moved to Tucson because I fell in love with a saguaro. It's a long story and a bad joke. Anyway, he's been using it as a handle to flirt with me ever since. He's cute and ancient and harmless, and I enjoy it.

"Hey, Pee Key," he says, knocking over his stacks of chips, "how much money I got here?"

I look at the disorganized pile of chips and say, "One twenty." I always know exactly how much money is on the table. I had counted Cisco's chips before he knocked them over.

Cisco giggles. He loves to test me. "What kind of shoes I got on?"

"Nikes." I had seen him toddle up to the table on a pair of black Nikes and a twisted, bone-handled cane.

"What kind of car is parked closest to the door?"

"Which side?"

"Left."

"White Oldsmobile with a handicap sticker."

Victor, listening in, says, "Course it's got a sticker. It's a handicap slot."

Cisco says, "How about a license number?"

I close my eyes. "880 AQE." I can't help it—I'm a show-off. Also, I'm counting on the fact that nobody's going to leave the game to go check that license number.

"You amazing, Pee Key. Sherlock Holmes."

I smile and flutter my eyelids. Yeah, I'm amazing all right, but Cisco and I both know that I can't read his play any more than I can read Sanskrit. He's one of those rare people who really do have a poker face. I never have a clue what he's thinking.

Victor, always looking for some kind of edge, says, "Ten bucks says you can't tell me how many lashes I got on my left upper eyelid, Peeky."

"Forty-seven," I say.

"Wrong. Pay up."

"Okay, but I'll have to pull 'em out to count 'em."

"For ten bucks? In your dreams."

"My dreams are *way* more interesting than that, Vic."

A few hands later Manuel pulls me off the table to make room for a new player. He sends me to fill a seat at a shorthanded $1–4 stud game. I lose twenty dollars in ten minutes, and I'm relieved when Manuel moves me to a red-chip game, $15–30 holdem.

This is where I can make some money. Four of the players are fresh blood, so I swing into my act as an ignorant, forty-something bimbo who will bet on anything.

"Come to mama," I say, pushing out my chest. The guy across from me is all eyes and comb-over. He's not a bad-looking guy— early forties, regular features, not fat—but the comb-over, the tic beneath his left eye, and the pulsing jaw pretty much ruin the package. I take an immediate dislike to him. I don't know why. Women's intuition. Or maybe it's his clumsy attempt at X-ray vision.

Denise, the dealer, smiles at me. "How's it going, Peeky?"

"I can't catch a break today," I say. "Deal me a winner." I am in the big blind this hand, meaning I have to make a forced bet of $15 before I see my cards. I toss out three red chips and look at my cards. A deuce and a five. Doesn't get much worse. I check out the competition. Nobody looks very happy. The next five players fold; the comb-over guy raises, and the next two players fold. It's just him and me now. I have the option to call or reraise. With these cards I should probably fold, but I have a feeling about this guy. I decide to defend my blind.

"Reraise," I say, slapping down six red chips.

"Again," says comb-over, raising my reraise.

Uh-oh. Maybe he's got a monster. I show my cards to Joe Garcia, who is sitting next to me. "What do you think?"

"One player to a hand," Denise says.

"Okay, I just call," I say.

Denise burns the top card, sliding it facedown under a chip, and flops the eight of clubs, nine of hearts, ten of spades. The comb-over guy's face shows nothing, but his right shoulder slumps and the fingers of his right hand close into a loose fist. A classic tell.

Most amateur players think of tells as magical signs—obscure little mannerisms that enable a skillful player to read another player's mind. Things like how they stack their chips, whether they touch their face, whether their eyes dart to their chips after seeing the flop, or how they handle their cards. All that stuff is real, and occasionally reliable. But in most games, all you have to do is watch the other player and use a little common sense.

The comb-over guy's body language tells me he hates the flop. He's probably holding a couple of high cards. I put him on ace-king.

"Check," I say.

He bets fifteen, making an effort to look confident. Oh yeah. Pure Hollywood.

I slowly count out six red chips. "Raise," I say.

Nobody likes getting check-raised, especially when they've got crap. He glares at me, looking at my face now instead of my boobs. He thinks he's beat but he calls anyway. Most guys will call a check-raise, especially from a woman. They won't like it, but they'll call. I think it's a testosterone thing.

The turn card is a seven. I bet into him. He thinks about it, try-ing to put me on a hand. What could I have possibly check-raised him with on the flop? A big pocket pair? Trips? A straight? There are hundreds of hands that beat him, and he knows it. He reaches for his stack, searching my face for any excuse to call. He *wants* to call. He has an ace-king. Big slick. Two overcards. He *hates* to give it up.

If there is one secret of winning at poker, it is in learning to un-derstand and control the calling impulse—both your own and that of your opponents. I hold my ditzy smile in place and let him stew. I think maybe he has just enough card sense to fold here. Also, he would hate to get beat by me, and he knows he's got nada.

He makes a rude noise with his lips and throws his hand away, facedown.

"Nice hand," he says, trying to reassure himself that I did, in fact, have him beat.

"Does that mean I win?" I say.

Joe Garcia rolls his eyes. I toke Denise a red chip, then turn my cards faceup to give the comb-over guy a look at the sort of garbage

I play. He grunts as if he's been kicked in the groin and turns red around the neck.

A few rounds later I play an ace-jack of spades, flop a pair of aces, hit runner-runner spades to make a flush, and take the comb-over guy with his ace-king—again—for his last few chips.

"Honey, you better see your proctologist—I think you got a fuckin' horseshoe stuck up your ass," he says, his eye twitching.

I stack my chips, pretending I didn't hear that. People say some nasty things when they lose a big hand on the river. Tapped, he leaves in disgust. I don't blame him for being upset, but hey, everybody gets lucky now and then, even me. Minutes later I see him talking to Buddy at the pot-limit table. He points in my direction; Buddy looks over, sees me, and laughs.

A new player slaps five bills on the table and slides into an empty seat. "Dee me in. New deck."

"Hey, Tran," Denise says.

"The jackpot man," Joe says.

"I lucky guy." A chip runner appears and trades Tran a rack of red chips for his five hundred.

Denise shuffles the new deck. "You working tonight?" she asks Tran.

"I punch out. Now I take everybody money." He is still wearing his white shirt and bolo tie, but the tie is hanging loose and his sleeves are rolled up. Like most of the dealers at the Santa Cruz, Tran is a player, too. He is looking at me, his head tipped to the side. "How you doing, Pee-kee?"

"I'm Lady Luck tonight," I say, still stacking chips from the last pot. "What about you? You're the talk of the town."

"What is 'talk of town'?"

"The bee's knees, the real deal, jackpot johnny."

Tran grins. "I dee *big* jackpot."

"Two in a week, right?"

"Two time. That right." We lock eyes for an instant. He is asking me a question.

I choose not to answer.

A FEW HOURS LATER we have a rare Dooley sighting. He emerges from his office, red-faced, his abdomen swinging and sloshing with uncharacteristic vigor. Dooley Braun shows his face in the card room so rarely that most of the players don't even know what he looks like, even though there's a framed photo of him at the Card Club entrance: "Dooley Braun, Card Room Manager." The photo was taken back in the late 1970s. It shows a younger, slimmer Dooley sitting behind a half-million dollars in cash. That was the year Dooley won the main event at the World Series of Poker. He'd been a big name back then, but Dooley doesn't play on the tournament circuit these days. He was hired a few years back to manage the Casino Santa Cruz Card Club. I think the idea was that his reputation would lend the fledgling card room some legitimacy. He certainly wasn't brought on for his management skills.

Dooley Braun is more figurehead than hands-on manager. The real work is done by his assistant, Vergie Drucker, and security chief Blaise Hunt. Dooley mostly hides out in his office. No one other than Vergie knows what he does in there. Rumor has it he spends his hours looking at internet porn on his computer.

Dooley waddles quickly through the card room. Cisco, three-legging it on the same course, reaches out with his cane and raps Dooley on the hip. Dooley stops, the two men exchange a few words, smiling like old friends. Strange. I would not have thought those two would know each other. Dooley hitches up his sagging polyester trousers and they continue on together, disappearing down the short hallway leading to the Slot Palace.

Whatever it is between Dooley and Cisco, it has nothing to do with me. I've learned to just keep my head down and do my job. For instance, the likelihood that the jackpots are getting knocked off bothers me, but it's not my problem. Working for the Santa Cruz you learn to mind your own business or you go nuts. The casino is not run according to the laws of logic, the laws of the tribe, or the laws of physics. It's more like Las Vegas meets Dysfunctional Family meets the Great Spirit. Gambling has provided the Santa Cruz with much-needed money, but it has also brought political infighting, embezzlement, drug abuse, and all the other side effects of sudden wealth. Almost every adult member of the tribe now drives a new luxury SUV. Not all of them drive sober.

When I went to work at Casino Santa Cruz five years ago, I decided to read up on my new employers, so I got on my computer and started surfing. Amazing what you could find on the web, even back then. The average Joe now has more information available on his home computer than we did when I was working for the Phoenix P.D. twenty years ago. Back then, paper trails were actually made of paper. These days they're made of . . . I don't know what. Electrons.

After Robert died, leaving me with a young daughter and a modest pension, I did the single-mom-mourning-widow thing for about six months, nearly went out of my mind with boredom, then took a job working as a private investigator. Warren Castle, one of Robert's good friends from the Phoenix police, had retired a few years earlier and started his own P.I. firm, Castle Investigations.

Most of Castle's work came from ambulance-chasing lawyers. I must have interviewed ten thousand traffic accident victims and witnesses. It was interesting listening to all those versions of reality. I found that by asking the right questions, I could create my own version of the truth—or whatever version of the truth our client was seeking. Warren also had several criminal defense attorneys among his clients—in addition to protecting the interests of the bad drivers of the world, I helped get a few murderers, thieves, and rapists acquitted. I didn't feel so good about that, but it was interesting. Reasonable doubt is a remarkably useful legal concept. A reasonable person can doubt anything from sunrise to gravity.

I also ran a lot of background checks for prospective employers and cautious fiancées. Boring, but not as stressful as the live interviews. Most of it could be done on the computer. I didn't work for Warren anymore, but I still had my computer skills, such as they were.

I found several websites with information about the Santa Cruz Indians, as well as numerous news items. The facts surrounding the tribe's origins were foggy, to say the least.

Officially, the Santa Cruz did not exist until 1974, when a man named Hector Vega declared himself, his family, and twenty-six close personal friends to be the last remnants of a landless Native American tribe known as the Santa Cruz. Vega claimed that his people were the true descendants of the Hohokam, who were, in turn, directly descended from the ancient Toltecs of Mexico. Vega campaigned vigorously to have his tribe recognized by the state of Arizona and the federal government. He received little support from other Arizona tribes, and was publicly denounced by the Pascua Yaqui, who were waging their own campaign for federal recognition, and whose documentation was considerably more convincing. According to a letter to the editor in the September 2, 1974, *Arizona Daily Star,* the Santa Cruz were "nothing more than a gang of renegade Coyotero Apaches with delusions of grandeur." The letter, written by an attorney working for the Pascua Yaqui, sparked a rivalry between the two tribes that remains heated to this day.

Despite the fact that there were no historical documents to support his claims, Hector Vega was able to assemble a group of supporters, including a team of young, idealistic lawyers, and a friendly congressman named Alex Blackwell.

The Santa Cruz, according to Vega, had occupied lands west of the Tucson Mountains for sixty-four generations until being driven from their homeland in the 1600s by the Spanish. Since that time they had roamed the Southwest, fragmented and homeless, a people in exile. Vega's tale grew in complexity and pathos with each retelling, and in 1976, President Gerald Ford signed a document granting the Santa Cruz Nation status as a federally recognized tribe. He also, with the same strokes of his pen, put thirty-six hundred acres of BLM land east of the Roskruge Mountains, twenty minutes west of downtown Tucson, into trust for the newly recognized tribe.

A few months later the tribe leased eight hundred of their newly acquired acres to a development company owned, in part, by Congressman Alex Blackwell. Vega and his followers took up residence on the balance of their reservation, supporting themselves by selling off a few hundred acres every now and then to developers, many of whom were friends of Alex Blackwell. Hector Vega built a home in the Roskruge foothills at the western boundary of the reservation and disappeared from the public eye. The Santa Cruz became a living footnote to modern Arizona history, their numbers remained small, and except for the occasional land sale, no one paid them much attention. Until, that is, the passage of the Indian Gaming Act of 1993, when the Santa Cruz made headlines again by opening southern Arizona's first full-service casino.

Maybe it's a good thing. But I can't help noticing that the key management positions at the casino are still filled by Anglos. That's because the casino is not actually run by the tribe, but rather by a casino management company out of Wisconsin called Magic Hand Gaming. Magic Hand provides turnkey services—everything from financing, to negotiating gaming pacts, to supplying an experienced management team. In exchange, they get a piece of the action. I imagine it's a pretty big piece.

I ran a background check on Hector Vega, just for the hell of it. There were a lot of Hector Vegas, but the one I was looking for did not exist before 1973. If Vega really was a Coyotero Apache, that made sense—Apaches tread lightly.

The Hohokam, of course, had been ghosts for centuries.

The contract between the Santa Cruz and Magic Hand Gaming is about to expire. A few months ago Hector Vega's son-in-law Carlos Begay replaced Magic Hand CEO Bruce Johnson as casino president. A lot of the non-Indian dealers were grumbling that they were about to lose their jobs to tribal members, but it hasn't happened. I think the change in leadership was mostly symbolic. Only a couple dozen Santa Cruz work at the casino, and, with the exception of Carlos Begay, a tribal member by marriage only, none of them holds a management position. If the Santa Cruz are preparing to take over their own casino, they've got a long way to go. The tribal members all get a stipend from the casino profits. Last year it was close to $20,000 a quarter. They don't have to work. Most choose not to.

But like I say, it's not my problem.

NEAR THE END OF MY SHIFT, I'm still getting bounced from game to game. I go from $15–30 holdem to $2–4 stud to $6–12 Omaha high-low. Finally, Manuel sends me back to the red-chip game, which has lost a few players. Jenny Mai is dealing now. Tran is on a heater, half-hidden behind a mountain of red chips. He looks wired, talking rapid-fire Chinese—or something—on his cell phone. Beatrice, a hard-faced Asian woman about my age, has the two seat, and Lorenzo Palmero is hunched morosely over a small stack of chips in the one seat, next to the dealer. Sally and Suzy Fong, who claim to be distant cousins but look like twins, are sitting next to each other at the other end of the table. Ordinarily, I would not wish to play at a table where two of my opponents appear to be so closely related, but the Fong cousins—or sisters, or whatever they are—are such weak players that even if they were partnering-up I would get their money.

I sit down next to Sally and take the big blind. Tran glares at me as the cards are dealt, his eyes red, his knee going up and down like a triphammer. I don't understand why he is giving me such a baleful look. Maybe he's afraid I'll jinx his heater.

"I raise," he says, firing six red chips toward the pot. Sally and Suzy giggle and pitch their cards into the muck. Lorenzo groans and calls the raise. Beatrice folds.

Nobody plays a heater like Tran.

Jenny lays out the flop: an ace and two rags—a deuce and a six. Lorenzo shakes his head and checks sorrowfully. Predictably, Tran bets and Lorenzo folds, saying, "I can't catch a hand."

We all feel sorry for him. That's what Lorenzo wants.

As Tran rakes in the pot he turns to me and says, not all that friendly, "How come you here, Pee-kee? You working? We don't mind play shorthanded."

"I go where I'm told," I say.

Tran stares at me, red-eyed and intense. He shrugs and grins. "Hey, I just messing with you, Pee-kee. I on a big rush."

"I see that."

"Deuce-seven, I raise!"

Everybody laughs, even Lorenzo.

Jenny is shuffling for the next hand when an orange-haired clown walks into the card room holding a balloon bouquet. Manuel tries to stop him, but only halfheartedly. Card Club policy prohibits this sort of thing, but how do you say no to Bozo?

Tran tosses his car keys onto the table in front of Sally Fong.

"How about you go to my car. I leave my Walkman there."

Sally looks surprised, staring back at him.

"Come on, I buy you dinner later, okay?"

Sally says something in Chinese, Tran responds. She grabs the keys and walks quickly away from the table.

Jenny, the dealer, finishes her shuffle and squares up the deck, her eyes on the clown, who is threading his way through the card club, coming in our direction. The balloons read *Happy Birthday* and *Forty Is Sporty*. Somebody is about to get a clown telegram.

Darrin, at the back of the room, scowls and starts his ferret stalk. Darrin is more assertive than Manuel—he will have no problem kicking Bozo out of the casino. He's good at that sort of thing. But before Darrin can reach him the clown stops at our table, points a white-gloved finger straight at me, and starts singing "Happy Birthday." I just look back at him, grinning like an idiot even though it's not my birthday and I turned forty more than four years ago. I'm getting someone else's singing clown telegram. I just let it happen. You take what you can get.

The clown is on his second "Happy birthday to you," when the balloons get away from him and float toward the ceiling, toward the security cameras. The clown starts jumping up and down, his size-nineteen feet flopping comically, trying to get the balloons back. Darrin reaches him and grabs the clown's shoulder in mid-leap. The clown loses his balance and falls into Darrin.

That's when I notice the change in Jenny's face. Her eyes are dilated, her mouth is tight and hard, and she is breathing fast. Something has frightened her. The clown? I've heard of people who are scared of clowns, but I don't think that's it.

The clown is escorted out of the card room, people watching and laughing, a few of them calling out "Happy birthday" to me, but I am watching Jenny. Her shoulders are stiff as a mannequin's. Instead of pitching the cards with her usual fluidity, her hands move by jerks and starts. I lift the corners of my cards and see two black aces.

This deal stinks so bad I want to run for the restroom and wash my hands. I order my thumb and forefinger to flick my cards into the muck. My fingers refuse the order. I am simply not capable of folding pocket aces before the flop.

Jenny says, "It's on you, Peeky."

What the hell. If I'm going to play I'm going to play it right. "Raise," I say, pushing out a stack of six chips

Suzy and Lorenzo both fold. Beatrice looks at me with a little smile and calls. Tran mucks his hand and sits back, crossing his arms over his narrow chest, his jaw pulsing with heartbeat regularity. Jenny burns a card and lays out the flop: two queens and an ace.

I have the big full house, aces full of queens, a dream hand. I should stand up and walk away. Instead, I bet.

"Raise," says Beatrice.

There are only a few hands that might justify a raise here, but that doesn't really matter. I know she has pocket queens as surely as if I had X-ray vision. Jackpot hand.

"Call," I say.

The ace of diamonds comes on the turn, giving me four aces, the stone cold nuts. I push thirty dollars into the pot, Beatrice raises, I reraise, Beatrice thinks for a few seconds, making it look good, then calls.

I bet the river blind.

T HE LIGHT IS ON IN MY KITCHEN when I get home, so I know right away that Jaymie has had another fight with the Black Prince. I take a few extra lungfuls of the cool night air and let myself in. The newspaper is spread over my sofa, and an empty Fresca can is making a ring on the oak coffee table. I pick up the can and head for the kitchen. Sure enough, Jaymie is sitting at the table eating my Ben & Jerry's.

"That better not be the Cherry Garcia," I say, kicking off my pumps.

Jaymie pulls the spoon from her mouth, looks at her reflection in it, frowns. I don't blame her. She looks like hell.

"What difference does it make?" she says.

"The Chunky Monkey doesn't go with Vouvray."

Jaymie stabs the spoon into the carton, and skids it across the table. There are still a few spoonfuls left. I plunk my purse on the table and open the fridge. "You want a glass?"

Jaymie shakes her head. I uncork a cold bottle of Vouvray. This is my wind-down time, my transition between the job and the rest of my life. A glass of Vouvray and a bowl of Cherry Garcia. Don't knock it till you try it. But try it alone, not with your twenty-one-year-old daughter who is thinking of leaving her husband. I sit down and start on the ice cream. I get a cherry on the first bite, a good sign. Jaymie is picking at her thumbnail, brown polish, working her way up to something. She is wearing a sleeveless denim shirt, no makeup, four earrings in her left ear, long hair dyed the color of Mexican chocolate, and lipstick to match. Her eyes are huge and heavy with makeup. The look is pure Tejana, despite the fact that Jaymie hasn't got a Mexican bone in her body. I sip my Vouvray, soft as cashmere.

"How was work?" she asks, switching her attention from her thumbnail to a tiny scab on the back of her hand. She still hasn't looked me in the eye.

"The usual."

"You win?"

"I caught a few good hands."

"My mother the cardsharp." She laughs.

I sit back, suppressing a frown. I would be even more offended if I thought she knew what she was saying. I am not a cardsharp. I play a straight game.

She says, "My friends don't believe me when I tell them what you do."

She's trying to hurt me now and I don't understand why. "What's wrong with what I do?"

"You trick people out of their money for a living."

"I play by the rules. Fair is fair."

"If it was fair, you wouldn't always win."

"I don't." Enough of that, I decide. It's her pain, not mine. I say, "So how are things with the Black Prince?"

Jaymie gives a little jerk, like I'd goosed her.

"Don't call him that." For the first time she meets my eyes and I see a healthy flash of anger.

"What should I call him?"

"Eduardo. His name is Eduardo."

"I couldn't help noticing you're not at home in bed with him."

Her shoulders squirm.

"He hit you again?"

"My mother the detective."

"I'm just asking."

"No, he didn't hit me."

I know when a complete stranger is holding pocket aces or garbage, but I can't tell if my own flesh and blood is lying to me. I spoon the last of the Cherry Garcia into my mouth. Jaymie finds a spot on the table and tries to rub it out with the ball of her thumb. After about a minute of this I decide the hell with it, life is too short for me to waste any more of it torturing my offspring.

"How's your job going?" I ask, searching for a safe topic. Jaymie works at Food Conspiracy, the co-op up on Fourth Avenue. I think she nets about $350 a week, plus all the tofu and brown rice she can eat.

"Okay. Only they cut my hours."

"Might be a good time for you to go back to school," I say.

Jaymie gives me a look I know well. I decide to change the subject. "Some of the dealers are scamming the casino, hitting a few too many jackpots."

Jaymie looks up. "Really?"

"One of the dealers dropped a cooler into the game. We hit the jackpot next hand."

"What's a cooler?"

"A stacked deck."

"You saw her do it?"

"No. But I saw how she acted a few seconds later. And I saw how the hand went down. I think two, maybe three of the dealers are involved. And some of the players."

"Are you gonna turn them in?"

"Not me."

"Why not? It's partly your money they're stealing, isn't it?"

Jaymie is referring to the fact that the jackpots are built up with players' money, and that money is all supposed to be returned to the players in the form of jackpots.

"In theory, yeah, but it's not my job to play casino cop. Besides, I can't prove anything."

"I bet there's some sort of reward."

"Maybe." I open my purse, pull out an envelope, drop it on the table.

"What's that?"

"Check it out." I down the last of my Vouvray and watch as Jaymie lifts the flap of the envelope. I hear her breath catch in her throat. She fans out the seventy crisp hundred-dollar bills.

"They let me win a piece of one," I say.

S OMETIME AFTER TWO AM the bedroom door opens. I know
it's Buddy from the sour, smoky, casino smell, and because he
knows his way around my bedroom in the dark, and because
who else would it be? I watch his shape undressing. A few seconds
later he slides into bed.

"I don't remember inviting you over," I say.

"You want me to go in the guest room?"

"Jaymie's in there." I roll to the right, away from him, pulling
covers over my shoulder. "You reek."

"Yeah. That's 'cause I smoke."

"So how'd you do?"

"I came back."

"All the way back?"

"Most of the way. I'm still down a couple hundred."

That probably meant he was down a couple thousand. I listen
to his breathing and smell his sweat and tobacco. Forty-eight hours
at the poker table and he slinks into my bed without so much as
taking a shower. To make himself even less welcome, he launches
into a bad beat story, the last thing I want to hear.

"I got pocket tens, I raise, Yassir reraises me outta the little
blind. I know, I know. Christ, you think I don't know he's got to
have a hand? The way he bets, reraising out of the blind, I know
he's got something. I know. I know Yassir, I know how he bets. He

even does that little shoulder roll when he looks at his cards, and he only looks once and puts a chip on them for protection and never looks at 'em again. I know he's got a big pair. But maybe I'll catch a ten on the flop, so I call. Then ace-rag-rag flops and he checks it. I bet. He smooth calls. Something about the way he looks, I figure he's slowplaying a set of aces. Then I hit my ten on the turn. Worst card in the world. Now I got a set of tens and I gotta play it. He checks, I figure maybe I'm wrong about him having the trip aces, so I bet. He comes over the top of me with a big raise. Now I'm sure he's got trip aces but what am I s'pose to do? I got trip tens. I know they're no good, that the only thing can save me is the case ten. I got all the information, all the experience. I know the play, I know what I gotta do. So I'm thinkin' I'm gonna fold right there, the hell with it, and all of a sudden the son of a bitch starts singing "Stairway to Heaven" in that weird accent of his. Now, understand, I have never seen this behavior before, and I have especially not seen it from Yassir, and the only way I am going to find out what the hell it's about is if I call the goddamn bet."

I couldn't resist asking, "You called him?"

"Yeah. It cost me a thousand bucks."

"Jesus, Buddy."

"I know. So, an ace comes on the river and he makes a shitty little five-hundred-dollar bet. I mean, two large in the pot and the guy is asking me to donate. Fuck that. I got out."

"You folded your full house? After you'd just bet a thousand? Knowing you were beat? Just to find out what the singing was about?"

"Yeah, well, I had an out then—there was still a ten in the deck, so what the fuck. I knew I was beat no matter what, and so did Yassir. At that point I wouldn't have paid ten cents to see his cards."

"Buddy . . ."

"I know, I know. And I know why he was singing. He did it to make me change my mind. He could've recited Rod McKuen poems or wiggled his ears or just started making putt-putt sounds. Didn't matter. The question I had was, What the hell did he think I was thinking that he wanted me to think different?" Buddy is steamed all over again.

"It's all one big game, Buddy," I say.

"I know it is."

Something every serious poker player understands: you play one poker game per lifetime. It begins with your first hand; it ends with your last. The tables change, your opponents change, the rules will change, the stakes change, the cards run good, the cards run bad. You will take breaks measured in days, weeks, or years, but it is all the same game. If you have ever played a hand of poker, you are in it.

"Yassir will give you that money back in time. You're better than him."

"Yeah, but it still stings." Buddy laughs. "*You* had a good night," he says.

"Pretty good."

"Won a piece of that jackpot."

"Yeah."

After a few seconds he asks, "What was your share? Eight?"

"Seven, after toking Jenny."

"Pretty lucky."

"Luck had nothing to do with it. Jenny dropped a deck."

"Well, hell, I figured that. I just wasn't sure *you* knew it."

"It was pretty obvious. She must have done it just after the clown let go of those balloons."

"I wonder why they let you in on it."

"It wasn't intentional. Manuel sent me to the table just as the clown was on his way in with the balloons."

Buddy exhales sharply through his nose. "I'm surprised they authorized the payout."

"What could they do?"

"They could do whatever the hell they wanted. Fucking sovereign nation. But why should they give a shit? The jackpot fund is players' money. Doesn't cost the tribe anything. But it might cost you your job, Peek."

I sit up and turn on the light. "Look, I didn't ask for that seat."

"I didn't say you did." Buddy is sometimes handsome and nearly always cute, but right now he looks terrible—pale, purple bags under his eyes, two days of blond-white beard. "But maybe you oughta take a few days off."

"Why would I do that?"

"In case they get cracked."

"They?"

"You know who I'm talking about. Tran, Beatrice, the whole goddamn Vietnamese jackpot mafia. They're getting greedy, and they're gonna get cracked. You don't want to look like you're too friendly with them."

I don't want to talk about it anymore. "You know what I think?" I say.

Buddy lifts his eyebrows, making his eyes round. Even worn out and raggedy, he's still puppy dog cute.

"I think if you want to sleep here tonight you better hit the shower."

THE SOUND OF RUNNING WATER relaxes me. Buddy likes to take long showers, and at the moment I am grateful for that. I don't want to talk about the jackpot. I can't think about it anymore. It's a done deal.

But I can't think about anything else.

Knocking off a jackpot is simple. The players involved wait for a game to get shorthanded—it's easier to control the action that way, and the payout is split between fewer players—then the dealer drops the cooler into play and *presto!* Jackpot.

Of course, simple does not mean easy. Every table in the card room is under surveillance by one or more video cameras. When a jackpot gets hit, before any money is paid out, the tapes are examined by security. Pulling a sleight of hand in front of an audience is one thing, but it's not so easy to fool a camera. A crooked dealer has to be very, very good with his hands—or they need a distraction. A clown with balloons, for instance.

I don't miss much, but I never saw Jenny bring in the stacked deck. I was watching the clown, just like everybody else, as the balloons blocked the camera's view for one critical second. I wonder how they covered up the move for the other three jackpots. The clown gimmick would only work once.

The way I figure it, Jenny had the cooler set up for five players. But when Manuel put me in the game, the deck became worthless.

One extra player would mean a whole different card distribution. That was why Tran was so angry when I sat down. He had already called the clown on his cell, so to make the deal come out right he had to send Sally out to his car. I got the four aces meant for Sally, which beat Beatrice's four queens. Jackpot.

I took my share. What else was I supposed to do?

Maybe I should've blown the whistle. I don't need the money. I've got money. I have twenty thousand dollars cash in a shoe box in my bedroom closet. I've got a wad of cash stashed in a Cap'n Crunch box in my cupboard, and another roll in the saguaro cookie jar, hidden under a layer of stale Oreos. I even have a few hundred in a checking account at Bank One. Money's not a problem. I don't need the seven dimes and I don't need the trouble, but somehow when it came at me I couldn't not take it. Call it a personality defect, I just can't say no to cash.

Besides all that, I had no proof the deal was rigged. But I know what I know. And when it all comes crashing down, which sooner or later it will, I'm going to look as dirty as the rest of them. Maybe I am.

The only dealers involved, as near as I can tell, are Tran Lui and Jenny Mai. That's two dealers out of the two hundred or so employed by the Santa Cruz. Over the past week Tran has dealt three jackpots and scored a piece of another one, and now Jenny, who won the big share of the jackpot two nights ago, has also dealt one. Of the players involved, I'm sure that at least three of them—Beatrice and the Fong sisters—are part of the same crew. I also suspect Deng Nguyen, who was involved in this morning's seven-stud jackpot. That's a lot of people. Blaise Hunt, the Casino Santa Cruz security chief, is no dummy. He has got to be looking very hard at those last three jackpot tapes. There are just too many names in common.

Buddy is right. Paying out a jackpot doesn't cost the casino any money, but appearances are important, and the wrong buzz among the regulars can kill the card room action as sure as a nuclear bomb.

Tran and Jenny and the rest of the crew will most likely just disappear. They'll turn up in a few weeks at some other casino, knock off a few more jackpots, then move on to the next hunting ground.

Me, I should be losing sleep over my daughter's marriage. Instead I am lying in bed listening to my boyfriend humming to himself in the shower, and I am thinking that that $7,000 is going to be the most expensive pot I ever won.

I OOZE OUT OF BED ABOUT TEN, stagger into the bathroom, wash my face, frown at the old woman in the mirror. Forty-four. If the Black Prince wasn't such a jerk I might soon be a grandmother. I pull on an old Jose Cuervo T-shirt, a pair of black leggings, and my disintegrating huaraches. My hair is doing something Medusa. I decide to ignore it till after breakfast.

I look over at Buddy's slack, snoring face. He's a few years younger than me—forty last March—but he looks like he's got one foot in the grave. Those two- and three-day poker sessions suck the life out of a man.

Buddy lives to play holdem and he's damn good at it most days, but he doesn't know how to quit once he gets started. He'll sleep for most of the day, then head back to the casino around six. In between, I might get him to help me do a few things around the house.

I've known Buddy Balcomb since the day he showed up at Casino Santa Cruz eighteen months ago and single-handedly destroyed the pot-limit game. He took close to $30,000 out of that game his first week in town. Of course, his heater didn't last, the other players learned how to defend themselves against Buddy's balls-out style, and now he loses more often than he wins. But when he wins, he wins more.

Buddy crashes at my house three, four nights a week. I guess you'd call us lovers, although the last few weeks there hasn't been much lovin'. Something is going on with Buddy, something he won't talk about and something I can't puzzle out. It might be anything from a bad run of cards to prostate cancer—either way, I won't get a word out of him until he's ready. He's close that way. To Buddy, life is a hand of holdem.

Buddy has what you might call a checkered past. He told me all about it the first time we went out to dinner. He told me he'd been in prison for armed robbery.

"I was nineteen. I got cracked for robbing a Seven-Eleven," he told me. "How dumb is that? You can't get much more than a couple hundred bucks. Had this little thirty-two automatic, big man with a gun, never even knew if the thing worked. Three years in Florence, I learned my lesson."

"Thou shalt not steal?"

"Thou shalt not risk going to jail for a lousy couple hundred bucks."

He thought that was pretty funny. I'm sure he was kidding. Buddy is more honest than ninety-five percent of the people you meet in church. Whatever he did when he was a kid was a long time ago. Buddy's not a criminal anymore. He's a gambler.

Buddy has an Airstream parked on a chunk of desert out by Ajo. I drove out there once. That was enough. Buddy is not what you would call a homemaker. But we kind of think the same about some things, and when he's not all knotted up inside he can be a lot of fun, and we've gotten used to each other.

I shuffle out to the kitchen following the sour, acrid odor of coffee left too long on the hot plate. Jaymie is gone, but she has left the yogurt carton standing open for my convenience, and a pile of mango peelings beside the sink. I pour out the burnt coffee and start a fresh pot, then set about watering my plants while the coffeemaker gurgles.

About ten years ago, on impulse, I bought a beautiful orchid at the Cactus Company, a neighborhood flower shop and nursery. I read the pamphlet that came with the plant, then called my sister

Nancy in Iowa and waxed poetic about the magical and aesthetic qualities of orchids. Three weeks later my beautiful orchid collapsed into a puddle of black slime. I dumped it in the trash and put the whole orchid thing out of my mind. A few weeks later another orchid was delivered to my door—a birthday present from Nancy. I've been killing orchids at the rate of one a year ever since. She keeps sending me the things. Usually it takes me no more than six weeks to do one in, but the *dendrobium* I'm working on now has been with me for more than two months and is only now beginning to show signs of putrefaction. If Nancy ever makes good on her threat to fly out here for a visit I'll have to drop several hundred dollars to re-create the orchid collection she thinks she has bought me.

The coffee is ready just as I over- or underwater the *dendrobium*. I'm sitting down with my first steaming mug when the doorbell rings. It's probably just the mail carrier with a package—I'm always ordering stuff—but I take a moment to tie back my hair before I open the door.

A short, slim Asian man wearing tiny, dark sunglasses looks up at me. He is dressed all in black, a fashion statement rarely made here in sunny Tucson.

"Yes?" I ask. My thought is that he is at the wrong house.

"Pee-kee?" he says as if not sure it's me.

I recognize the voice. "Tran?" I have never before seen him outside the casino.

"You don't look like you," he says, looking over his sunglasses and flashing a grin. Tran has two standard facial configurations: a frozen blank he wears while dealing or playing, and an all-out boyish grin that appears and disappears abruptly during social discourse.

"That makes two of us. I don't think I've ever seen you without a white shirt on."

"You see me working."

"That's right." My mind is scrambling, trying to figure out what he is doing here. I am afraid I know, but I can hardly believe it.

"You got a minute?" he asks.

I step back, making room for him to enter and he glides in. I get the feeling that he could walk through the bars of a jail cell by turning sideways.

"Coffee?" I ask, leading him toward the kitchen, the room where I feel most safe.

"Okay." He follows, a spindly shadow.

Tran takes his coffee with four heaping teaspoons of sugar. I watch him take a sip.

"How you doing?" he asks, wearing his stone face now.

I shrug, waiting for him to explain his presence.

He says, "You win some money last night?"

I notice a slight quaver in his voice. I sit back and cross my arms and nod. Here it comes.

"Pretty easy money, huh?" His slim fingers are in motion, exploring the coffee cup. He is nervous. If we were playing cards I would raise him now.

I say, "I'm not so sure."

"Very easy money." He bobs his head vigorously. "Jenny say you leave her a nice tip."

"Ten percent."

"Very generous."

"It's part of the game."

Tran grins and nods, liking that. "So, we okay then, huh?" He sips coffee, peering at me over the tops of his shades.

I just look back at him, still not sure where this is going, but he is done talking. I finally say it. "Are you here to ask me for a piece of it, Tran?"

"No way, José." Stone face. "I ask for Sally. Fi-ty percent."

"You want half."

"Fi-ty percent. For Sally."

For a moment I am uncertain what to do. I have the money, but is it really mine? Tran wants half of it for Sally; Sally will probably kick half of that back to Tran . . . but it's not their money, either.

"Forget it," I say. "I didn't ask to be involved."

Tran blinks. After three seconds he says, "Sally be very upset." He shakes his head. "I thought you cool."

"I'm very cool."

"Somebody do you a favor, you appreciate it."

I shake my head.

Tran sighs. He gets up and heads for the door, then turns back and asks, "But you not say anything?"

I nod. It feels all wrong, but I nod.

10

I AM MOPPING THE KITCHEN FLOOR—something I do once every couple months whether it needs it or not—when I hear water running in the bathroom. A few minutes later Buddy shows up in the kitchen, washed and shaven, begging with his amazing grin for a fresh cup of coffee. It's not quite noon, which is early for him. I set aside the mop and pour some beans into my antique coffee grinder. It used to belong to my grandmother back in Wichita, Kansas. Still works. Buddy sits down at the kitchen table and watches me turn the crank.

"I love to watch you move," he says, his grin tilting left. His face awake is nothing at all like his face asleep. When he smiles, his cheeks move up and his eyes shimmer and you see him eight years old on Christmas morning. "You are a goddess."

I roll my eyes. It's one of Buddy's lines. I know he's just trying to butter me up. When is the last time you saw a goddess mopping the floor in huaraches and a Jose Cuervo T-shirt? But he says it so good, showing all those teeth, that I can't help but catch a warm buzz inside.

"I tell you you're beautiful lately?" he says.

"Not in the last ten hours." I pull the drawer from the grinder, tip the ground beans into a filter, and drop the filter into the coffeemaker. Buddy watches.

"I must be slipping. You are beautiful." He looks right at me, right into me, and he is smiling that perfect big happy I-want-to-lick-your-face smile and it is impossible not to believe him. The last time I looked at myself in the mirror I did not see a beautiful woman, but that was then. I start the coffeemaker and get Buddy's favorite mug out of the cupboard.

"I dreamed we were on a poker cruise," Buddy says. "You won this monster hand, like a million bucks."

"I wouldn't mind living that dream."

"You were amazing." He is looking full at me, looking as if I am the most wonderful thing to behold in all the universe.

I hand him his mug of coffee. He takes a cautious sip, then smiles again. "Best coffee I've ever tasted."

"You are so full of shit," I say, but I am smiling, too.

"That's true," he nods. "But it's friendly shit."

"You hungry?"

"Not really." He thinks for a moment, staring up at my chest. "You got any pears?"

"Pears?"

"I would eat a pear."

"Sorry, we're fresh out of pears today."

He shrugs. "Here I was starting to think you were perfect. Now I find you got no pears."

"How about a banana?"

"No thank you."

"Bowl of cereal?"

"You know what I'd like?"

"I give up."

He grabs my hand and pulls me down onto his lap. "I'd like a little Peeky for breakfast."

I laugh. "You are incorrigible."

"Yes, I am full of shit and I am incorrigible, whatever that means, and I am ready to rock and roll your lovely bones from here to eternity." He kisses me and his callus-free gambler's hand slides up inside Jose Cuervo and cups my breast, soft and warm. "So what do you think about that?"

I think it's no time to be thinking anything.

"Buddy, can I ask you a question?"

"Hmm?" Buddy turns his head to look at me.

"Were you sleeping?"

"I was resting my eyes," he mumbles, sleepily.

"It's two in the afternoon."

"What's your point, beautiful?"

"I have a question."

"Shoot."

"What are we doing?"

Buddy gives that a moment, then says, "We are lying in bed, limp with joy after our erotic congress." He raises his eyebrows. "Did I get it right?"

I laugh, but I persist. "I mean what are we doing with our lives?"

"Oh, that." He rolls onto his side and props his head on his hand. "I got a question for *you*. How come you always ask questions like that at otherwise perfect moments?"

"I don't know." I really don't. Maybe being so comfortable and sated brings with it a pang of guilt. I just have to poke and prod. "When should I ask?"

"I don't know. How about never?"

"I don't think I could do that. You going to answer?"

Buddy regards me with an uncharacteristically sober expression, searching my face for a way out. He says, "Let me ask *you* a question. What do you want?"

"Do you mean out of this conversation?"

"Out of life."

"Justice," I answer without hesitation. It is something I've thought about. "I want everybody to get what's coming to them. I want my share of pocket aces. I want my share of jackpots. I want my share of you."

Buddy's mouth has curved into a wry smile.

"Don't *you* want that?" I ask.

"Not me, baby. I want more."

"More than what?"

"More than my share."

"So what are we doing?"

"Having this very weird conversation."

"C'mon, Buddy."

"Okay. The answer is, what we're doing is, we're living. Getting by. Having a good time while we're still able to enjoy life. Taking our share. That's what we're doing."

"What about in twenty years? Are we still going to be playing cards for a living?"

Buddy flops back on his pillow. "We might not be around in twenty years."

"You'll be sixty. That's not so old."

"I dunno, Peek." Staring at the ceiling. "I've been feeling pretty mortal lately."

Something in his voice scares me. I imagine cancer. "Is there something you're not telling me?"

"You?" He grins and looks at me and his blue eyes take on that Buddy sparkle and the moment of near honesty is past. "I tell you everything, baby."

THE NEXT FEW DAYS things feel like they're settling back to normal, both at work and at home. Jaymie makes peace with the Black Prince, my *dendrobium* shuffles off its mortal coil, and the only bad beat to get dealt is a little three-thousand-dollar high-low stud jackpot that I'm pretty sure is legit. Sally is pleasant, as always, and shows no sign of being upset with me. I'm hoping that Tran and his bunch are going to cool it for good—or better yet, just leave town—but they keep showing up.

Blaise Hunt has been spending more time than usual on the Card Club floor. All the employees get edgy when the security chief is around, like prairie dogs eyeing a hawk on the horizon. Hunt wears the same uniform as the regular security guards. Just one of the boys, except that he sports an oversize Dirty Harry–type revolver on his belt. He also has the disconcerting habit of zooming his little button eyes in on one person and staring for several seconds at a time. Tuesday night I catch him looking at me. I try to fend him off with a big smile, but he just keeps on staring the way a cat stares through a window at a bird. I endure it for a minute or two, then flee to the restroom. When I come out he is gone.

Shortly after that I get on a heater and win three racks of red chips playing $20–40 Omaha high-low, a thousand of which I lend to Buddy, who is stuck bad at $30–60 holdem. Nothing unusual there. Buddy taps out a few times a year, but he's a good enough player he always comes back.

I win again on Wednesday, and break even Thursday, the end of my workweek. My net for the week, including the jackpot, is a personal record of $10,610.

On Friday morning Buddy gets up early.

"It's not even noon yet," I say. "What are you doing up?"

"I got this thing I gotta do," he says with typical Buddy vagueness. "Oh, and I got your money." He pulls a roll from his pocket and peels off $1,000. "Thanks for the float."

"Anytime." I trade him a mug full of coffee for the cash.

"You aren't working tonight, are you?" he asks.

"You know I don't work Fridays. Why?"

"No reason." He kisses me. "You know how beautiful you are?"

"No."

"Mucho beautiful. I gotta go." He is out the door with his coffee mug. Ten seconds later I hear his car back out of the driveway.

I'm watching something called "The Ten Worst Shows Ever on TV" when the phone rings. I almost don't pick it up, but then I think it might be Jaymie. It's not. It's Bert Lyman, one of the other Santa Cruz props, calling to tell me about his bowels, which are in an uproar due to a bad tuna salad sandwich. I listen until I can't stand any more details, then interrupt him.

"Bert, I'm sitting at home watching clips from 'The Gong Show.' You want me to take the rest of your shift?"

"Well, I was kinda sorta hopin'."

"I'd be happy to."

"Y'know, I kinda liked that 'Gong Show.'"

"You got cable?"

"Sure I do."

"Turn it to the Nostalgia Channel when you get home."

"You're my kinda woman, Peeky. Listen . . . uh-oh, I gotta go . . ."

"Go, Bert. Go."

Drawing to a straight in a lousy little $4–8 stud game I am down $200 and cursing Bert Lyman for eating that bad tuna salad when a cloud of sweat and beer breath crawls up behind me. I try to ignore it. Bad smells are one of the hazards of playing in a public card room. The dealer spins out the sixth card. One opponent pairs his door card, the other snags a fourth heart, and I catch a blank. There's a bet and a raise. I fold and turn to see who or what is befouling my air.

It is Eduardo Montana, the Black Prince, my son-in-law, glaring at me. He's got two days of beard and a huge bruise on his cheekbone. Behind him, I see Theo the floorman coming with a security guard.

"Eduardo?" I try to sound casual.

"You know where she is at?" he says, his voice flat. He is holding himself in.

"Jaymie?" I laugh, God knows why. "I have no idea." I really don't.

"She didn't come home last night. She didn't go to work." His eyes are red-rimmed and puffy and I go from fear to pity.

"Maybe she needs some time to herself," I try to sound calm, but now I, too, am wondering where she might be.

Theo puts a hand on Eduardo's arm. "Excuse me, sir, but I'm going to have to ask you to leave."

Eduardo shakes him off. "I just wanna know she's okay," he says.

I start to tell Theo that I can handle the situation, but it's too late. The security guard grabs Eduardo, trying for an arm lock. Eduardo slips the hold easily. His right fist hooks across his abdomen and up, catching the guard on the point of his chin. The guard staggers back, surprised. Drunk or sober, Eduardo knows how to handle himself in a fight. By then a second guard has arrived. Eduardo charges, driving a shoulder into his ample gut, knocking him backward into a stud table. Theo and the first guard pile onto Eduardo—everyone in the room is on their feet now, maneuvering for a better view or trying to get out of the way. I hear some muffled thuds, a grunt of pain, and then see Eduardo break free and make a run for one of the emergency exits at the far end of the Card Club. He hits the door hard, a flash of sunset silhouettes him, and he is gone. One of the guards runs in pursuit, the other is jabbering excitedly into his radio.

Theo, holding a bloody handkerchief to his nose, asks me who *was* that guy.

"My son-in-law," I say. Despite all, I can't keep the note of pride out of my voice. I know they won't catch him.

Two hours later the incident is forgotten except by Theo, whose nose is two sizes larger now. I am winning steadily at a $6–12 holdem table when the next awful thing happens: Mutter Blodgett has a heart attack at the pot-limit table.

Of course, no one knows at first that he's having a heart attack. Mutter just sort of doubles over and pushes his chair back. I am sitting at the next table, not eight feet away. The dealer calls for the floor, and Theo comes over and tries to talk to Mutter, who is clutching his gut, eyes squeezed shut in pain. Theo can't get a word out of him. Then Mutter's eyes get big and roll up into his head and he falls off his chair.

Theo gets on the PA and asks if there's a doctor in the house. I happen to know there are at least three, but the only one to give up his seat is a Mexican gynecologist named Fernando something. It takes him about ten seconds to get Mutter on his back and start CPR. I watch Mutter Blodgett's prodigious abdomen pulse as Fernando pumps his chest, four hard thrusts at the sternum, then the mouth-to-mouth. Several people have gotten up and are forming a crowd, leaning in close over Mutter and the doctor. Theo is on the PA asking everybody to go back to their seats. Most of the lookylous return to their tables, but a few, entranced by the spectacle, won't budge. A pair of hulking Santa Cruz security guards come in, yammer self-importantly into their shoulder-mounted radios, and move the gawkers. They take up positions on either side of Mutter and stand there watching. The doctor recruits one of them to take over the chest compressions, while he continues with the mouth-to-mouth. Theo and Manuel are moving the other pot-limit players to another table at the far end of the casino. Someone touches my shoulder—it's Cathy, the dealer.

"Six dollars to you," she says. I look down and see two cards in front of me. The other players are looking at me, waiting for me to call the bet or fold. I look at my cards and see a pair of queens. Not bad. I throw them away.

The doctor and the security guard have gotten into a rhythm: thrust . . . thrust . . . thrust . . . thrust . . . breathe . . . breathe . . . breathe. . . . Every other sequence, the doctor places his hand on Mutter's throat, feeling for a pulse.

Thrust . . . thrust . . . thrust . . . thrust . . . breathe . . . breathe . . . breathe. Mutter does not look good to me. His belly is white and slack. I can see one of his hands. The fingers do not look like they will ever fondle another ace. Thrust . . . thrust . . .

Again, the dealer demands my attention. I have two fresh cards. I look at them. Ace, king of hearts. This time I call the bet. I am raised by Tommy C. in the small blind. Tommy will raise with anything, so I am happy to call. The flop comes deuce, four, king. Tommy bets; I raise to isolate him. We go to the river, me betting all the way but not improving. Tommy turns over pocket jacks and I take the pot.

A grunt of effort from the security guard interrupts my chip stacking. I realize with a start that for almost half a minute I completely forgot that a man was dying not ten feet from my right elbow.

. . . thrust . . . breathe . . . breathe . . .

"Your big blind," the dealer says. I put out the mandatory six-dollar bet.

It takes Santa Cruz Fire and Rescue nearly half an hour to arrive with their cardio equipment. The doctor is still working, but it
is not looking good for poor Mutter. The two medics, both grossly
overweight themselves, seem unfamiliar with the equipment, but
they do their best and within a few minutes what is left of Mutter
has electrodes taped to his chest and a respirator over his mouth.
They work on him for another half hour before loading Mutter
onto a gurney and wheeling him out of the casino. I am as sure as
anything that he is dead, and I am up more than four hundred dollars. As soon as he is out the door a cleanup crew moves in and I
leave the table to escape the penetrating howl of the carpet cleaner.
I go outside for a bit of fresh air.

It's not so fresh. Donny Keyes is standing under the edge of the
canopy smoking a cigarette and staring up at the marquee lights.
Several bats are feeding on a cloud of insects.

"How's it goin', Peek?" he asks, looking down at me. Donny almost played for the Lakers once, or so he claims. A lot of gamblers
used to be almost famous, to hear them talk.

"I'm hanging in there," I say.

Donny has been propping at the Santa Cruz three months now.
He once told me he loses $300 a week on average, which takes a
serious bite out of the $416 he nets in salary as a prop. I wonder
why he doesn't find another job, but I think I know the answer. He
figures himself $116 a week to the good, which makes him a win-
ner. That's how some of these guys think.

"Hell of a night," he says. "First a fight, and now Mutter croaks.
Worse thing is, shit happens in threes. I might just go home early
before something else happens."

I laugh.

"I'm serious, Peeky," he says. "I were you, I'd get a case of the
flu and head for home, too."

"I never knew you were so superstitious."

"Just 'cause I'm superstitious don't mean it don't never rain
shit." He takes a deep drag on his cigarette and sends a plume of
smoke toward the wheeling bats. "The room has a wicked feeling

tonight." He flicks his cigarette butt away. "Maybe I don't feel so good. Must've been something I ate."

"You have any of that tuna salad?"

"I guess that must've been it."

We head back inside. I've got a couple of hours to go on my shift. A few minutes later I notice Donny talking to Theo. Theo is shaking his head and Donny is pointing at his gut, twisting his morose face into a grimace of intestinal agony. Theo throws his hands up; Donny turns and walks out of the card room.

The pot-limit game loses its steam without Mutter's donations. Pretty soon it breaks up and the players settle into smaller games. I wonder again why Buddy isn't there to keep it going. He's usually a fixture on Friday nights.

I've never believed that stuff about things happening in threes, but Donny was right about one thing. The room has a wicked feeling tonight.

BY TEN-THIRTY there are twenty-six tables going—a big night, even for Friday. I put the Black Prince and Mutter Blodgett out of my mind and settle in to the rhythm of the game. I'm up a few hundred so I decide to tighten up a notch, hang on to my winnings. I've got less than two hours to the end of my shift, and I'd like to make it a perfect week: no losing sessions. I can feel myself relax as I make the decision.

That's when the third thing happens.

Usually when some event occurs in a poker room I feel it before I hear it, and I hear it before I see it. This one is no exception. I look up from my cards, not sure what I'm looking for, and see two guards wheeling a cart up to the cage. They stop just as they are pushing the cart through the security door. One of them says something into the radio strapped to his shoulder. He points excitedly toward the exit and the other guard dashes back through the card room, nearly colliding with a blue-haired clown. Another clown? This is not the same clown that brought me the balloons. This one has a pointy red nose and a patchwork bag over his shoulder. The clown stops in the entrance, looks after the guard, shrugs comically, then flounces past Manuel and Theo with a huge red-lipped smile.

The clown pulls a bladder horn from his patchwork bag and gives the room a friendly toot. He is wearing blue gloves to match his hair. The toot produces a ripple of awareness; a few heads look up and watch as he weaves through the tables toward the back of the room. Then a second clown, this one with a rainbow wig, comes in and starts talking to Theo at the podium. He wants the microphone, but Theo, smiling uncertainly, is holding it out of the clown's reach. The clown slaps the sides of his head in mock frustration. Manuel is laughing.

The blue-haired clown stops in front of the cashier cage and starts to dance, feet slapping carpet, blue-gloved hands flapping in the air. A second wave of awareness rolls through the Card Club— half of the players are watching the first clown, some are focused on the second, only a few remain oblivious to the circus.

In the cage, Dolores Cortes is smiling uncertainly. Her assistant, Camilla, is laughing, pleased with the distraction from the usual grind of counting other people's money. The guard is watching the clown, too, a strained smile pasted upon his face.

The clown pauses in his dance and reaches into his bag. He beckons them all to take a closer look. Dolores and Camilla move their faces close to the barred front of the cage. Even the guard leans in for a look. The clown pulls out a small handgun and fires three times, as fast as hands can clap. A hole appears in Dolores's forehead, the other bullet hits Camilla in the face, just below her right eye, her mouth still open in a happy grin. The third shot takes the guard in the neck. He staggers back, clutching his throat, blood spurting.

For a single heartbeat we are still, waiting for the punch line, then the card room erupts in panicky voices, players running, diving for the floor, crawling. One man makes it to the emergency exit but the instant he opens the door he is knocked back into the room by two more clowns carrying guns. I hear more shouted orders but I can't see because by then I have crawled under a table. I am hearing my husband's long dead voice: *Don't be a hero.*

Hero? I say. *What hero? What the hell do you think I'm gonna do here?*

Heroes get killed, he says.

A weird cartoon voice comes over the PA system. "Don't move and you won't get hurt!" It's the rainbow-haired clown doing a Donald Duck voice.

Joe Garcia, cowering next to me, says, "Fuck that." He starts crawling toward the second emergency exit, twenty feet away.

"Everyone on the floor facedown *now!*" says Donald Duck. "Anybody moves is dead."

I see Joe stop. For one complete second the card room is silent, then I hear another gunshot followed by a collective moan of terror. Hurried footsteps, clowns on carpet, and I see a pair of sneaker-clad feet hustle past. I'm telling myself to stay put, but as scared as I am I'm curious to see what's going on. I edge out from beneath the table and raise my head.

Two clowns are inside the cashier cage. The clown with the rainbow wig and the Donald Duck voice is standing in front of the board, holding the microphone in one hand and a long-barreled handgun in the other, looking out over the room. Something about the familiar way he holds the mike sends a shiver through me. I hear a shuffle of feet on carpet behind me and turn my head slowly. The fourth clown, rubber mask, orange hair, very close, holding a small handgun, it looks like a .32 auto, the sort of backup gun a cop straps to his ankle. He is wearing yellow rubber gloves, the kind I use for cleaning the oven. On each side of his bulbous purple nose, through holes in the mask, I see pinhead pupils on blue irises. I put on my terrified, harmless, middle-aged woman face. It's no stretch at all.

The clown makes an agitated motion with his free hand, wiggling his fingers, motioning me to put my head down. Something clicks in my brain, something about that finger wiggle, but I am too scared to look at it. I get down and I stay down. The carpet, which I have always thought of as mauve, is actually made out of blue, green, red, and pink fibers. The Donald Duck voice rakes our ears again.

"Nobody move for five minutes. Anyone who leaves this room

before that will be killed." He adds, "Thank you for your coopera-
tion."

Within twenty seconds I feel the people start to stir. I hear
voices, rising in volume, and then, once it feels safe, the high-
pitched clamor of hysteria. I slowly rise to my feet, my head passing through an invisible cloud of fear and burnt gunpowder. I sit at
the table and, having no other ideas in my head, I load my chips
into my purse. Six winning sessions in a row. All I want now is to
get home alive. I can't think; I don't want to know. I move toward
the exit, keeping my gaze averted from the cashier cage, following
an invisible line on the carpet. I have to be out of that room, even
if Donald Duck and his crew are waiting on the other side of the
door with a pistol. The people milling about are a blur. In a few
places people are gathered, looking down. One group parts and I
see Tran Lui crumpled, motionless, on a carpet glistening with
blood. Two security guards rush in holding guns, shouting "Don't
move! Don't move!" which is exactly the wrong thing to say. They
are as scared and confused as the rest of us—maybe more so, because they have no idea what happened. I keep moving toward the
main entrance, staying close to the wall. People are pouring out
through the emergency exits. A guard tries to stop them. He waves
his gun above his head. I don't know what he's thinking. He is jos-
tled and his gun goes off. This causes some people to drop to the
floor and others to stampede. I am one of the stampeders, not a
thought in my head, and then I am falling, my hands hitting carpet. I try to get up; I'm knocked down. I roll to the side, trying to
get out of the way, but all I see are legs and then one knee coming
at me and everything flashes gray.

I COME TO SITTING UPRIGHT on the sofa in the lounge with someone holding a cool wet towel to my temple. I turn my head to see who is helping me, hoping it's Buddy. A woman's hand, pale with short nails. Not Buddy. Martha Green.

"Take it easy, sweetie," she says in her soothing Irish accent. Her face is smooth until she smiles, when dozens of fine wrinkles appear around her eyes. "Let's let the ambulance boys have a look at you."

"I'm okay," I say. My entire head is throbbing. I look around. About twenty cops and security personnel are milling about. Security Chief Blaise Hunt is standing near the center of the card room. His gray hair, cut in a flat-top, seems extra-bristly. The rest of him is much the same: stiff, squared-off, solid, crisp. Hunt is talking to a large man dressed in a dark suit. The man's black hair is pulled back tight into a ponytail held by a turquoise clasp. He turns his head and I recognize Carlos Begay, the Casino Santa Cruz president. This is only the second time I've seen him in the card room. As I watch, he turns away from Hunt and strides quickly out of the room. Hunt says something into a radio mounted on his shoulder. His black eyes scan the room. They find me and pause for an instant, pricking me, then move on. Two paramedics are rolling someone out on a gurney. The face is covered.

"What happened?" I ask.

Martha says, "There was a robbery."

"I know that. I mean . . ." I point at the stretcher. "Who?"

Martha is the most unflappable person I know. You could chop off her hand and she would say, "Oh dear, now look what you've gone and done."

"That would be Tran," she says, calmly.

The image of Tran standing at my front door is immediately followed by the memory of seeing him dead on the floor, blood soaking into the carpet. "No," I say, trying to undo the past. It doesn't work. Tran is still dead. "What about Dolores and Camilla?" I still see Camilla laughing as the slug punches a hole in her cheekbone.

"I'm afraid they're both goners as well. The security guard, too."

"Four people. My God." I bite hard on my knuckle and the pain drives away my thoughts, but an instant later they return. My mind riffles through a catalog of images. I bite harder and for another brief moment I think I have avoided remembering, but it is too late, the images batter through and spread themselves before me, a nightmare slide show.

. . . *pointy red nose, blue wig, Dolores and Camilla with red holes in their heads. Donald Duck's voice, the multihued carpet, the purple-nosed, blue-eyed, yellow-gloved clown, motioning me to get down. A sea of legs and hands and knees coming at me . . .*

I make my living by noticing little things: the flicker of an eyelid, the throbbing of a vein. A pupil dilating. A hand shaking. My mind is a catalog of tics, twitches, tremors, and mannerisms. I remember faces and I remember the things that people do with their bodies. I see how people walk and sit and hold their cards and smoke their cigarettes. I can tell you how many moles Mutter Blodgett had on his face—nineteen. I notice how long a player looks at his cards and how he bets, and I remember what it means, and because of this I am very good at what I do.

But right now I want to know nothing.

The Santa Cruz Tribal Police are talking to everyone, working their way from the front of the room to the back, where Martha and I are sitting. Blaise Hunt is with them. I wonder who is in charge. They are going ask me questions. They are going to ask me what I saw. What I know.

Martha Green is sitting with her arms crossed over her breasts, staring into the distance. She is not thinking about me anymore. Maybe she's thinking how lucky she is to be alive. Maybe, like me, she's trying not to think at all. I am holding the towel to my head. It is no longer cool, but it is something to do with my hands.

I will tell them I saw clowns with guns. I saw two girls die. I heard Donald Duck quacking. I know nothing more. They will let me go home.

The paramedics reach me first. I let them do their little tests. I am alive, they decide. I am not bleeding. My vital signs are all normal. They seem a bit disappointed.

I try to leave after that, but the police make me wait another hour. By the time they get to me they are tired and bored with asking the same questions and getting the same unhelpful answers, over and over again. Blaise Hunt stands behind them, watching and listening as I respond to their questions. I give them only a frightened middle-aged woman who wants to go home, officer. She just wants to go home.

The sky is bright in the east when I finally totter out of the casino and try to remember where I parked.

14

THERE ARE TWO PEOPLE waiting for me at home. Buddy's ten-year-old Buick is parked in my driveway. Prince Eduardo the Black is sleeping in his pickup truck across the street. I pull in alongside Buddy's car. Eduardo wakes up, climbs groggily out of his truck, and starts across the street. I pretend I don't see him and head for the front door. He picks up his pace, coming across the lawn now. I wonder if he's going to grab me. He's probably wondering the same thing. I save him the decision by sticking my can of Mace in his face just before he gets to me.

It works great. He stops like a mime hitting an invisible wall, his hands coming up to protect his face. "Don't!" he says with such intensity that I'm sure he's been pepper-sprayed before.

"Back off, Eduardo."

"I just want to talk to you." He has a cut lip to go with the bruise on his cheek, courtesy of Casino Santa Cruz security.

"This is not a good time. Go home. Go to bed."

He licks his lips. He wants to rush me, to bowl me over and tear up my house looking for Jaymie. But he won't. He isn't that far gone, for one thing. And he doesn't like pepper spray.

The door opens behind me. I see in Eduardo's face that he is hoping it will be Jaymie, and I can see from the way hope leaves his eyes that it is not.

"There a problem here?" Buddy asks.

Eduardo backs away. "No problem, man." He looks defeated. I feel sorry for him all of a sudden and say, "Eduardo?"

He stops.

"I'm sure she's all right. You call me later, okay?"

He nods and walks quickly to his truck. Buddy and I watch him drive away.

"You okay?" Buddy asks.

"The card room got robbed."

"I heard. It's all over the news."

Why isn't he hugging me?

He holds the door open. I walk past him into the familiar smell of my home. It feels both large and close. I head straight for the fridge and pour myself a glass of Vouvray.

Buddy follows, his body language that of a virgin bomb disposal technician. He doesn't know what to do. What's to know? Put your arms around me. Squeeze me. I don't offer him any wine. Buddy doesn't drink. He grabs himself a Fresca and follows me into the living room. I sit down on the sofa.

"You sure you're okay?" He stands over me, his hands all over the Fresca can. I can smell him. He's nervous. What does he think I'm going to do? Fall apart?

"Don't worry, I'm okay." I sip my wine. It doesn't taste right. Wine is not what I need right now. I don't know what I need. I set the wine aside. I am looking at Buddy's knees and they seem to be several yards away. I feel strange, both large and small at the same time. Did the paramedics give me something? I don't remember any pills or shots. Maybe I have a concussion after all.

"I was right there, Buddy. Right in the middle of it. I saw Dolores and Camilla get shot."

"Jesus . . ."

"But I'm all right."

"They said some people were shot. They didn't say who."

I look up. His eyes are red and wet. I say, "Tran Lui and a security guard were killed, too."

He looks away, his mouth compressed.

"Buddy?"

"What?"

I pat the sofa cushion. "Sit down."

He sits.

"Put your arm around me."

He raises his left arm and lays it across my shoulders.

"Now give me a hug."

His arms wrap and squeeze me, and I am holding him, and I cry at last.

Buddy is like a lot of men in that he can't have physical contact without getting turned on. This time, to his credit, he holds me for twenty minutes before making the transition from mourning-the-dead to taking-care-of-business. Maybe sex should be the last thing on my mind, but I need the flesh-on-flesh contact. There is nothing quite like desperate, needy screwing to make a gal feel alive.

I fall into sleep almost immediately afterward, sinking like a swimmer being sucked into a whirlpool. By the time I open my eyes again the room is bright with midday sunlight. Buddy is sitting up, getting out of bed. He looks back and sees that I am awake. I start to get up, too, but he waves me back, wiggling his fingers, telling me to lie down and go back to sleep.

I stare at his hand, recognizing the gesture. He pulls his hand back and I see an instant of alarm in his face—then his features snap into poker mode, frozen and blank.

It's too late. Buddy can read me as well as I can read him.

I sit up, completely awake now.

"I was just gonna make us some coffee," he says, standing up.

"That was you," I say.

"What? What are you talking about?" He knows he can't bluff me, but he has to try.

"Don't bullshit me, Buddy." It's so clear now. I can see his eyes through the clown mask. On some level I must have known it was him even as it was happening. I saw it, but I couldn't let myself know it.

He is giving me his blank nothing look now, waiting. I say, "My God, Buddy. What have you done?"

"What do you mean?"

"You killed four people."

He shakes his head. "No. Not me."

"Four people are dead."

His poker face collapses and he looks away. "It wasn't supposed to go down that way."

"How was it supposed to go down? One dead? Two dead?"

Nothing.

"Why did you do it?"

His face gets very hard. "I had no choice, Peek. You really don't want to know more."

He's right, I don't want to know. I feel horrible, the way I'd feel if I found out I had a parasitic worm feeding on my liver.

I pull my knees up and wrap my arms around my legs. "I think you better leave."

Buddy shuffles his feet.

"Get the fuck out of here, Buddy."

A FTER BUDDY LEAVES I am too upset to sleep, but there is nothing for me elsewhere. I curl up in bed, fighting off images of clowns with guns, trying my damnedest to find my way back into oblivion. It doesn't work. I keep seeing the robbery, over and over again. Buddy in his clown suit, telling me to keep my head down. The clown with the pointy red nose making deadly holes in Dolores and Camilla. The clown with the rainbow wig and the Donald Duck voice . . . I know him, too. I knew him from the way his head jutted forward from thin shoulders. The way he held the microphone. The ferretlike stalk. And the voice, beneath the Donald Duck quack, a nasal undertone.

Darrin McConnell, the floor man.

The card room was robbed by one of its own employees. And my boyfriend.

An hour passes, then two. A sudden raucous noise rattles my head. I claw at the phone more to stop it ringing than to answer it.

"Hello?" My voice sounds like a raven's croak.

"Peeky? This is Eddie."

"Eddie?"

"Eduardo. You said I could call you, okay?"

I remembered saying something like that. "Oh."

"Look, can I talk to you?" He sounds sober.

"Isn't that what you're doing?" I sit up. The bed is a mess. The top sheet is twisted into a knot; the cotton blanket is wadded up against the headboard.

"I mean, can I come over and talk to you?"

I don't say anything right away. I try to think of what I have to do that afternoon.

Nothing. What do I usually do on Saturday afternoon? I have no idea. My mind is blank. A visit from my son-in-law does not seem like such a bad thing.

I say, "Give me an hour, okay?"

"Thank you, Peeky." He sounds pitifully grateful. This is the Jekyll side of Eduardo. When he is not all Latin fire and bluster and beer he can be a sweet, bashful, almost timid young man.

One hour to the minute, Eduardo is at my door. He is wearing a clean, maize-colored dress shirt, jeans, and ostrich cowboy boots with a matching belt. His eyes are still bloodshot, but his cheek is less swollen now. He has a butterfly bandage over the cut on his lip, his black hair is carefully combed straight back, and he is holding a bag from my favorite South Tucson *panadería*.

"I brought you some things," he says, handing me the bag.

I take the bag and he follows me into the kitchen, where I have a pot of coffee brewing. Eduardo accepts a mug and doctors it with milk and sugar. I put the Mexican pastries on a plate. We sit down, me in my usual chair, Eduardo where Jaymie was sitting just a few nights ago. He tells me he likes to visit my house because it feels so comfortable. He tastes his coffee, winces as it stings his cut lip, and tells me what a great cup of coffee I make. It occurs to me that he hasn't heard about the casino robbery. I don't say anything. What good could it do? I let him do the talking, let him try to butter me up. Part of me enjoys it, even though I know he is just telling me what he thinks I want to hear. At least it takes my mind off Buddy. He asks me if I've heard from Jaymie.

I shake my head.

Eduardo's face crumples slightly. "I'm worried about her," he says.

"Maybe she's worried about you," I say.

He shakes his head hard. "No, I mean like she could get hurt, you know?"

"You mean like she might get punched in the face by her husband?"

Eduardo colors and points his finger at me. "One time! One time I hit her."

"You cut her lip open. She had to get stitches."

"One time." His neck is turning red and the vein on his forehead is pulsing.

"What about the black eye? What about the bruises on her neck?"

He thumps his chest with a fist. "I did not do those thing." Eduardo's English is perfect, except when he is drunk or upset.

I shake my head. "She's scared of you, Eduardo. She's probably afraid to go home."

"That's not why she is gone. She is afraid I will stop her, that is what she is afraid of. I will stop her."

"Stop her what? Leaving?"

He shakes his head and I feel the weight he is carrying inside it. "You don't know what it is with us, do you? The last few months. She don't tell you, of course. Is just, Eddie is the bad guy. Eduardo beat up women. You know, maybe I hit her once, okay? Maybe I had a reason to hit her. I don't mean like it's *okay*, I just mean it's like you can understand how come I do it, you know?"

I stare across the table at him, giving him the same nothing look I use to bluff a rock off an ace-king.

Eduardo continues. "What it is between a husband and wife is private, you know? But sometime, sometime you got to tell things you don't want to, okay?

I am wishing that he would stop talking. I don't want to hear this, whatever it is.

"See, Jaymie, she got a problem, you know, with dope."

Staring into Eduardo's bloodshot eyes, I feel every muscle in my body go tense. I want to jump across the table and shove the words back down his throat but I am frozen in time. It amazes me the depths to which a man will sink. I can hardly believe that he is sitting in my kitchen making excuses for beating my daughter.

"She like to get high," he continues, seeing that I will give him nothing back. "She's into, you know, smoking crack and stuff." His eyes are shiny, as if he is about to cry.

I curl my lip to show him I don't buy his act. "My daughter is no crackhead. Why are you lying to me?" I say.

"I am not lying to you." A flash of anger cuts through his tears. "She got a problem."

"As far as I can see, you're her problem."

He shakes his head, his lips white with pressure. He reaches into his pocket and comes out with a glass tube about two inches long.

"You ever see one of these?"

The tube looks familiar. I have seen them in the parking lot at the casino, but never gave them a second thought—just another bit of garbage, like cigarette butts or gum wrappers or empty Tic Tac boxes. A few weeks ago I'd found one in the side pocket of my blue leather jacket. I assumed that it was a used perfume sample, or something else relating to personal hygiene, something Jaymie had left when she'd borrowed the jacket. I had tossed it into the trash without a second thought.

"You know what it is?" Eduardo asks.

"Not really . . ." I have that sickening feeling; like the feeling you get in the seconds before the doctor gives you the results of your mammogram, or when you sense a lover is about to break up with you.

"Is a crack vial." He sets it on the table. "I find it in her purse. She tells me she quits and then I find it in her purse." His eyes are angry and hurt and full of tears. His skin is pulled close to the bone. I sit back and close my eyes to protect myself from the emotions flooding his face. Things are sorting themselves out in my head. I see Jaymie showing up at three AM with a black eye and finger marks on her neck, telling me that Eddie beat her up, but something's not right in the way she tells it. And why did she look so wasted lately, as if something had sucked the life right out of her? Anemia, I told her. You should see a doctor, I said. She laughed.

I say, "How long have you two been using?"

He shakes his head. "No, no, no. I don't do that stuff. Just a little beer."

"A lot of beer."

"Okay, only that's *it*. I don't do no dope, okay?"

"Then how did Jaymie start using?"

"She always like that stuff. You know. Before I know her. Even in high school I think."

It was true. I knew she'd smoked pot in high school, and once she'd been arrested with a bunch of other kids for cocaine possession. Lots of kids mess around with drugs in school—I know I did—but most grow out of it. Jaymie hadn't been in trouble in almost three years. I thought she'd left her wild youth behind, but if Eduardo is telling me the truth, Jaymie never stopped using. She just got better at hiding it.

"Isn't it— How does she afford it? Isn't that stuff expensive?"

He lowers his chin and looks away.

"Do you give her money for dope?" I ask, still trying to blame it on Eduardo.

He shakes his head. "No, Peeky. I think she get it from you."

I HAVE NEVER BEEN GOOD about keeping track of my money. I just keep it in my purse until the roll gets too big—I don't like to carry more than two thousand dollars—and then I stash it. My intentions are good. I mean to put it in my bank account, but never get around to it. I've probably got thirty grand in cash hidden around the house. Maybe more.

A couple thousand dollars? I'd never miss it. I wonder which of my many stashes Jaymie has been raiding. Probably the Cap'n Crunch box, or the saguaro cookie jar, or both. Jaymie inherited my sweet tooth. She might have been looking for a quick sugar fix and instead found a fat roll of hundreds. All those times she dropped by for a visit. Stopped by to see her lonely old mom. Good daughter. Attentive daughter. I think of us sitting in the kitchen talking and I get up to use the bathroom. She waits for the door to close, then goes for the Cap'n Crunch.

I am in the bathroom, trying to calm down enough to rejoin Eduardo. I do not like the way I feel. They say that when it comes to their kids, parents have an infinite capacity for self-deception. I always figured I was the exception, and here I find out that I've been financing my daughter's crack habit.

For a moment I am falling into myself. I want to curl up and shrink. But Eduardo is in the kitchen and Jaymie is out there somewhere. I force myself to step back, to see this new reality. For the moment, I pretend that she is somebody else's daughter, a young woman who needs help. This way I can think about it.

I look into the mirror expecting red eyes and cheeks streaked with tears, but it seems that I have not been crying at all. My features are composed and lacking all expression. Perhaps I am hysterical. I stare at my reflection for a time, then rejoin Eduardo in the kitchen.

Eduardo is standing at the back door looking out through the screen at my poor, neglected garden.

"I'm sorry," I say.

He shakes his head. "You got nothing to be sorry about. You don't know."

"I should have. In any case, I know now. Do you know where she is?"

"No. I thought I did. This place down in South Tucson, just off of Sixth Avenue, where she use to go. You know, where she can get high. See, I would not let her do it at home. No dope, that is our house rule. So she go to these places. Anyway, I don't see her all day and then her work calls and wants to know where she is and so I went to this place looking for her and the guy answers the door, he say he don't like me coming looking for her all the time, and"—he touches his cheek—"we get into it a little, you know?"

I nod. I can imagine.

"That's when I go to casino and see you."

"After a few beers."

"I have to calm down." He makes a lopsided, cut-lipped grin. "That don't work so good."

"It usually doesn't. Where do you think she is?"

"I don't know. But I'm gonna find her. I am telling you this so, if she show up here? You let me know."

"Maybe I should help you look."

"You do not want to go to these places."

"I used to be a cop, Eduardo. I can handle myself." I don't mention that it was mostly desk work.

He shakes his head. "I will call you when I find her."

After Eduardo leaves I sit on the sofa for a long time fighting the black hole that is sucking at my guts. Eventually I force my body to stand and move through the house, doing things that need doing. I water the living plants, discard my dead orchid, and refill the hummingbird feeder. I clean the bathtub. I count the money in my cookie jar and the Cap'n Crunch box. There's even more than I thought, close to twenty thousand.

I should put it in the bank. Maybe Monday. In the meantime I put it with the rest of my money in my Nine West shoe box, the only stash I'm sure Jaymie hasn't found, and add the box to the twenty-odd Nine West, Ferragamo, and Bandolino boxes in my bedroom closet. Jaymie might not hesitate to reach into my cookie jar, but I don't think she'd go digging through my closet. We don't wear the same shoe size.

As I work, my thoughts skitter like beads of water on a griddle, touching everywhere but settling nowhere. All I know to do is stay busy, keep moving until the skittering stops. I pull the refrigerator away from the wall and clean behind it. I dust the light fixtures. I'm about to attack the bathroom grout with a toothbrush when I notice the time. Six-thirty. I know that this time is important, but for a few dizzy seconds I do not understand its significance . . . then I remember.

Work. I have a job. Saturday night, I'm supposed to be at work by seven.

It seems impossible. Is the casino even open? How could they be open for business after what happened? I think about it for a few seconds. Of course they'll be open. They never close. The gamblers would be there with their money. The cashiers—not Dolores; not Camilla—would be exchanging chips for cash. The dealers would be spreading their games. There would be seats to fill. They would need their prop.

I consider calling in sick. It's too soon to go back. There will still be blood on the carpet. And I have this daughter, this little girl who might need me. Then I look at the toothbrush in my hand and the mildew-stained grout in the shower. I imagine my hand shuffling chips, lifting the corners of freshly dealt cards, making a bet, and suddenly I feel calmer. The purity and order and comfort of the game calls to me. Check, bet, call, or raise. So simple, so seductive.

Eduardo has my cell phone number. He can reach me as easily at the casino as here.

I set the toothbrush on the edge of the sink and go to work on my face.

ON MY WAY INTO THE CARD CLUB I realize that I haven't eaten in hours, so I take a quick detour to the employee lounge to hit the vending machine. I'm eating a Snickers bar when my eyes sweep across the wall and get caught by the words *Drug Abuse*. I get up and take a closer look. It's a cardboard pouch pinned to the bulletin board containing several flyers promoting a company called Addiction Services Counselors. The front of the flyer reads:

Want to Quit?
Just ASC!
Addiction Services Counselors
Tucson's Oldest Intervention and Referral Service.
The First Step Is Yours. Just ASC!

I guess addiction is a hazard of working in the gambling industry. So is bad copywriting. I stuff one of the flyers in my purse. I don't know how deep Jaymie has gotten into this drug thing, but if she can't quit on her own, she might need help. I polish off the Snickers, wash my fingers, and head back to the Card Club, where a harried, frightened-looking Richard Frye is working the board. Richard is normally unflappable, a good quality to have in his position, but today he is clearly stressed.

"Peeky. My God," he says. "Were you here?"

"I was." I look over the room. It looks reassuringly familiar. I blink, and see after-images of clowns.

Richard is shaking his head. "It could've been any one of us."

"It was bad." My eyes move to where Tran was sitting when he was shot. The carpeting has been replaced, and the table is full of Omaha players.

"Who's working the floor?" I ask, tearing my eyes away from the square of new carpeting.

"Marisa and George."

"Where's Darrin?"

"He didn't show. Vergie called him, but there was no answer." That's a tremendous relief. I don't think I could have faced him.

"Who is George?" I ask.

Richard points across the room to a stocky, pink-faced man. "He used to work up at Gila River. I think he just started this morning. Hey, you hear about Donny?"

"Donny Keyes?"

"Yeah. He got himself banned. For beating up a slot machine."

"You're kidding. Donny? When did this happen?"

"Friday night, same time as the robbery. I guess he just lost it. Security had to haul him out kicking and screaming."

Strange. I thought Donny had gone home that night with a phony case of the stomach flu. Besides, I never knew Donny to play the slots.

"Unbelievable," I say.

"So we need to hire another prop. Know anybody?"

"Not really. You need me anywhere right now?"

"Table six could use some support."

I look at table six. A five-handed $3–6 holdem game. I take a seat, my face twisted into a false smile, and let the other players check me out. I imagine how I look to them. Middle aged. Not quite pulled together. Desperate. Harried. Possessed.

I succumb to the rhythm of the game—shuffle, deal, bet, raise, call, fold—numbing my mind to thoughts of murder and clowns and Buddy and Jaymie and crack vials. There is nothing quite like a poker game to make the rest of the world go away.

I am an hour into my shift when Richard touches my shoulder and tells me that Blaise Hunt wants to see me in his office.

In all the years I have worked for Casino Santa Cruz, I have never exchanged a word with Blaise Hunt. He has always been a silent presence, powerful and aloof. I don't even know how to find his office, and neither does Richard. I approach the security guard at the Card Club entrance. He directs me to the elevator near the telephones at the back of the Slot Palace. I never knew there was an elevator there. I ride it up to the second floor, where a slight, Irish-looking security guard leads me down a short hall to Blaise Hunt's office.

Hunt's office is spare and clean, consisting of little more than a long metal desk with two straight-backed side chairs parked in front of it. Hunt is sitting in an oversize swivel chair, staring at me across the desk. He points to one of the side chairs. It bugs me that he did not stand up to greet me when I entered the room, so I sit in the other one. Hunt rotates his chair to compensate.

"How are you doing, Peeky?" he asks. I'm a little surprised that he is using my nickname, as we have never been formally introduced.

"I'm doing fine," I say. "Blaise."

He shrugs off my familiarity. "That was a terrible thing yesterday," he says.

I nod.

"You were right in the middle of it," he says.

"Everybody was in the middle of it."

"I was there when the police were talking to you."

"I didn't have much to tell them."

"Are you sure?"

"I told them what I saw."

He gives me ten seconds of silence. I wait him out.

Hunt's right shoulder rises in a faint shrug, the same shrug a player holding the stone cold nuts might deliver just before regretfully pushing out a bet he can't lose.

"I don't believe you," he says.

I consider reacting with outrage, with confusion, with innocence. I go with ditzy.

"That's what my daughter said. She said, 'I don't believe this happened to you.' "

Hunt presses his lips together and inhales through his nostrils, gathering strength. "I mean, I don't believe you told the police everything you know," he says with mock patience.

"They asked me what I saw, and I told them. It was awful. Those poor girls. It was awful what I saw. . . ."

Hunt stares at me. For several seconds he is as utterly motionless and full of potential as an uncut deck of cards. I think that in a game of $30–60 holdem Blaise Hunt would be a tough opponent to read. Not impossible, but difficult.

"Did you recognize any of them?"

"Who?"

"The men in the clown suits."

I shake my head.

"Really?" He seems perplexed.

I am perplexed, too. Why am I protecting Darrin McConnell? Am I afraid Darrin will lead them to Buddy? I shouldn't care. Buddy is a thief, a liar, and an accessory to murder. It's over between us. How could I ever trust him again? How could I have trusted him enough to let him into my bed?

Problem is, you don't just stop loving someone.

Hunt has his eyes fixed on me. I am wearing a confused smile. It is not entirely an act.

"Yellow gloves," I say. Hunt raises his eyebrows a scant quarter inch. Is he encouraging me, or is he doubtful? I expand on the yellow glove theme. "One of the clowns had yellow rubber gloves. Like for cleaning the oven."

Hunt waits for more. I shrug and smile.

He says, "You aren't able to identify any of them?" Is he asking me, or telling me? I notice a minute upturn of the corners of his lipless mouth. Do I amuse him, or is he covering up his frustration?

"Sorry."

"You didn't recognize Darrin McConnell?"

"Darrin?"

"You didn't recognize him? It seems everybody else did."

"He was one of them? But they were all wearing masks!" I'm trying hard to look surprised and not doing it very well.

"McConnell has a distinctive walk. Three of the dealers and two customers suggested to us that he was the clown with the microphone. What do you think, Peeky?"

I nod as if it is coming to me. "It could have been. Did you ask him?"

"Do you know where I can find him?"

"I don't really know Darrin."

"That was not my question."

"No, I don't know where he is."

"How about your boyfriend?"

I crinkle my brow. "You mean Buddy?"

"Yes. Where was he on Friday night?"

I pretend to think. "I think he went home."

"To his trailer, or to your place?" Hunt has been doing his homework.

"I don't know. He was at my place when I got home. Maybe he didn't feel so good. I heard there was a problem with the tuna salad."

"You disappoint me, Peeky."

I give him befuddled.

"You won a nice jackpot the other day," he says, coming at me from a different angle.

I smile happily. "Yeah. That was great."

"Very lucky." He smiles back, and now I see genuine amusement.

"Very lucky," I agree, smiling inanely.

"Too lucky, you might say."

I bristle at that. Even though I know the jackpot deal was rigged, I had nothing to do with it. I'm innocent. Since ditzy isn't working, I decide to attack.

"Look, I play cards here forty hours a week," I tell him. "At thirty hands per hour average, that's sixty thousand hands a year, or seven thousand of my dollars added into the jackpot fund. I should see an average return of about two and a half jackpot shares a year, with an average payout of twenty-eight hundred dollars. Until last Friday, I hadn't caught a piece of one in nineteen months. I don't call it lucky. I call it fourteen months behind the curve."

Hunt has retreated behind his face. Some people just don't like getting slapped with numbers.

"We know Jenny dropped a deck, Peeky."

"Then you know more than I do. I didn't put myself in that game. Manuel sent me there because they were shorthanded. It was out of the blue. I got lucky. I got my share of a jackpot."

"We will be talking to Manuel as well."

"What are you insinuating?"

"How well did you know Tran Lui?"

"Tran? Not well."

"You ever see him outside of work?"

"Not socially, if that's what you mean."

The skin around his eyes relaxes. He thinks he's trapped me. "You never had any contact with him outside this casino?"

"I didn't say that." Could he know that Tran visited me at home? I decide to play it safe. "He stopped by my house yesterday."

"Why did he do that?"

"It's a funny story," I say, wondering what is about to come out of my mouth. "See, when I got up to leave that day I accidentally picked up Tran's cell phone and dropped it in my purse. You know how some players leave their phone sitting on the rail? I must've thought his phone was mine. I got home and hear this different ringing sound coming from my purse. I answer the phone and it's Tran. He stopped by that afternoon to pick it up." It sounds convincing to me, but all I'm getting from Hunt is dead fish.

He says, "And Jenny Mai?"

"I don't know her any better than I knew Tran."

"Then why did they feed you that jackpot?"

"I have no idea." But I think it quite strange and frightening that Blaise Hunt seems to be trying to link the jackpot scam to the robbery.

"Is there anything else you want to tell me, Peeky?"

"No. Except I think you've got a lot of nerve accusing me of such a thing."

Hunt laughs unpleasantly, then thanks me for stopping by. I am on my way out the door when he speaks again.

"Oh, Peeky?"

I look back.

"I'm afraid you're fired."

I struggle to make sense of his words. "Fired? Me?"

Hunt is smiling. I think he actually means it to be sympathetic, but it's the ugliest smile I have ever seen.

I say, "But I didn't do anything."

"Possibly true. You took the money and you didn't do any-thing."

I turn and walk silently out of Blaise Hunt's office, my face in flames.

I am in the elevator when it occurs to me that Blaise Hunt is not my boss. Did he have the right to fire me? The tidal wave of shame I felt upon hearing the words *you're fired* becomes anger. Hunt doesn't have the right to fire me. Technically, my boss is Dooley Braun, the Card Club manager. Dooley hired me. Dooley initials my performance reviews. Memos to Card Club employees always bear Dooley's loopy signature. And the sign at the en-trance reads: "Dolan F. Braun, Card Room Manager."

I get out of the elevator and head straight for Dooley's office. I walk right past Vergie's desk, ignoring her squawk of protest, and open the door. Dooley is sitting behind his desk staring into the screen of his laptop. He looks up with a muddled frown.

"Are you firing me?" I ask. I sound a little hysterical, but only because I am.

Dooley blinks at me; his eyes focus. "Hi, Peeky," he says. He smiles. Dooley once had a wide, sharklike smile that gave his opponents nightmares. These days his teeth look dull and weak. "What's going on?" he asks.

"You tell me. Am I fired?"

I am grasped from behind by four meaty, ungentle hands. Dooley's impotent bulk recedes as they pull me back out the door.

"I guess so, kid," Dooley says. "Sorry."

One hulk on each side, I am propelled through the card room toward the front door. I see the players' shocked faces staring at me. We almost run into Cisco, who is tottering out from the men's room. He looks startled, which is more expression than I have ever seen on his impassive features. I hear him say "Pee Key . . ." as we pass. Richard, working the board, stares at me uncomprehendingly. The guards walk me out the glass doors and down the shallow flight of concrete steps and release me. I can feel their eyes on my back as I walk across the parking lot to my car. I get into the car and start it with a sequence of distant and robotic motions. I drive, imagining the babble of voices in the card room weaving fresh tales to account for my banishment. They will talk about me for minutes, maybe longer, but only between hands. The cards never stop coming. Soon they will be speaking of other matters. In a month or so, someone might ask, "Whatever happened to that lady prop? What was her name?" And someone sitting across the table might say, "Her name was Peeky. She got fired. They say she was playing partners." Or copping chips. Or marking cards. Or wanted for murder in Oklahoma. Or dead of cancer. Or any of a hundred other stories they would invent to account for my sudden absence. A year from now their memory of me would be gone completely, erased by time and the cards.

I drive carefully, as if taking a driving test, doing my best to insulate myself from my feelings. When I fall apart, I want to fall apart at home.

18

FOURTEEN YEARS AGO on the Fourth of July my husband, Robert, got up in the middle of the night to take some Pepto-Bismol. Twenty minutes later he hadn't returned to bed. I found him sitting in the kitchen doubled over, his face dead white and beaded with sweat.

"Are you okay?" I asked him.

"I'm fine," he said, "except I think I got a weasel in my gut."

It was his last and least successful attempt to joke his way around life's challenges. Three hours later he was dead on the operating table. They said his appendix had burst, that he'd gone into toxic shock, that his heart had stopped, that they had tried everything to save him, that they were very, very sorry for my loss. I remember standing there in the hospital clutching Jaymie, seven years old, the only solid thing left in the universe. I remember walking out of the hospital to my car feeling like Moses without God, without his people, walking through the Red Sea alone, holding back the walls of water by sheer force of will.

That is how I feel now. I am walking through a tunnel of dark water and it is closing behind me. I park my car in my driveway and get out and walk through the tunnel, holding it back. I reach my front door. I fit the key to the lock and I step inside and set my purse on the little Mexican tile table by the door. Now what? Turn on the light? Too bright. Vouvray and ice cream? I shudder at the thought of alcohol and frozen fat. I wish I had a hole I could fall into and . . . just fall.

In a way, this is even worse than losing Robert. At least then I knew it wasn't my fault. Robert died by the hand of God. But I was fired because of who I am, what I did. And my daughter is using crack. Who is to blame for that if not her mother?

This time, the tunnel walls are slick with self-loathing and doubt.

I toe off my shoes and shuffle to the sofa and sprawl. The only light is from a streetlamp filtered through half-closed blinds. Slowly, gingerly, I begin to let the walls close in.

"Peeky?"

The sound of the voice, so close, sends an electric jolt through every part of my body. My heart thuds. I snap forward, getting my feet under me; my arms shoot forward in a protective gesture.

"It's me. Buddy."

"Jesus, Buddy." I put my hand on my chest. My heart is slam-dancing.

"Didn't mean to scare you." He is sitting in the club chair across the room, a faint stripe of streetlamp light banding his cheek.

"What are you doing here?"

"Waiting for you."

"I didn't see your car."

"I parked over on Sunset. I'm afraid they might be watching your house."

I say nothing. We are separated by ten feet of dead air. I can see part of his cheek, the corner of his mouth, and a glint of eyeball. He is sitting very still.

"Are you okay?" he asks.

"I just got fired."

"Oh . . . shit. I'm sorry."

"You should be. It's your goddamn fault."

"But you didn't—"

"Shut up, Buddy."

"Okay. Sorry."

"What do you want?"

"Just to tell you . . . I have to go away for a while. Maybe Mexico."

I get a flash: Buddy on the beach, tropical breezes, Cuban cigar, suntanned young woman fanning him with a palm frond.

Buddy says, "This thing I got involved in, I got a bad feeling about it."

"It took you till now?"

"I don't trust these guys."

"You don't trust a pack of murdering thieves? *Por qué?*"

He shifts in the chair and the stripe of light moves off his face onto his shoulder. He says, "You remember a few weeks ago I played in that holdem tournament up in Phoenix?"

"You took third place."

"I also ran into a guy name of Woody Stumpf."

"Woody *Stump*?" I hear myself say. "You've got to be kidding."

"I wish I was. You met him, you know."

"I did?"

"Last week. He was in the club checking things out. You busted him out of a fifteen-thirty game. Blew him off a winning hand, then laid a bad beat on him. He was pissed."

I think back. "Does Woody have a comb-over?"

"That's him."

"If he hadn't got his eyes stuck on my tits he might've won."

"That's Woody." Buddy laughed. "He just about shit when I told him you were my girlfriend. Anyway, Woody and I used to run together back in the day. Remember I told you about robbing that Seven-Eleven? I didn't tell you everything."

"You lied to me? I am shocked." That's a lie, of course. I am being ironic. I am unshockable. I am an ice cube; I am in stasis.

"Woody and I were working together back then. And . . . well, a man got killed." He is leaning forward now. "Up in Tempe. During a robbery."

I was wrong about being unshockable. "You killed somebody?"

"It was an accident, Peeky."

"You killed somebody robbing a Seven-Eleven?"

"We weren't just robbing C-stores, Peek."

"But . . . you went to jail for robbing a Seven-Eleven."

"That was the job I got nailed for. But Woody and me, we were doing banks. About a dozen of 'em before I got smart and gave it up."

I stare at him for a moment, then stand up and walk into the kitchen and flip on the light and pour water into a tall blue Mexican glass and stand at the sink and drink half of it. I hear Buddy follow me to the kitchen. I turn. He is standing in the doorway with his arms at his sides wearing the white linen shirt I bought him last Christmas. The shirt looks great but he looks awful—pale, unshaven, baggy-eyed.

"We were in a Bank One in Tempe," he says. "Easy in, easy out. Woody was working the tellers and I was at the door, making sure nobody left and nobody was coming. This guy, this customer standing in line, I notice he's standing sort of funny, holding his arm down by his side. Something about him bugs me. So I point my gun at him and tell him to get down on the floor, and his hand comes up, and he's got a gun." Buddy shakes his head. "Why did he do that?"

"So you shot him," I say.

"What else could I do?"

"That could've been Robert standing in line at the bank."

"Your husband? I thought he died from appendicitis!"

"It *could* have been him."

Buddy squeezes his eyes closed and turns his head away. He holds the pose for a few seconds, then gives his head a violent shake, throwing off the memory.

"Anyway, we got the hell out of there. Thirty-six hundred bucks. Later I read in the paper that the guy died. Turns out he was an off-duty security guard, trying to be a hero." He shrugs wearily. "I been seeing his eyes ever since. I was probably the last guy on earth to see those eyes when there was still something in them."

Buddy searches my face. I give him nada.

"That was the last time," he says. "The Seven-Eleven thing was a year old at that time, but I got nailed for it a few weeks later because the clerk, the guy I'd robbed, spotted me one day, followed me back to my apartment, and set the cops on me. They had some nice surveillance camera shots of me, dumb-ass barefaced kid with a gun, and nailed me for the C-store job. But they never put any of the bank jobs on me, 'cause Woody and me always wore disguises."

"Dressed as clowns?"

"We didn't do the clown thing. I had a fake beard and brown contacts. Woody liked to put on these plastic snaggleteeth, made him look like Austin Powers."

Some small part of me wants to laugh, but most of me wants none of this to be true. Buddy is still standing with his arms hanging limp at his sides, filling the doorway yet somehow looking small and beaten. I can't imagine him robbing a bank.

"I quit after that. But Woody, he thought he was Jesse James. Still does."

"You didn't quit, Buddy. You just robbed a goddamn casino." I am holding the water glass with both hands, massaging its smooth, hard surface.

"I had to, Peek. Woody had this deal set up and he needed help. He threatened to turn me for killing the guy up in Tempe if I said no. He kept the gun I used—he was supposed to dump it, but he stashed it. With my fingerprints on it. Woody's the kind of guy who'd do that."

"He'd be turning himself in, too."

"Woody's already got a murder rap hanging over him. You can find his picture in the post office. He killed a guy a few weeks later during another bank job. He gets arrested now, he's screwed either way. Me, I've been living clean close to twenty years. I've got you, I got my half acre, my Airstream, I got friends, I got a few bucks put away. I got a life here—or at least I did. I'm not going to jail, Peek."

"Am I supposed to feel sorry for you?"

"I just don't want you to hate me."

I wish I could. "People are dead," I say.

"I know that. But I'm still not going to jail, Peek. Even if I deserve it."

He is standing there in the doorway, arms limp. I wish he would cross them, or lean against the doorjamb, or put his hands in his pockets. The feelings I have roiling around inside me coalesce into something I recognize, dimly, as anger. I want to hurl myself at him, but my hands are locked on the water glass. I turn to drop the glass in the sink but instead I throw the glass at him with all my strength. It shatters on his chest; water and shards of blue glass rain onto the tiles. Buddy doesn't move. He doesn't even seem surprised.

He says, as if nothing happened, "I'm supposed to meet Woody tonight to split up the money."

"Don't go then."

"I have to. If I don't show up, he'll come looking for me. Believe me, you do not want a guy like Woody looking for you."

"Fine." I hear air whistling through my nostrils.

"After that, like I said, it's probably gonna be Mexico for a while. Maybe Costa Rica."

"The farther the better." I am so angry I don't care if he goes to Timbuktu, wherever that is.

A look of pain crosses his face. "I'm really sorry about all this, Peek. I'm sorry about your job, I'm sorry about everything."

I nod, unable to offer him—or myself—more comfort than that.

"Look . . . you want to come?"

"What?"

"I don't mean right now. I mean, we could meet up. After things cool down."

"You're joking."

"Money's got no smell, Peek. We could live real good south of the border. There's even a poker scene down in Costa Rica."

"Get the fuck out, Buddy."

He stands breathing loudly though his nose for a few seconds, then crosses the kitchen and steps out the back door. I wait until I hear the alley gate slam shut, then let the walls of water close upon me.

BEING ALONE AT NIGHT is not a bad thing. The house is quieter, the sounds and smells are all my own, the bed is bigger, and I have only myself to care for. If you have friends and family, someone you can call, it is not so bad. But who do I have? Jaymie, my missing drug addict daughter. Buddy, my outlaw boyfriend. *Ex*-boyfriend. My poker friends. Only now the casino is off limits. I wonder how many of them will have time for me now.

I am wrung out. My eyes are a mess, swollen and raw. My nose is tired of running and my stomach hurts and my chest is sore. What doesn't hurt? My legs. My legs have come though all this just fine. I've always had good legs.

I could call my brother up in Flagstaff, but we don't get along so good. He's joined some holy roller church up there and thinks I'm Satan's spawn, working for the heathens, gambling for a living. I hardly know him anymore. I can't imagine what sort of conversation we might have if I told him my boyfriend was an armed robber. Nancy, my accomplice in orchid mass murder, would be sympathetic, but I don't think I could stand the contrast between her perfect Midwestern family life and my disastrous existence.

I don't need anybody, I decide.

I try that for about thirty seconds, then pick up the phone and call Eduardo. The phone rings a dozen times. Why doesn't he have an answering machine? I slap the receiver down and look at the clock. It's not even eleven. How many hours till daylight?

Too many. Far too many.

What does a forty-something woman do at eleven p.m. on a Saturday night when her life is falling apart? I turn on my computer and log on to a poker site. I've got a couple thousand in my online account, so I sit in on a $15–30 game and play a few rounds. As usual, I quickly become bored and frustrated. I'm a people player. The virtual experience doesn't do it for me. I log off and stare at the blank screen. I could find a live game at the Desert Diamond or at Casino del Sol. But at either of those places I'm certain to run into someone I know. I want to be with people, but I don't want to talk to anybody.

I take ten minutes to make myself beautiful. The results are not all I had hoped for—my eyes are still a mess—but what the hell. I hop into my car and drive.

The Gila River Casino is located ninety miles northwest of Tucson and twenty miles south of Phoenix. Poker players from both cities are drawn to Gila by the cash-added tournaments, assorted perks, and the fact that many of them have been eighty-sixed by all the more conveniently located casinos. Consequently, the players at Gila have a reputation for being both cheap and irascible. I consider myself to be neither, although my new status as an angry and unemployed prop and mother of a crackhead might eventually get me there.

The parking lot is about half full. I drive around awhile, searching for the perfect slot. I am not superstitious, but I do take my parking seriously. Where I park affects how I will do at the table. It really does. No, really.

Okay, maybe I'm a little superstitious. More likely, I'm a practical self-actualizer. Maybe by parking with care I am doing something to put myself in a mental state conducive to playing cards well. So I thread the rows until I see a spot that has that certain something, and I wheel my Miata into place. It feels right. I check myself in the rearview mirror. My eyes still need work. I open my purse to get at my makeup kit, then change my mind and slide a pair of oversize shades onto my face. Much better. Go get 'em, girl.

There are only seven games going in the card room: two $3–6 holdem, one Omaha game, one $15–30 holdem, and three little stud games. There are two open seats at the $15–30 table, so I slide in, buy $500 in chips, and pay the big blind.

I don't usually wear sunglasses at the table. It's not my style. But the shades do offer certain advantages, the greatest one being that you can study the other players openly.

The player to my left is a three-hundred-pound black man wearing several pounds of jewelry including a dozen gold and silver rings on his fingers, at least as many bracelets, and a gold necklace made of links as big around as my pinky. I peg him for an overly aggressive player, and he fires a raise into the pot to prove it. Four of the other players call, which tells me they don't respect his raise. I look at my cards. Eight, nine of spades. It will cost me $15 to see the flop, and there is $165 already in the pot. I like the price the pot is laying me, so I call.

The flop comes ace-king-trey. I check, the bangled guy tosses out a bet and gets a couple callers. I fold. The turn brings a rag, a nothing card. The bangled guy bets again and is called by a skinny, professorial-looking guy wearing a maroon ASU windbreaker. I've seen him before. His name is Roddy. He plays the poker tournaments down at the Santa Cruz and I've never seen him turn over a hand that wasn't the nuts or close to it. The river brings a jack, and the bangled guy fires again. Roddy looks at the pot, looks at his cards, shrugs, and says, "I raise, Moaf."

The bangled guy, Moaf, frowns and says, "You got to be kidding me." He lifts the corners of his cards and scowls. "What you got, man?"

Roddy, not an expressive man to begin with, remains opaque. Of course, I now know exactly what he has. It seems obvious, but

Moaf squirms in his chair, bracelets jangling, then says, "Okay, I pay you off," and tosses six chips into the pot.

Roddy turns up an ace-jack of diamonds—exactly what I expected. Moaf slams his palm down on the table, hard, and throws his pocket queens faceup into the muck.

"Easy, Moaf," says the dealer.

Moaf looks away. "Sorry, man," he says, drumming thick fingers on the felt.

Non-poker players are often astonished by the way a good player can read another player's hand. There's nothing magic about it. Reading hands is a matter of logic, deduction, personalities, and betting patterns.

I knew what Roddy had because I'd played with him before, and because of the way he bet his hand. Anything less than an ace-jack suited, he would have folded on the flop, or would not have been in the hand at all. A better hand, he would have raised earlier. Okay, maybe he could have had ace-queen, but with two of the queens tied up in Moaf's hand, it just wasn't that likely. Besides, he wouldn't have raised on the river if the jack hadn't helped him. No one at the table was surprised by Roddy's ace-jack. Except Moaf.

Seconds later we are looking at a new deal and the hand is forgotten by all, except Moaf, who continues to sulk for the next several hands.

The other players at the table are typical $15–30 players. I've seen a couple of them here or there but most I don't know. I am one of them. I settle in, feeling contentedly anonymous behind my shades.

In the back of my mind I note that I haven't thought about Jaymie since I sat down. I check my cell phone to make sure it's on. No messages. I bury it in my purse and sink back into the game.

There is a feeling that sometimes comes over me at the card table. It is as if I am underwater. The air is thick, and people move slowly, and the cards seem to float through the air. It is a good and comfortable place to be. The water is warm and familiar. I let probability wash over me, I let time flow through me, I bend and twist with the currents, watching, feeding.

It is almost noon when I pull into my driveway. The nice underwater feeling is long gone. My shoulders ache and my eyes are burning. I am home again but nothing has changed. Or has it? I am still jobless, but maybe Eduardo has found Jaymie. Maybe other good things have happened. It's possible.

I pick up the Sunday paper from the front step and let myself into the house. Buddy is not sitting in the living room waiting for me. I go to the kitchen. Jaymie is not eating the last of my Cherry Garcia. Alone again.

I've been up for twenty-four hours, but I'm too jazzed from the drive to sleep. I pour myself a glass of wine and sit down at the kitchen table. I think about the $460 I won up at Gila. The good feeling usually produced by won money fails to appear. I look at the newspaper. My eyes jump from headline to headline. "Campers Blamed for Chiracahua Blaze." "Crosswalk Fatalities Double." "Two Dead in Santa Cruz Shootout." "Nogales Tunnel Collapse Kills Four."

I sip my wine and turn to the crossword puzzle. One across, four letters: player of old tunes. HIFI. One down, six letters: former mermaid. HANNAH. Thirteen across, four letters, Elvis ___ Presley . . .

. . . oh shit.

I turn back to page one.

Two Dead in Santa Cruz Shootout

Violence erupted on the Santa Cruz Indian Reservation late Saturday night, leaving two men dead. According to tribal police, both men were wanted for questioning in the Friday-night robbery and murders at Casino Santa Cruz.

Responding to reports of gunfire, tribal police entered the small adobe home on South Pescadero Road at 10:00 p.m. and discovered the bodies.

According to neighbors, more than a dozen shots were fired. One man was seen leaving the premises.

"It sounded like a war," said one neighbor, who asked not to be identified.

The deceased have been identified as Darrin Edwin McConnell, 36, of Tucson, and Juan Allones, 44, who was renting the home. McConnell was an employee of Casino Santa Cruz.

According to an anonymous source close to the investigation, police found clown masks and costumes similar to those used in the robbery of Casino Santa Cruz. Police also recovered several weapons, an undisclosed amount of cash, and a small amount of marijuana.

Two other suspects in the casino robbery remain at large.

The Santa Cruz Indian Reservation, located 20 miles west of Tucson, is the smallest Indian reservation in Arizona.

I have to read the article twice before I am sure that Buddy's name isn't mentioned.

"Run, Buddy, run," I say.

I think I found her, Peeky."

Eduardo is standing on my front steps. His jaw is twitching. I am barely conscious; the only thing holding me together is my bathrobe.

"Is she okay?"

"Depends on what is okay."

"You want some coffee?"

"Sure."

I step aside to let him in. "You'll have to make it yourself. I have to get dressed."

I go back to my bedroom. It is three o'clock in the afternoon, which means I slept all of two and a half hours. I kick off my slippers and shrug out of the bathrobe. My body looks pale and flaccid. I should exercise more. I should join a health club. I should have raised my daughter better.

A few minutes later, hair tied back, teeth brushed, dressed in a green nylon track suit that makes me look a little like Kermit the Frog, I join Eduardo in the kitchen. He hands me a mug of coffee.

"She is staying at this place up on Redington Pass," he says.

I feel dull and disengaged, as if none of this is real. I sip my coffee. Too hot and too strong. Just what I need.

"Did you talk to her?"

"No. I talked to this guy I know, Mannie, says he saw her out there. Peeky, I think we got to go get her. I think if we both go, maybe she will listen to you."

Redington Pass, between the Santa Catalina and Rincon Mountains, is serviced by a single unpaved camelback road that leads from Tucson to the small town of Redington, twenty-five miles to the northeast. The road is mostly washboard interrupted frequently by cattle grates, washes, and rogue boulders emerging from the roadbed. I ride with my fingers white on the door handle as Eduardo's truck skitters over the uneven surface. Twenty minutes ago we were driving past art galleries, Safeways, sushi joints, and Starbucks; now we are in the high desert, driving through parched, hilly grasslands dotted with scrubby mesquite and yucca. Five miles outside the Tucson city limits and it feels like the wild west.

Eduardo's pickup truck has four-wheel drive and a good spare tire. I know this because he told me so. "Don't worry," he said, "I got four-wheel drive and a new spare." I wasn't worried till he told me that. Now I'm worried. I'm a city girl. I get a flat tire, I call AAA. Out here my cell phone won't even work.

If they ever run a highway into the area it'll be covered with condos and fake adobe houses within a decade, but for now, with the nearest freeway forty-five minutes away, the pass remains relatively undeveloped. The dirt tracks that branch off from Redington Road every half mile or so lead variously to working ranches, weekend cabins, squatter camps, meth labs, or nothing at all. Paul McCartney has a ranch out here. So do the White Power Alliance and Calvary Christian College.

We come up over a rise and nearly plow into half a dozen rangy, long-horned cattle. Eduardo stomps on the brake. We chatter to a stop on the washboard surface and wait for the cattle to amble off the roadway.

"Look for a sign says Triple T Ranch," Eduardo says. "Supposed to be on the right." The last member of the herd stops and turns its head to face the truck. It is looking right at me. Eduardo honks and revs the engine; the beast shakes its head and moves off. Eduardo puts the truck back in gear.

"Jaymie's staying at a ranch?" I imagine my daughter riding a horse, healthy and suntanned, roping cattle.

"No. We go past the Triple T sign, one half mile, then turn left onto an unmarked road. Mannie says it is a quarter mile off the road."

"How do you know this guy Mannie?"

"I grew up with him. Mannie is a nice guy, but mostly he is a fuckup." Eduardo shoots me a look. "Sorry."

"Don't worry about it."

"Is just that Mannie is, you know, a stoner. He like to get f— He like to get high, you know?"

"So is this like a crack house?"

"I don't know. Mannie, he was out there buying some kind of shit. I don't like to know, you know?"

Three cattle grates later I spot the TTT Ranch sign hanging from a gate. Eduardo resets his odometer and we keep going. A mile later we have not yet seen the promised cutoff to the left

"How reliable is this Mannie?"

"Not very. Hey, look there." Another gate on the right displays a second TTT Ranch sign. We continue on, and shortly come upon two cars parked alongside the road. One of them is Jaymie's Honda with all four wheels missing.

"Somebody grabbed her wheels. You don't want to leave a car parked out here." Eduardo points out a tire-marked track to the left heading down into a shallow, rocky arroyo. "Probably she walked in."

"Is that what we do?"

"No way." Eduardo puts his truck in fourwheel drive and eases it over the edge of the road into the arroyo. After about fifty yards of slow, steep going over a jumble of small boulders the track levels off; we follow it around the base of a hill, two tire tracks cutting through grassy meadow, then into a grove of juniper and scrub oak. We come out in a small grassy bowl about fifty yards across. Eduardo stops the truck.

On the far side of the clearing a weathered, cedar-sided mobile home is tucked in beneath a rocky embankment. A black SUV and two motorcycles are parked in front. Also in front is a chaise longue made of aluminum tubing and nylon webbing supporting a very thin, very tan, very naked young man. Actually, he is not entirely naked if you count the sunglasses and cowboy hat, which he tips back a few degrees to look at us.

We sit in the truck, engine idling. I don't know what Eduardo is thinking, but I hope he's thinking something. After a few seconds he nudges the truck forward, pulling up close behind the SUV. He rolls down his window.

"Hey," he says to the guy on the chaise.

The naked man says nothing. Now that I'm getting a better look at him, I'm thinking he's more boy than man, maybe eighteen. Possibly younger. His hair is bleached to near white, his skin tanned to a precancerous umber.

Eduardo gets out of the truck. I get out, too.

"How you doing?" Eduardo says.

The boy's right shoulder twitches, possibly a shrug.

"Nice place you got here," Eduardo says. "Nice and private."

"It ain't mine," says the naked boy.

"Jaymie around?" Eduardo asks. His voice nearly cracks with the strain of keeping a casual front, but I don't think the kid notices. Eduardo steps closer, his shadow crosses the boy's genitals. "I asked you—" Eduardo takes a step back. "Hey," he says softly, holding his hands out, palms forward. I look past him and see that the kid has something large and silver in his hand. A revolver. It looks enormous, far too big for his scrawny wrists and spidery hands.

"Easy with that," Eduardo says.

The kid isn't pointing it at us, he's just holding it and smiling.

"That's a big one," Eduardo says.

"Forty-four Mag," the kid says.

"Clint Eastwood."

The kid grins. "You see that can over there?" He gestures with the gun barrel to where an old red coffee can is balanced atop a rock about fifty feet away. "You see it?"

We both nod. The kid raises the revolver, holding it with both hands. He squints down the barrel, his mouth tight with concentration, then pulls the trigger. The sound slaps my eardrums and for an instant I am back at the casino eating carpet, only this gun is much bigger and louder and sharper-sounding.

"You missed," says Eduardo.

"Got five more," says the kid.

"But you were close."

"That don't—"

The screen door to the mobile home slams open; a tall, bearded, thick-chested, ponytailed, tattooed, red-faced man wearing greasy jeans, black laceup boots, and a leather vest storms out, fists balled.

"God damn it, Feeb. What in hell did I tell you about shootin' that—" He stops, looking at Eduardo, then at me. "Who the fuck are you?"

I step toward him. A guy like this, you never want to back up. "I'm Jaymie Montana's mother," I say.

The man frowns and tips his head. "No shit?"

"No shit," I say.

"Christ, I'd a thought you'd be this old broad."

Despite all, I get a little tingle from this dirtbag's left-handed compliment. "Is she inside?"

He shrugs and watches me through squinting blue eyes, trying to put me on a hand.

I say, "We're here to take her home."

"You sure she wants to go?" he says easily, still studying me.

Out of the corner of my eye I can see the kid, gun resting on his smooth brown belly, watching us. Eduardo, just behind and to the right of me, is radiating coiled energy. I send him a telepathic message to stay cool.

"Let's ask her," I say, stepping toward the open door. The man hesitates, then steps aside and makes a theatrical gesture, inviting me to help myself.

As I reach the open door I hear the ponytailed man say to Eduardo, "So what the fuck are you? The bodyguard?" I turn back and catch Eduardo's eye. He makes a hand motion, telling me to go on in without him. I take a breath and enter, prepared for anything: Jaymie chained to a bed; Jaymie shooting dope into her arm; Jaymie being gang-raped by a daisy chain of Hells Angels; Jaymie covered with open, oozing sores, lying unconscious in her own filth.

The smell inside is Pine-Sol and cigarettes. It takes a few seconds for my eyes to adjust. I am standing in a tiny entryway facing a print of a bald eagle flying across the face of a mountain peak, the snow, trees, and rocks on the mountain arranged to suggest the stars and stripes of the American flag. To my left is a small kitchen. The counters are clean and uncluttered, the linoleum floor has been recently waxed, and the sink is empty. On the other side of the entryway is a room with a sofa and three upholstered chairs, all facing a large-screen TV. Again, the room is neat and clean, sullied only by a bamboo bong on the tiled coffee table and a girl—blond, thin, maybe sixteen, maybe thirty—curled up in one of the chairs, reading a copy of *Vogue*—not the latest one, the one before that. She looks up at me. A trace of curiosity flickers in her eyes but fails to ignite.

"Where's Jaymie?" I ask her.

She shrugs and drops her eyes back to the magazine.

"What's your name?" I ask.

She looks up, rediscovering me. "Tracy," she says.

"What are you doing here?"

"I live here."

"This is your place?"

"Me and Max."

"Who's Max?"

"You don't know Max?"

"Is he the big guy with the ponytail?"

"That's Max," the girl says.

"Where's Jaymie?" I ask again.

Her eyes shift to the doorway at the opposite end of the room, then back to me. She rolls her shoulders and falls back into her magazine.

The doorway leads to a hallway with three doors on the right. I look into the first small room and am hit with a cloud of rotting sneakers, wet ashtray, unwashed body, and cheap cologne. A young man with a shaved head and several jailhouse tattoos is sprawled across a queen-size futon, snoring. The bed is a mess, sheets twisted and not very clean. The kid is wearing nothing but a pair of ragged jeans. I back out and close the door. The next door leads to a laundry room. The floor is covered with dirty clothes. A cadaverous young woman with stringy blond hair is sitting on the running washing machine wearing nothing but panties and a sleeveless T-shirt, painting her toenails black.

"Hey," she says, looking up. Her eyes were heavily made up maybe twenty-four hours ago; now they are shards of blue and pink set against a smear of black.

"Hi," I say.

"Waiting for my jeans," she says, flashing a smile. Her teeth are beautiful, remnants of a recently healthy past, but her gums are red and inflamed. I ask her about Jaymie.

"The Mexican girl?"

"She's not Mexican."

"Whatever." She points to the room next door.

21

JAYMIE IS SITTING ON THE EDGE of the bed wearing cargo shorts and a loose linen blouse. Her eyes widen when she first sees me, then go dead a millisecond later.

"What?" she says, affecting disinterest. Her eyes hold mine for an instant, then slide away. Her long hair is messy and dull.

"Are you all right?" I ask. She looks like she hasn't eaten in weeks—was she that thin the last time I saw her? Maybe I just didn't notice. I'm seeing her now with different eyes.

"I'm fine. What are you doing here?"

"What do you think?" I ask. On the end table I see a half-empty pack of Kools, a box of tissues, a disposable lighter, and an ashtray. Leaning against the ashtray is a blackened, bulbous glass object that I'm pretty sure is some sort of pipe.

"I don't know." She takes a cigarette from the pack. Her hands are shaking.

"When did you start smoking again?" I ask.

"I never really quit," she says. "Just around you." She lights up, inhales deeply and fires two jets of mentholated smoke out through her nostrils. It seems to calm her. "What was that bang?"

"One of your friends shooting off his gun."

She rolls her eyes. "That idiot Feeb."

"Jaymie," I say, "what are you doing out here?"

"What am I doing here? What are *you* doing here?"

"Looking for you."

"Yeah, well, you found me. Congratulations."

"What is this place?"

"A friend's."

"Some friends you got."

"They're not so bad." She finds an ingrown hair on her knee and starts picking at it with her fingernail.

"You haven't answered my question."

"What question?" She manages to draw a drop of blood.

"What you're doing here. You just disappeared. You haven't been at work in three days. You're going to lose your job."

"Some job. Ringing up tofu and bulgar." She rubs out the blood droplet with the heel of her palm, remembers that she is holding a cigarette, and takes another deep drag.

"Jaymie, is this a crack house?"

"*Crack* house?" She looks up and laughs, giving me the same incredulous look she gave me when she was sixteen years old and I mispronounced some rock star's name. "Jesus Christ, Mom, have you been watching reruns of 'Cops' again?"

You don't know how uncool it is possible to be until you've raised a teenage daughter. I thought we were through that phase. Apparently not. I point at the glass pipe on the table.

"Then what is that?"

She looks at the pipe and shrugs. "I smoke a little weed to help me sleep. I'm not a goddamn nun, y'know."

"Look at you. You're skin and bones. You look awful."

"That's what you came out here for? To tell me I look like shit?"

"I know you've been stealing money from me."

Her eyes go dead. She crosses her arms and brings the cigarette to her lips, looking past me at nothing. She takes two furious puffs on the cigarette. The ash is more than an inch long.

"I'll pay you back." The ash drops onto her lap. She doesn't notice.

"That's not why I'm here. I came to take you home."

"You wasted your time." She lifts her legs back onto the bed, leans back against the headboard, and takes another drag off the cigarette. "I'm not going anywhere."

"Yes you are," I say. My voice sounds good: solid, level, without a quaver. "Eduardo and I did not drive all the way out here to go back without you."

Her face changes. "Eddie's here?" She looks scared, and for a moment I think that she's afraid of Eduardo. "Where?"

"He's waiting outside with your friends."

"Who? Max and Feeb?" She swings her legs back onto the floor.

She's not afraid of Eduardo; she's afraid *for* him.

"Look," she says, "you got to go. Eddie, he's gonna get himself in trouble. You don't know him."

"I know him better than I used to. I know him well enough to know that he's not leaving here without you. And neither am I."

"This is bullshit," she says, brushing past me. I follow her out of the room, past the girl in the living room, and out into the afternoon sun.

Eduardo, Max, and Feeb are standing right where I left them. Jaymie walks straight toward Eduardo, shouting, "Why don't you let me alone!"

Eduardo takes a step toward her, reaching out. Jaymie stops, spikes her cigarette into the dirt in front of his feet, and crosses her arms tight across her chest. For an instant they stand frozen, then she whirls and walks quickly back toward the doublewide. Eduardo starts after her.

"No," I say, using the same forceful voice I'd used on her as a toddler. It works—on both of them. They stop moving as if I've cut the power switch.

"Get in the truck, Jaymie," I say.

She shakes her head slowly, but doesn't move. Max is smiling in a way I do not like. Eduardo is looking around, measuring his distance from Max and the naked kid with the gun.

"Take it easy, Eduardo," I say.

"Yeah," says Max. "Take it easy, Ed-WAHR-do."

I say, "Jaymie. Get in the truck."

"You should just go, Mom."

"If you don't get in that truck right now, I'm going to pick you up and carry you." I haven't used that threat since she was seven.

Her shoulders slump. To my amazement, she starts walking toward Eduardo's truck.

Max, watching her, says, "Hey, Feeb, you think you could hit that old truck from where you're sittin'?"

"Sure."

"Prove it."

Feeb raises the gun, aiming at Eduardo's truck. Jaymie is halfway there, only a few degrees outside his line of fire. I feel a shout rising from my throat but Eduardo is closer, and he's already moving. He launches himself toward Feeb but is intercepted by Max, who plants one of his black laceup boots hard in Eduardo's midsection. Eduardo goes down, rolling into and over the kid on the chaise. The gun goes off; Max aims another kick at Eduardo, loses his balance, and falls into the tangle of bodies and nylon webbing. I look at Jaymie, who is watching, openmouthed, apparently uninjured.

Time slows. This is nothing like the robbery at the Card Club. Back then I was a mouse, surviving by making myself small and doing nothing. This is different. I don't have time to be afraid. Several things are happening: Eduardo, tangled in the twisted remains of the chaise, is on the ground trading punches with Max. Feeb is staggering to his feet, excited and scared, the big revolver heavy in his right hand. Jaymie is making a high-pitched sound, almost a squeal. And I am in motion: one, two, three strides, like wading through chest-high water. Feeb's arm is coming up with the gun, aiming it toward Eduardo and Max, looking for a clear shot. I dive, grabbing for his right arm. I miss the arm but my shoulder hammers into his midsection. Air explodes from his lungs and for one disassociated moment I am grateful for my extra twenty pounds. He goes down and I roll over him, groping for the gun. I pin his wrist to the ground and yank the revolver from his limp grasp. All he's thinking about right now is oxygen.

Max and Eduardo are still going at it. Jaymie is screaming at them to stop. I point the gun in the air one-handed and pull the trigger. The kick is nothing like the genteel slap of my little nine millimeter; it nearly dislocates my shoulder, my right wrist goes numb, and everything changes. Jaymie's scream evaporates, replaced by the ringing in my ears. Max and Eduardo fly apart and scramble to their feet, both of them bleeding from the nose. The skeleton of the ruined chaise is still attached to Eduardo's left leg.

I point the gun at Max's belt buckle. This time I'm holding it with both hands, the way I was taught.

He holds up his palms and says, "Heeey . . . Jaymie's mama! You don't want to do that!"

Look out everybody. Crazy old broad with a gun. I let the gun barrel drop a few degrees and pull the trigger, blowing a divot in the ground between his boots. *Knows how to shoot.*

"On your knees or die," I say.

Max drops to his knees, and locks his hands behind his head. He knows the routine; no surprise there—practice makes perfect.

I swing the gun on the naked boy, who is on his feet now, his unimpressive penis attempting to withdraw entirely into his body.

"You, too."

He follows Max's example.

Eduardo shakes the chaise off his leg and limps toward Max.

"Stay where you are, Eduardo," I say, my voice coming from deep inside my chest. I don't want him between me and Max. Right now I'm in control of the situation. I want it to stay that way. I move to the left, getting Max and Feeb lined up so I can cover both of them. Max's face follows me like a radar dish.

"You some kind of lady cop?" he asks.

"Something like that," I say. I tell Eduardo to get Jaymie in the truck. He doesn't like that. He wants to kick the shit out of Max, and he can hardly bear to take orders from a woman, especially in front of another man.

Max notices this. "Better do what she says, Ed-WAHR-do," he says, hoping to provoke Eduardo to go for him. He is thinking that a little scuffle might alter the balance of power. Eduardo looks as if he might go for it.

I move closer to Max and cock the hammer with a very satisfying and audible click.

"I don't mind shooting you," I say.

"Don't!" Max says.

I catch Eduardo's eye and wink at him. The wink takes him by surprise, and I see a bit of tension drain off his shoulders. I jerk my head toward Jaymie, who is frozen, sagging, and confused. Eduardo follows my look, licks his lips, and walks over to her. Amazing what a well-timed wink can do to a man.

I return my attention to Max, who is watching me warily.

"You got what you come for?" he says.

I move as close to him as I dare, which is about eight feet. I've got the gun, but Max is big and fast. I am taking no more chances with him.

"My daughter is off limits," I say. "You understand? I don't want her back here. Not ever."

"Why tell me? Tell her."

"I'm telling you. If I find out she's been back here, I'll aim higher. You understand what I'm saying?"

"Yeah. You're threatening to blow my dick off."

"Actually I was thinking I'd kill you."

"What am I supposed to do if she just shows up?"

"You better hope she doesn't. You so much as take a phone call from her, you'll be hearing from me."

Max tries a smile. "I can't answer my phone now?"

"You got caller I.D.?"

He nods.

"Use it."

"Okay, Jaymie's mom, whatever you say. Anything else?"

"Yeah, one more thing. What do I have to do for you to take me seriously?"

"You got the gun, Mama. How can I not take you serious?" He grins, thinking he knows something about me.

He's wrong. He doesn't know how close I am. No Arizona jury would convict me for shooting my daughter's drug dealer. On the other hand, I never killed anybody. Maybe I'll shoot him just a little. Wound him. Show him I'm serious. I look over his prone body. Shoot his hand? Too creepy. A leg shot? Problem with that is that a .44 Magnum is so powerful that any wound near a major artery might be fatal. Best just to shoot him in the foot. He'll lose some toes, but he'll probably survive. I sight along the barrel.

"Hey . . ." Max says. *"Hey!"*

"What?" I ask, lining up the sights with his boot. With only two shots left in the cylinder I can't afford to miss.

"What are you doing? Are you crazy? Quit *pointing* that thing at me!"

I lower the gun slightly and look at him. His forehead is shiny with sweat and his pupils are huge.

"Are you trying to say something?" I ask.

"Look, I don't want any part of your daughter. Not now, not ever, okay? And if she ever does call me, I'll make sure she knows that. Seriously. I want nothin' to do with her. Or you."

"You wouldn't lie to me now, would you, Max?"

He shakes his head hard. "Swear to God. I never want to see either of you again."

This time I believe him.

Eduardo drives slowly through the scrub oak and up the arroyo, blood drying on his upper lip, his jaw pulsing. Jaymie, stiff as a Gumby doll, sits between us staring through the windshield. I am holding the gun between my legs and thinking about what just happened.

In poker, bluffing is way overrated. You don't make money by bluffing. Most players do it too often and at the wrong times. But even those whose sense of frequency and timing is impeccable are often terrible bluffers, because they don't know the secret of the successful bluff, which is, quite simply, to not be bluffing. You fire one barrel—push out a stack of chips with some sort of garbage hand—you've got to be willing to follow it up with another bet. That's what does it. It's what you're *willing* to do that scares your opponent. If you don't believe in yourself, how can you expect anybody else to believe you?

That was what made an impression on Max. I would have shot him. I almost did.

If you're not crazy enough to drop the bomb, what's the point in having it?

22

B Y THE TIME WE PULL into my driveway the sun has dropped behind the Tucson Mountains. The neighborhood has taken on a flat, shadowless look. I climb out of the truck painfully, bent like an old lady, feeling bruised in all my muscles. I can't imagine how Eduardo must feel. Jaymie follows me out, looking as numb as I wish I felt. Eduardo stays in the cab, looking at us, waiting for an invitation.

"You want to come in?" I say.

He shrugs, and I realize that he was hoping Jaymie might want to go home with him.

"Come on in," I say. "Wash your face."

"Hey," Jaymie says. She is standing at the edge of the driveway looking toward the house.

"Hey what?" I ask.

She says, "You always leave your front door standing wide open?"

I have never been raped, thank God, so I can only try to imagine how it must feel to be so violated, but it must be something akin to this: my home upended, befouled, vandalized, destroyed. Leather sofa cushions slit, handfuls of batting pulled out, shelves swept clean, their contents broken and scattered, tables and chairs upended. I hear Eduardo behind me, saying something, then rushing past me, checking the kitchen, then the bedrooms. They've knocked everything off the mantel. I am paralyzed, staring at a pile of gray, chunky ashes on the hearth amid the shards of Robert's urn.

Eduardo touches my shoulder.

"They're gone, Peeky." He has the phone in his hand. "I'll call the police."

There is a great hollowness inside me, slowly filling with something vile. I move through the remains of my home, into my bedroom—mattress slashed and gutted, drawers flung, contents of my closet strewn across the floor. My eyes skitter across the wreckage and land on a shoe box, Nine West, empty. I stand staring at it, blinking. Forty thousand dollars, gone. The loss of the money doesn't hit me as hard as the violation.

I move like a zombie down the hall and into the kitchen, past the looted cupboards, stepping on broken plates and emptied boxes. The saguaro cookie jar has lost an arm. Eduardo is talking into the phone. I stand paralyzed and hollow, hearing his low voice but not understanding what he is saying. He hangs up and says something to me.

"What?" I say.

"Are you okay?"

"No."

He doesn't know what to do. I turn away and go back to my bedroom.

My jewelry box is empty, its contents scattered on the floor. They didn't take my jewelry? I am insulted. My laptop has been knocked off my desk. I pick it up, plug it in, and hit the start button. No more online poker for me. Then I remember the guns. Robert's old service revolver, and the nine-millimeter LadySmith he gave me for my thirtieth birthday, the last present he ever gave me. The drawer of my bedside table is hanging open. I kick through the wreckage and find Robert's .38 tangled in a pile of underwear, rejected by the burglars. I look a little longer and finally conclude that they took my LadySmith. I walk back to the kitchen, holding the .38 in my hand.

Eduardo is standing at the kitchen sink staring out the window at a pair of hummingbirds feeding.

"The police are coming, Peeky."

"Good."

"Is anything missing?"

"Everything. My money. My gun."

"Your gun is in your hand," he says.

"This is Robert's gun. Mine they took."

"Oh." He frowns. "How much money?"

"A lot."

"You know who did this?"

I shake my head. Maybe the hummingbirds know. The hollowness is less acute now, the space filling quickly with something I now recognize as anger. I take a deep breath. What good is anger with no one to direct it at? I have no idea who these people are, or what they wanted from me. Maybe it was some of Jaymie's junkie friends . . . no, they would not have left behind the TV, the stereo, the jewelry. Or maybe they would, once they found the forty grand. Another idea intrudes. Could it be something to do with Buddy?

My thoughts thud. Buddy. My card player instincts start buzzing. Something to do with Buddy. But what? Buddy wouldn't tear up my house. Maybe it was his friend Woody. Maybe Woody thought Buddy had stashed his share of the loot here.

Or maybe it was a random break-in. A couple of kids getting lucky with a Nine West shoe box.

"Peeky?" Eduardo's voice. "Maybe we should wait outside."

I follow him through the house, my feet dragging through the remains of my life, groping with fuzzy, murderous thoughts, but I can't hang on to them. I sit down on the front step, more confused than ever.

"Peeky?" Something in his voice snaps me to attention.

"Peeky . . . where's Jaymie?" Eduardo is looking at the empty driveway where he had parked his truck.

23

I WAKE UP ON A TWENTY-YEAR-OLD sofa bed that I once owned, dreams of being interrogated by hooded, smiling monks fresh in my mind. I am conscious now, but the monks are still pressing the Iron Bar of Agony into my spine.

I gave the sofa bed to Jaymie three years ago when she moved into her first apartment. The fact that I am suffering on it now means that I am in the spare room at Eduardo and Jaymie's rented town house on Harrison Road, where the sofa bed has been employed for the past year in its less painful sofa configuration, for watching television. I open my eyes and slowly extract my body from the rack. The monks fade, still grinning beneath their dark hoods.

Eduardo is in the kitchen making coffee. His face alone is enough to wake me up. He has bruises and cuts in every stage of healing, from angry red to deep purple to bilious yellow. Three fist-fights in one week does not flatter a man.

He pours me a mug of coffee. His knuckles are cut and bruised, too.

"You sleep okay?" I ask.

"Not much."

"You think she went back to Max's?"

He shakes his head. "I don't know. Maybe I go look."

I notice the .44 revolver I took from Feeb sitting on the

counter next to a box of shells. I don't much like that Eduardo took the trouble to go out and buy ammo.

"I don't want you going out there alone, Eduardo." I add milk and a couple teaspoons of sugar to my coffee. Usually I drink it black, but today I need a little sweetness and comfort.

"Maybe I go with some friends."

I sip my coffee, thinking that the last thing Eduardo needs is to have his face pounded again. Or to get himself shot.

"We should just call the police," I say.

"And tell them what? My wife left me? What they gonna do?"

"We could ask them to drive out there, knock on the door."

"Tucson cops, they don't go that far out. We would have to call Pima County, and they would ask, 'Is she adult? Is she prisoner?' No. They would do nothing. I go with some friends. I got a friend with a wrecker—even if she is not there, we get her car." He tips his head toward the gun on the counter. "Maybe I give that kid his gun back."

"Maybe get yourself killed."

"I don't think so."

"And what if you find her, then what? We can't hold her prisoner. She needs to be in a drug treatment program. Before we go chase her down again, we need a plan. Where do we take her? How do we convince her to go? If we just go grab her again, she'll run away the first chance she gets. We have to get on the phone and find out what our options are. See what sort of help is available." I am impressed by my own clearheadedness. I think it's a result of some primeval motherhood gene: when your child is in danger, you can't afford to fall to pieces. That comes later.

Eduardo is trying to figure out how to sip his coffee, looking for a part of his mouth that isn't too sensitive. After a few wincing efforts, he sets the cup on the counter to let it cool.

"So who do we call?" he asks.

I open my purse and take out the "Want to Quit?" brochure I picked up at the casino.

As we drive south on Alvernon in my Miata, it occurs to me that in the past eighteen hours I have hardly thought at all about Buddy, or the casino robbery, or being fired. Now Jaymie's problems and my own burglary have made all that other stuff seem unimportant. Just about every situation has its advantages, I suppose.

Eduardo, looking cramped and uncomfortable in the passenger seat, asks, "You ever put the top down?"

"The day I bought it. It messed up my hair."

"You bought a convertible and you never put the top down?"

"Everybody makes mistakes."

Addiction Services Counselors is in a long, low, block building several hundred yards south of Old Vail Road. At sunrise, it would be literally in the shadow of the Arizona State Prison. I wonder whether they have some arrangement with the Department of Corrections, or if it's a psychological ploy, or simply a matter of cheap land having been available. Probably a little of each.

We are greeted by a long-haired, tattooed young man who, but for his cheerful smile and healthy appearance, would have fit right in with Max and his bunch out on Redington Pass. He ushers us back to Teresa Alvarez's office.

Alvarez looks much as I had pictured her during our phone conversation: attractive, about my age, Mexican or Native American, long black hair, full figure, and a guarded smile. She is wearing a U of A sweatshirt and blue jeans. We sit in her office and I tell her about Jaymie. She has heard it before, but has the good manners to hear me out, sitting forward in her chair with her hands clasped as if in prayer. I talk for a long time, occasionally interrupted by clarifications or amplifications from Eduardo. When we finally run out of things to say, Alvarez unclasps her hands.

"Do you feel that Jaymie is at a point where she is willing to accept help?"

"Yes," I say.

Eduardo says, "Not even close."

Teresa Alvarez smiles and waits. After a few seconds I incline my head toward Eduardo and say, "He's probably right."

"So she thinks she's handling it."

I nod.

"In that case, we have two choices," Teresa says. "We can perform an intervention. A group of family and friends, those closest to her, and a facilitator, which we can provide, will sit down with her and convince her to enter a treatment program . . ." She explains how the intervention works, the costs involved in a treatment—I am stunned by the numbers—and so forth. It sounds good. It's decisive, it's proactive, it's *something*. I am sitting forward in my chair, an eager student.

"But I have to tell you," she says. "If Jaymie doesn't really want to get off drugs, her chances of success are poor."

"How poor?" I ask.

"Everyone is different."

"Give me the odds."

"If she goes into treatment under protest, I'd say less than one in ten. With crack or meth, maybe worse."

I sit back in my chair, stunned. "Twenty-six thousand dollars for what amounts to a gutshot draw?" I say.

Alvarez's face arranges itself into an expression both shocked and amused. She doesn't say anything for a few seconds, then says to me, "We have a program for gamblers, too."

"I don't gamble," I snap.

At that, Teresa Alvarez starts laughing.

"What's so funny?"

"You sound like my father. I suppose you're a poker player?"

"That's right."

"You usually win?"

I nod.

"Good for you. Anyway, what I said about your daughter is the simple truth. Back in the eighties, interventions were the next big thing in treating addictions, but they don't work as well as we'd hoped. The addict has to want help. If you brainwash them into it, your chances of success are small. It is, as you say, an inside straight draw at best."

"You said we have two choices."

"Yes. The other one is to wait."

"Wait for what?"

"Wait for her to bottom out. And no, I don't know where her bottom is. For some people it's running out of money. For some it's losing friends, or family. Or waking up in a strange bed not know-ing how you got there. Everybody's different. When I checked my-self into a program twelve years ago, my moment of truth was looking at myself in the mirror and noticing that I was missing one of my front teeth. Had no idea where or when I lost it." She looks away. "Most people, it's about losing control—or losing the *illusion* of control. It's that moment when they realize they can't fix them-selves."

"Some people, it's when they die," I say.

She nods. "Some people."

"I don't think I can wait that long."

"Most can't."

I drive mechanically, wishing for something to happen that I can respond to directly: a flat tire, a traffic accident, a heart attack. Eduardo is sitting with one foot on the dash and his bruised chin buried in his chest. His eyes are dark and wet, his whiskered jaw is pulsating.

"So now we got to pick a place for her to go," he says.

"Yeah. If we can come up with the money. I don't suppose her insurance would cover it?"

"What insurance?"

Of course. A part-time co-op cashier wouldn't have a health plan. The same goes for former casino employees, I realize. One more thing to worry about.

"The money's not important," I say, wondering if I really be-lieve that. Twenty-six thousand dollars. How long would it take me to win that much at the poker table? I could drive up to Vegas and prey on the tourists. Three or four weeks of $30–60 holdem might do it. If I played flawlessly. If the cards fell my way.

Or I might bust out the first night. I have only eighteen hun-dred dollars in my purse and about five hundred in my checking account—not much of a bankroll.

"I can get the money," I say, as if saying it out loud might make it be true.

Eduardo looks at me.

"She's my daughter," I say.

24

W HEN EDUARDO TOLD ME he could borrow a wrecker
from his job, I envisioned the reincarnation of Emi-
liano Zapata astride an engine of destruction, something like a domestic version of a military tank. But it turns out a
"wrecker" is just a truck that will carry a car. It comes equipped
with Marco—a scrawny little guy with "Sixth Avenue Motors" em-
broidered across the back of his greasy coveralls—and a nearly
spherical young man they call Cheeps. Standing in the shadow of
the wrecker, Eduardo explains the situation to them. At least that's
what I think he's doing. It's all happening in rapid-fire *español*. I'm
standing on the outskirts, picking up a word here and there. I
think I'm getting the drift. They're going to drive out to Redington
Pass, load up Jaymie's car, then walk in through the arroyo and "extract" Jaymie. "Extract" is Eduardo's word. I think he's been watching too many movies.

"I'm going with you," I say.

"There's no room in the truck."

"I'll follow you."

"No," he says. "It is too dangerous."

"That's not your problem. It's my choice."

"No." He makes a squirming motion with his shoulders. I've
seen that before. He is uncomfortable, but he's made his stand.
"Peeky, we might have to go fast, you know? I don't . . . ah . . . you

might, you know . . . ah, crap. I don't want to have to worry about you, too, you know?"

That sets me off. "Were you worrying about me yesterday when you were getting your ass kicked?"

"Yes," he says, getting red in the face. "And I was not getting my ass kicked. I had him."

"You had nothing. If I hadn't been there that kid would've blown a hole in you."

"If I hadn't been all worried about you, I wouldn'ta got myself in that position in the first place."

That makes no sense whatsoever. I'm about to tell him so, but I see a glint of desperation in his eyes. He doesn't want me busting his *cojones* in front of his friends. I pause, take a breath, and force myself to calm. These Latin egos are so damn fragile, I don't know how their women keep them from shattering daily.

"Okay," I say, backing down. "But you stay in touch. If you find her, call me on my cell and I'll call Teresa Alvarez to set up the intervention. We'll meet back here."

"Okay," he says, looking relieved.

The three pile into the wrecker and drive off, leaving behind a cloud of blue smoke.

As I open the front door a small, optimistic part of me is hoping that a crew of Brownies showed up to clean while I was staying with Eduardo. The fantasy lasts for a few milliseconds, then dies at the sight of my living room. The sheer awfulness of it hits me all over again, and I sag at the knees. I back out and close the door and sit on the steps to breathe.

As I am searching for the courage to go back inside, I notice Mandy Krause, the octogenarian nut job who lives across the street, staring out at me from her window. She spends hours of every day sitting there working her crossword puzzle books and keeping a rheumy eye on things.

I cross the street and knock on her screen door, one of those high-test perforated steel jobs that are so popular in the Southwest. It takes a good minute and a half for the inside door to open. I see Mandy's shadow behind the screen.

"Yes?"

"Mandy, it's me, Peeky. From across the street."

"Peeky! How are you, dear?" She undoes some latches, then pushes the screen door open. Mandy is wearing her usual outfit: a lilac-colored housedress with a rosary made from pink glass beads hanging around her scrawny neck. The dress displays several prominent stains—it looks like tea, raspberry jam, and tomato sauce. Her cloud of white hair has drifted almost entirely to the left side of her head. The house exudes a distinctive odor—a potpourri of roses and apples layered over something not so nice. Mandy does not invite me in, to my considerable relief.

"I'm fine," I say.

"I was worried, dear. I saw the police visiting you last night."

"Yes. Someone broke into my house."

"Oh dear!" She lets go of the screen door and claps a hand to her mouth. I grab the door to keep it from closing.

"I'm sure the police will catch them soon," I say quickly, not wanting to alarm her any more than is necessary.

"Whatever is this world coming to?" Her eyes fog over and her lips part. "It is all foretold, you know."

"Yes, I'm sure you're right."

"We are being punished for our sins." By *we* she means *me*.

"Mandy, did you see anyone at my house yesterday afternoon? Did you happen to notice anyone?"

"I mind my own business, dear."

"I know that, Mandy. I just thought maybe you happened to glance out the window and see something."

"I don't know . . . when did you say?"

"Yesterday. It's important, Mandy."

"Let me think," she says, touching the side of her chin with her finger, enjoying the attention. "There was a man in a pickup truck.

I have seen *him* several times." She lowers her voice. "A *Mexican* man."

"That would be my son-in-law," I say.

"I've also seen a man in a white car, many times." She gives me a slit-eyed look. "All night, he stays."

"Yesterday, Mandy. Between three-thirty and six."

She taps her chin. "Well . . . there was a blue car. Or maybe it was gray. It was parked in front of your house for some time. Yesterday was Sunday, you know. My show was on then, so I really didn't pay much attention. You have so many visitors!"

"Did you see who was driving it?"

"No, dear."

"Do you know what kind of car it was?"

"It was quite large, as I recall. Oh! I nearly forgot. I have a *present* for you!" She shuffles off, leaving me in the doorway.

A minute later she returns with several brochures clutched in her hand.

"These are for you, dear." She shuffles through the brochures, then hands me one titled "Chastity: A Liberating and Joyful Virtue." "This one is quite good." She picks out another—"My Lord; My Lover: A Positive Approach to Abstinence." "Oh yes. This one is a bit racy, dear. I'm sure you'll enjoy it." The third brochure shows Jesus Christ standing on a hilltop preaching to a group of kneeling women. It is titled "Jesus and Sex."

"Um . . . thank you, Mandy."

"You're welcome, dear. We are all of us God's creatures."

I head back across the street determined to attack the mess in my house dispassionately and systematically. There are strategies for dealing with this sort of thing. The World Trade Center, now there was a mess, but they took it one step at a time and slowly cleaned it up. That's what I have to do. Take it one room, one section of one room, one square foot at a time. At least I won't find any corpses. I hope. I steel myself and head back into the house. I am a cleaning machine: efficient, heartless, unstoppable.

The first thing I do is throw away Mandy's brochures, then head for the bedroom, ground zero. My bed is destroyed, the pillows slashed and emptied, dresser drawers thrown and shattered, clothing scattered and trampled. My jewelry—rings, earrings, and bracelets—is strewn across the room. Is there anything I want to keep?

I start stuffing things in garbage bags—slashed pillows, sheets, clothing, makeup, anything that might have been touched goes in the bag. I throw away handfuls of costume jewelry, keeping only the few things Robert gave me, when a pair of gold hoop earrings destroys my momentum.

Did Robert give them to me, or did I buy them for myself?

I can't remember. I squeeze my mind for the memory, trying to force it out, but I draw a blank. All I know is that I've had the earrings for a long time. Too long. I toss them in the garbage bag, then change my mind and dig them out. They might be worth fifty or a hundred bucks. Money that could go toward Jaymie's treatment. I could have a yard sale, sell everything. What would it all go for? A couple thousand? What am I worth on the open market?

It hits me then how this drug thing spreads itself from one person to another like an infection, and how it all comes spiraling back to money, and I remember then that the earrings had been on sale for $9.99 at Macy's. They were gold plate and I bought them myself.

I throw them back in the garbage bag and sink to the floor, cursing the faceless man or men who raped my home, cursing my errant daughter, cursing Blaise Hunt and Dooley Braun and everything else in my crappy, gone-to-hell life.

I am about to melt into a directionless blob when I hear the front doorbell.

There are two men on the front steps, one on my side of forty, the other fifteen or so years younger, both wearing Men's Wearhouse suits and polyester ties—Jehovah's Witnesses or cops, I can't tell the difference anymore. Either I will be invited to God's heavenly kingdom, or downtown for questioning. Or maybe they caught the guys who trashed my house. Somehow I doubt it.

The older man fixes his face in a grim, bad-news smile. "Ms. Kane?"

He knows my name; that makes him a cop. I nod.

He shows me his badge. "I'm Ben Falka with the Tucson Police." He motions to the other man. "This is Officer Martinez. May we come in?"

I make room for them to pass through the doorway.

Martinez says in a high, boyish voice, "Holy shit, what happened here?"

I almost laugh. *Holy shit?* I guess they're not here to follow up on the B and E.

Falka gives his younger partner a look, then expresses the same thought in somewhat more formal terms.

"Have you had a break-in?" he asks.

"My cat had a bad day."

Martinez looks around nervously, no doubt expecting to see a pet cougar.

"A couple of your guys were out here yesterday," I say. "I thought maybe you came to tell me you'd arrested somebody for this."

Falka shakes his head at the mess. "We're, ah, from a different department."

"What department is that?" Their discomfiture is making me feel better, I don't know why, maybe because I'm pretty sure by now that they haven't come to arrest me.

"You mind if we sit down?"

"Help yourself," I say, pointing at the cushionless sofa.

Ben Falka, tall and bony with graying, thinning hair, sits at one end of the sofa, his butt so low to the floor that his knees stick up as high as his shoulders. Martinez, with the compact and rigid body of a weightlifter, perches on the far sofa arm. At this moment, I can see, they both wish they were someplace else.

"Would you like something to drink?" I ask. "A glass of water?"

"Water would be great," Falka says. Martinez declines with a shake of his head. I fetch a glass of water for Falka, then sit down across from them on the only undamaged piece of furniture in the living room, a painted Mexican side chair. I cross my legs, striving for nonchalance. Falk sips his water, smiles, clears his throat, and consults a small notebook.

"Ms. Kane . . . may I call you Patty?"

"Call me Peeky."

"Peeky. Yes. Are you acquainted with a Herman Balcomb?"

That takes a second to get through.

"You mean *Buddy*?" This is why Buddy didn't want to tell me where he was going. So I wouldn't have to lie to the cops when they came looking for him. "Sure, I know Buddy. We used to be— We went out for more than a year. But I haven't heard from him lately. I think he moved out of state."

Both men are staring at me. Something dark and prickly is happening in my belly.

"Things weren't working out," I say. "Buddy's a pretty independent guy."

Falka looks at his hands. They are nice hands; he could have been a doctor. Martinez has shifted his eyes to a place on the wall behind me. My sense of dread becomes overwhelming.

Falka says, "I have some bad news, Peeky."

I am hugging myself. I close my eyes. His next words come from a distant loudspeaker.

"We found Buddy last night. He's dead, Peeky."

I wish I hadn't told him my nickname. Or Buddy's. It would be so much easier if a Ms. Kane were to receive this information about one Herman Balcomb.

I say, "Where?"

"His body was found in Pantano Wash."

"In the wash? Did he drown?" I don't know what I'm saying. It hasn't rained in weeks; the washes are bone dry.

"Peeky, do you know anyone who might have wanted to hurt Buddy?"

"Everybody liked Buddy," I say reflexively.

"He was shot."

Time passes. A few minutes or a few seconds, I don't know. I need time to think. My mind is shutting down. Of course, I have a general idea who was responsible for killing Buddy, but I am not going to trust these two, this Falka and Martinez, until I know more.

I say, "I thought he was gone."

"What do you mean?" Falka asks.

"I thought he'd left town. I talked to him . . ." My hand drags across my cheek and comes away wet, surprising me. I usually only cry at small, silly things: a bird hitting the window, a sappy movie, an old song. "He said he was leaving town."

"When was that?"

"Saturday. I think."

Falka writes something in his notebook.

"How did you know to come here?" I ask.

Falka says, "He had one of those cards in his wallet. You know, 'In case of emergency please contact'? He also had a photo of you."

I know the photo, the only good one anybody ever took of me. I didn't know he carried it in his wallet.

Martinez is staring off to the side. He won't let himself look at me. How can a guy who chases crooks for a living be so chicken-shit? I pity the wife, if he has one.

I say to him, "Do you know how to talk?" My voice comes out loud and brittle.

His eyes skitter across my face, startled. "I'm sorry for your loss," he says, his eyes resting safely on his knees. His voice is high and soft, and I instantly feel awful for snapping at him. I think he must work out to compensate for his effeminate voice. Maybe that is also why he became a cop. I feel myself reaching out to him emotionally, then I catch myself and a wave of fury obliterates the empathic impulse. Suddenly I am furious, angry at all of them— this high-voiced cop, his phlegmatic partner, the late Buddy Bal-comb, Woody Stumpf, Eduardo, Jaymie, *everybody*. Why won't they leave me alone to play holdem and eat Cherry Garcia and watch my orchids die?

"Please leave," I say, tears acid on my cheeks.

Martinez, who apparently picked up on my moment of feeling for him, starts to say something, but Falka touches his arm and stands up.

"We're very sorry, Peeky, but we need you to come down to the morgue to identify the body. Do you think you could do that?"

I nod. I don't know what else to do.

Twenty minutes later we are in the morgue and they are pulling back the sheet and the instant I see his face a tourniquet wraps my skull, impacting my thoughts, jamming them together so hard that nothing moves. There is nothing but the face. I blink, and nothing changes.

"Peeky? Are you okay?"

I need something. I have no idea what it is, but I need it des-perately. The edges of my vision are being constricted by a purple halo, getting smaller.

I feel a hand on my back. A voice. "Breathe." My body turns. Falka's lips move. "Breathe, Peeky."

That's it, the solution to my problem. I open my mouth and air rushes out. My knees buckle, but I don't fall. He is holding me up. I suck in a lungful of cold morgue air and my head clears.

"I'm okay," I say. Falka nods, but he keeps his hand on my arm.

I turn back to the corpse. I'm glad he didn't get shot in the face. He was not a bad-looking man. His mother must have been proud of him, at least up to the point where he started robbing banks.

"That him?" Falka asks, his voice barely audible. "Is that Buddy Balcomb?"

I nod. "That's him."

Ben Falka drives me home in his government-issue Ford. He tries to make small talk, but I am deep into my role as the bereaved consort and say little. All I can think about is Buddy. The only thing I know for sure is that he is not lying dead on a slab in the county morgue. That dubious privilege is reserved for one Woody Stumpf, who died with Buddy's wallet in his hip pocket, and who looks much better without his comb-over. I wonder if Buddy killed him. I think maybe he did. My Buddy, now twice a killer. Do I love him less? Perhaps, but the mantra that fills my mind as I ride west on Speedway with Ben Falka at the wheel is, simply, *Run, Buddy, run.*

I CHECK MY CELL as soon as I walk into my house. I was so distraught when the police gave me the news about "Buddy" that I forgot to bring it to the morgue with me. There is one message, from Eduardo.

"Peeky? It's Eddie. Listen, we got out there and she is gone. I mean, her car is gone and nobody is home, okay? But don't worry, I am going to find her. I will call you, okay?"

"Okay," I whisper. My brief spell of joy at learning Buddy is alive evaporates. I look around at the mess. "This is your fault, you piece of shit," I say to Buddy or myself.

I know I'm in no shape to deal with it now. I need to get out. Drive up to Gila and play some cards. The soothing repetitiveness, the anonymity, the purity of the poker table draws me like a junkie to OxyContin. Maybe Teresa Alvarez was right. Maybe I do have a problem.

I imagine myself behind the wheel heading west on I-10. I'll call and have them put my name on the $15–30 holdem list. I can see the casino off to the left, exit 164. I know right where I'll park my car.

What am I thinking? My daughter is missing, maybe in serious trouble. I'm unemployed. Unidentified persons are breaking into my home for reasons I can only guess at. My house is a disaster area. My felonious boyfriend is on the run. And it's rush

hour. It would take me two hours to get to Gila River this time
of day.

But I've got do something.

I am sitting on the cushionless sofa still doing nothing when,
an hour later, my doorbell rings again. I have got to have that thing
removed.

I peek sideways past the blinds, expecting to see Falka and Martinez again, but this time it's a woman: young, slim, composed,
and well dressed. Everything I used to be. Her black hair is
thick, and straight, and pulled back into a ponytail. Her eyeglasses have crisp, squarish black rims. Her gray suit looks Ar-
mani and probably is, her heels are definitely Manolo, and she is
wearing a turquoise choker that would look ridiculous on anyone who was not both Native American and strikingly beautiful.
There's no way I can compete with this package, so I open the
door without bothering to check myself in the mirror.

The woman does not say anything right away. She gives me a
careful look, then looks past me at the ruins of my living room. I
give her credit for nearly maintaining a disinterested expression,
but a slight compression of her lips gives her away.

"I had a little entering and a lot of breaking here," I say.

She nods. "So I see." Her voice is low and soft.

"What can I do for you?" I ask.

"Are you Peeky Kane?"

"I'm Ms. Patricia Kane, yes."

"I'm sorry. Ms. Kane."

"Call me Peeky."

She smiles. I think.

"What can I do for you?" I say.

She hands me a card. *Gayle Rosalia Vega. Attorney at Law. The
Santa Cruz Nation.*

"You're a lawyer?" I say. "This can't be good."

Gayle Rosalia Vega, Attorney at Law, raises one perfect eye-brow. Members of disadvantaged minorities who make it through law school are seldom amused by lawyer jokes. I don't know what I was thinking.

"Peeky, I am not here as an attorney." I wonder if she speaks so softly in the courtroom. She says, "I have come here at the request of my grandfather. Hector Vega."

I'm not sure I heard that right. "Hector Vega?" I say. The elusive, reclusive Hector Vega? Founder and leader of the Santa Cruz, the biggest little tribal nation in the Southwest?

I say again, "Hector *Vega*?"

Take a random survey in greater Tucson: of those who have heard of Hector Vega, half will say he's dead; the other half will say he was never alive. The only photo I ever saw was from back in 1974, I think, when he was fighting for federal recognition of his tribe. The photo had been taken in front of the federal courthouse in Phoenix, where Vega had been testifying. He was a handsome man, long black hair tied back with a red bandanna, eyes hidden behind aviator shades, a thin cigar held delicately between his teeth. I remember it because for years, every time Hector Vega made the news, they ran that same stock photo. I always thought of him as a cross between Howard Hughes and Thomas Pynchon, a camera-shy recluse locked up safe and crazy in some rez version of Xanadu.

"Grandfather asked me to invite you for dinner," Hector Vega's granddaughter says, her full lips giving the words an ironic spin.

"I . . . I'm not . . . dinner?" I gesture feebly at the mess behind me, and at my clothes, and at the universe, and then I get even more confused. "Why?" I ask.

"This is not a bad thing," she says. "He is looking forward to seeing you."

"But I don't know him. I mean, you know I just got fired from the casino."

Her eyes remain steady; her shoulders rise in a faint shrug. "My grandfather does not always share his reasoning with me," she says in her quiet, soft voice. She is speaking the literal truth, I realize, but lying by omission. A useful artifice for any good lawyer. She might not share all her grandfather's thoughts, but she damn well knows what this is about.

"I'll need more than that," I say.

Our eyes touch, and she shrugs again. "He wishes to offer you a job. That's all I can tell you."

"I see," I say, although I don't see at all. "Doing what?"

"You will have to talk to my grandfather about that. We can drive out there now, if that is convenient."

"This really isn't a good time for me. As you can see, I'm a bit discombobulated at the moment—"

"It will be very casual—just you and Grandfather."

This is just too strange. "Where?"

"His home. On the rez."

I need about a week to think about this, but Gayle Rosalia Vega, Attorney at Law, Hector Vega's granddaughter, is standing on the stoop waiting.

I say, "You aren't going to tell me anything more, are you?"

She smiles. I sigh.

"Okay then, come on in." I open the door wide and back up to give her room. "I think I'd like to follow you in my car. Save you a trip back here."

"I don't mind."

"No, really. I'd just as soon have my car. I'm planning to run up to Phoenix tonight anyway, it'll be quicker if I leave from the rez. Can you give me twenty minutes to change and put a face on?"

"Of course," she says.

"Have a seat if you can find one," I tell her. I head for the bathroom, where I remember seeing a tube of lipstick on the floor next to the toilet.

26

I FOLLOW GAYLE VEGA'S BMW out the Ajo Highway past the casino exit, past Three Points, past the Tucson Rifle Club. Just before we enter the Tohono O'odham rez we turn right onto an unpaved road I never knew existed. The BMW disappears in a cloud of dust. I turn up the air-conditioning, but I can still taste grit. My little ragtop is not exactly climate controlled—dust seeps in everywhere.

We are heading straight at the Roskruge Mountains, toward a part of the Santa Cruz reservation I've never visited. Actually, I've never visited any part of the rez, except for the casino.

The road snakes around a foothill bristling with saguaro. The BMW slows, the dust clears, and we are climbing a series of steep, paved switchbacks. I am wondering why they paved a road way out here when the house comes into view. It was not a road, but a mile-long driveway. And not just a house, but a sprawling, flat-roofed adobe-and-stone hacienda that looks as if it grew naturally from the surrounding stone.

Gayle Vega parks beneath the spreading branches of a mesquite tree. I pull in next to her and stare at the house with its broad eaves, oversize windows, and stonework that manages to look both casual and precise.

"I didn't know Frank Lloyd Wright built houses out here," I say as I get out of my car.

The lawyer laughs, and I see that she is even more beautiful than I had realized. She is more relaxed now that her mission is accomplished. Back on home territory.

"It was designed by one of Wright's students. Grandfather loves it, but there is always something leaking or broken. In that sense, it is very authentic."

I follow her down a flight of wide stone steps into a shaded courtyard ringed with potted plants, mostly tropical varieties that I don't recognize. She pulls on the iron handle of a heavy-looking polished mesquite door. It swings open silently and easily, and we enter.

There is nothing quite like the feeling you get stepping out of the dusty desert heat into a cool, clean, moist home made of stone, earth, or adobe. A lot of Mexican homes have it, but most of the homes in Tucson, even those with adobe exteriors, come with the drier, harsher cool produced by conditioned air and Sheetrock walls. This house was built by someone who understood desert living. The floor in the entry area is ceramic tile—not that shiny stuff, but thick, porous tiles that get better with age. You can see the traffic pattern in the tiles; it looks a thousand years old, like the Mayan stone plazas at Chichén Itzá. Tiny skylights in the saguaro-rib ceiling accentuate the mottled, aged look of the tiles, creating a cool but well-lit interior. As soon as the door closes behind us my pores open, my eyes unsquint, and my rib cage relaxes, allowing my lungs to fill completely for the first time in several days.

"Nice," I say.

"Yes, it is."

The inside walls are waist-high adobe topped with glass panels: a see-through house. The interplay of light, shadow, earth, stone, and glass manages to both excite and reassure. From the entry area, I can see all the way through the house to the western horizon. Sunsets must be spectacular here.

"How big is it?"

"I don't know. Twelve thousand square feet? More, if you include the outbuildings and patio areas. You could get lost."

"Nice," I say again. You wouldn't know it by my dump, but I've always had a thing for big, beautiful homes. I've subscribed to *Architectural Digest* for years, but I don't get many chances to walk around inside its pages.

"I'll see if I can find Grandfather," she says, and glides off down one of the long, low hallways, her heels making soft ticking sounds on the unglazed tile.

And then it is very quiet. This house absorbs sound. I look around at the carved mesquite benches that line the walls, and the intricately tiled table in the corner, and the brightly painted and gilded Blessed Virgin Mary statuette set into an alcove across from the front door.

I am drawn by the light at the far side of the house. I walk down a short hallway through what appears to be a meeting room and descend a shallow flight of steps to a semicircular atrium with a polished stone floor and one wall made entirely of glass, looking out into a miniature slot canyon, open at the far end, framing a spectacular view of the Aguirre Valley to the west.

After that first stunning eyeful, I see that the canyon is not a natural feature, but rather an artifact, a terraced desert garden dotted with dozens of cactus varieties. A narrow stream trickles down one wall and along the canyon floor. I find a glass door in the window wall and walk out into the garden.

The transition from inside to outside is jolting. The sun ricochets from the canyon walls, instantly drying my lips and eyes. I pull my sunglasses from my purse and slide them on. Much better. I follow the stream, drawn by the view. The canyon is smaller than it looks; it is no more than sixty or seventy feet long. The stream flows into a pond about ten feet across. At the far edge of the pond is a wooden bench looking out over the valley. An old man wearing jeans and a grimy white T-shirt is squatting between the bench and the pond, fishing a dead goldfish from the surface with a long-handled nylon net. He examines the fish through thick eyeglasses, shrugs, and flips it over his shoulder.

The goldfish sails out into space. He looks up and I recognize him.

"Ayyy . . . Pee Key. You came to see my cactus garden."

"How are you doing, Cisco?"

"Me?" Gripping the back of the bench, he pushes himself up, his face rigid with effort. "I'm old as Geronimo, Pee Key."

"I'm right behind you."

"You? I got daughters older than you."

"You always were a gentleman."

Cisco grins, and we just stand there looking at each other for what seems like a long time.

"So," I say, looking around, "this is quite the garden you've got here. How long have you been working for Mr. Vega?"

"Long time," he says, still grinning. "You playing any cards, Pee Key?"

"Up at Gila. I got myself eighty-sixed from the Santa Cruz." He shakes his head, grin fading. "Why they do that?"

"I guess Blaise Hunt just took a dislike to me."

"Ayyy . . . who could not like you, Peeky?"

We both laugh. I could never put one over on Cisco. The old man has a built-in bullshit detector. He circles the pond, looking for more dead fish, using the long-handled net as a cane, his legs swinging around each other in his full-diaper gait. He stops between me and the pond and bends over to examine something.

"That a fish?" He points at a floating leaf.

"It's a leaf," I say.

"Huh." He stands up straight, or nearly so. "I thought maybe it was a leaf. But I don't see so good lately. You want to see my new cactus?"

"Sure. Only, I'm supposed to be meeting with Mr. Vega. I maybe should get back inside."

Cisco is looking at something behind me.

"Granddaughter," he says.

I turn and see Gayle Vega standing behind me, one eyebrow slightly raised, a faint smile curving her lips.

"I see you found him."

P EE KEY, YOU LOOK LIKE you swallowed a bug." Cisco is laughing, and I am trying to see Hector Vega in his features. At first it won't come, then my brain adapts—his wrinkles smooth out, his hair grows longer and darker, and his thick plastic-rimmed glasses become aviator shades.

"I didn't recognize you," I say, "Mr. Vega."

"You call me Cisco," he says. "And I will call you Pee-Key-who-swallowed-a-bug."

Gayle Vega is smiling, but her brow is wrinkled.

"Grandfather, have you been gambling at your own casino again?"

"I never quit," he says gleefully.

Gayle Vega rolls her eyes.

"Your grandfather," I say, "is no gambler." I look at Cisco/Vega. "He's a kick-ass poker player."

"I kick ass," he confirms.

Gayle shakes her head and smiles.

"Let's go inside," Cisco says, hooking a hand around my arm. For a moment I am confused, thinking that he intends to pull me along, then I realize that he is looking for support. We follow the stream back toward the house, Gayle walking a few paces before us, Cisco's hand locked on my elbow.

"Night-blooming cereus," Cisco says, stopping and pointing out a spindly, gray-green cactus. "They call her Queen of the Night. Hard to grow up here. See the flower?" A short stalk ending in a bulbous bud juts from the body of the cactus. "Tonight, maybe, she will open. One night only. Desert special." Cisco cackles and we move on. A few steps later he points out another group of cacti, a row of low, lumpy growths lining a ledge on the canyon wall. "Peyote," he says. "In case you want to get messed up." His cackle becomes a prolonged giggle, making me wonder whether he's been eating some himself.

Gayle holds the door open for us and we move into the cool interior of the house.

"We will eat in the card room," Cisco says.

"I'll let Maria know."

"Fry bread, powdered eggs, and commodity cheese," he says. "Show Pee Key how good we eat out here on the rez." There is an edge to his voice I've never heard before, a glimpse of the Hector Vega in Cisco.

"Yes, Grandfather." She glides off. How she does that on four-inch heels I will never know.

The "card room" is forty feet by twenty, with a ceiling so low I can reach up and touch it. The outside wall is interrupted by seven wide, low windows looking toward Tucson. A poker table stands at one end of the room. The table is an oblong covered in green baize, just like in the casino, but instead of a padded vinyl rail, this table is framed in polished mesquite with silver inlays.

"Nice table," I say. "I bet you don't play three-six holdem on this one."

"Sometimes we do," says Cisco. He tugs me away from the card table. "We sit over here, okay?"

Near the windows is a small, crude table made of pine planks and two-by-fours. It has been painted several times, most recently yellow. It looks as out of place in this spectacular home as a milking stool in the White House.

Four mission-style chairs with cushioned seats surround the table. Cisco sinks gratefully into one of them, and I take the chair opposite.

I run my hand over the tabletop.

"Family heirloom?"

"Kitchen table. I made it, I was nineteen." He raps a knuckle on the yellow surface. "This was where we started."

I'm not sure what he means.

"The Santa Cruz," he says. "Me and Yani, may she rest in peace, sitting right here eating fry bread and commodity cheese. Course, we were up on the San Carlos then."

"The Apache rez?"

"Table was green then, green like Yani's eyes. She painted it yellow when Rosie was born." He spreads his fingers, his hand flat on the table, and closes his eyes as if absorbing its essence. "It's a good table."

A stocky, black-haired woman appears bearing a tray. She sets a pair of crystal glasses and a matching water pitcher on the table, along with a bowl of exceptionally large cashews.

"You like cashews?" Cisco asks.

"I do." I take a cashew to prove it.

"Many years ago I promised myself when I was rich I would always have cashews."

It sounds like a reasonable goal. Me, when I get rich, I will never run out of Cherry Garcia.

"Is Rosie your oldest?" I ask, pouring each of us a glass of water.

Cisco nods. "Rosie first, then Maria, then Alma, Teresa, Veronica, and Elizabeth. All girls."

"How many grandchildren do you have?"

Cisco smiles at the table. "Eighteen." His expression falls. "Seventeen, now. Dolores was killed last week." He looks up. "In the cage. She was only nineteen."

"I'm sorry."

"Yes."

We sit in silence out of respect for the dead. The backs of his hands are dark and wrinkled all the way to his fingertips, but there is a delicacy to them. I have always admired Cisco's hands, but never more than now, seeing them resting on this table he made.

"Mr. Vega . . ."

"Cisco."

"Cisco." I need to do something with my hands, so I grab a couple more cashews. "What am I doing here?"

"Eating cashews," he says.

"They're very good."

"I order them from Harry and David."

"Your granddaughter said you wanted me to do some sort of job."

Cisco nods. More silence. He will get to it, whatever it is. Indian time has always baffled me. I feel like an impatient schoolgirl. I sit quietly waiting. Maria brings in another tray, this one covered with small dishes—chips, cilantro, finely shredded white cheese, olives, crema, pickled serranos, chopped tomatoes, and two salsas: green and red. Cisco sits back and watches happily as she sets the dishes in the center of the table. As soon as she leaves he starts eating chips and salsa. I follow his example.

"You want a beer?" he asks. "Wine?"

"Water is fine." I think I need to stay sharp.

Maria returns with plates for us and more food: tamales, enchiladas, roasted peppers, tortillas, machaca, frijoles, and a salad of shredded cabbage and cilantro. The table is crowded edge to edge.

"This looks great," I say.

Cisco is piling food on his plate, a little bit of everything. He lays down a base of tamales, enchiladas, machaca, and beans, then mounds cheese, peppers, olives, cabbage, tomatoes, crema, and salsa on top. Maria makes a sound with her lips, shakes her head, and walks off.

"My daughter disapproves of my eating habits," Cisco says. "She says I am a pig." He digs in, scooping a forkful of food into his mouth. I serve myself a lesser quantity of food, avoiding only the serranos, which make me sweat.

Everything is excellent, especially the tamales. An ordinary tamale is heavy as a brick and nearly as digestible. These are perfectly wonderful, a light batter filled with an unlikely mixture of pork, olives, carrots, and raisins.

"Maria's a marvelous cook," I say. "Is she Gayle's mother?"

"Gayle is Alma's. First grandchild to graduate from college. Smartest of the bunch, so far."

"She is beautiful."

He nods, his mouth once again full. Maria is right—Cisco eats like a pig. A very happy, appreciative pig. I'm sure that Maria loves having her food devoured with such enthusiasm. In fact, it is hard not to eat quickly. The food is that good. Within ten minutes we are both stuffed.

"You didn't eat any cashews," I say.

He laughs. "I don't like them anymore. Once I could afford them, I ate too many."

He stands up, using the edge of the table for help, and toddles off, placing his feet carefully, leaving me to wonder again what I am doing there.

A few days ago this man fired me. Or, to be fair, a man who works for him fired me. I'm afraid he is going to ask me about the jackpot scam. Or the robbery. I could never fool him at the card table. I doubt I'll be able to do it now, even if I wanted.

I turn when I hear his shuffling steps returning. He is holding a long, thin cigar between the fingers of one hand, and a gnarled wooden cane in the other.

"Let's go, Pee Key. We don't want to miss the sunset."

"Pee Key, what do you see when you look at me?"

I look at him. We are sitting on the bench at the end of the canyon garden, the Aguirre Valley spread out before us, the sun a great orange blob settling upon the horizon. Cisco is smoking his cigar, and as I look at him it is the cigar that brings him into focus for me: I see a grayer version of the Hector Vega in that three-decade-old photo, a similar cigar fitting that same way into his weathered face.

"I see a leader who has accomplished much for his people," I say.

He laughs. "You humor me."

I say, "I also see a pretty good three-six holdem player. I always wanted to ask, how come you don't play the higher limits? You're good enough."

"You think so?"

"I know so."

"You are always right, Pee Key." He draws on the cigar, letting smoke trickle out and rise past his face. "I just play to keep an eye out."

"For what?"

He shrugs. "You never know."

"How is it I never knew who you were?" I ask.

"I never told you."

"Does anybody at the casino know you?"

"My son-in-law Carlos knows me. He does not like it that I play in the card room. He thinks it lacks dignity. My grandchildren who work there know me. A few others. Family. Mostly we keep it in the family." He points with his cigar. "Watch."

The sun has touched the horizon. It sags, melting into a puddle of deep maize. The sky above fades impossibly from yellow to blue, without a trace of green.

Darkness falls quickly in the desert. I have never understood why this is so. There are no languid evenings with the light slipping slowly away like those I remember from my Midwestern child-hood. Here it stays bright until the sun touches the horizon. Min-utes later the stars will be visible, and the grateful night creatures will creep and skitter and slither up out of the washes and arroyos. The smell of Cisco's cigar blends with aromas of mesquite and euca-lyptus. We watch until the last lunule of sun winks out.

Cisco reaches out a hand in the near dark and rests it on my forearm. The hand on the arm is a powerful gesture. Those who know how and when to use it go far in life.

"Pee Key, how come you won that jackpot?" His voice is soft, but I feel as though he just shouted in my ear.

"It just happened," I say.

"Tell me."

And so I do. I lay out the scene for him—how Manuel put me in the shorthanded game just as the scam was about to go down. I tell him who was sitting where, and how the clown showed up with his balloons, and how the betting went. I tell him everything. When I stop talking, Cisco releases me and leans back and smokes some more.

"Do you want the money back?" I ask. Not that I have it.

He shakes his head. "It would only cause more trouble. You got lucky, Peeky."

Did he just call me *Peeky*? What happened to Pee Key?

"No point in asking for bad press. We get enough already, what with the robbery and all."

Cisco says nothing for a very long time. I hear the faint, distant sound of coyotes laughing. I feel my nails digging into my palms.

"How is Buddy doing?" he asks.

I think I know now what I am doing here. I think he knows Buddy had something to do with the robbery. He is using me to get to Buddy.

"He's dead," I say.

It is almost imperceptible, but I sense Cisco's shoulders sink a few eighths of an inch. If we were playing poker, and if he was someone other than Cisco, I would say he missed his hand. But the fact that he is Cisco might mean there is another message in those slumping shoulders.

"The police came this morning," I say in a wooden voice. "I identified the body. He was shot."

Cisco remains absolutely still for several seconds. "I am very sorry," he finally says.

28

I<small>T IS AFTER MIDNIGHT</small> by the time I arrive at Gila River. I slide into a low-key $15–30 holdem game and watch the cards go by. I don't know any of the other players. Some of them know what they're doing. Ace-ten under the gun, I dump it. Pocket nines? The pot gets raised in front of me, into the muck they go. I fold hand after hand, slipping into my Zen mode, waiting for the cards to offer me odds I can't refuse.

I really shouldn't be here. My daughter is missing, my house is a disaster, and I don't have enough money to be playing $15–30 holdem. But the alternative—going home—is too much to bear. I need the rhythm of the cards.

I let the game flow through me. Ace-king, I raise from middle position. The other players look at me and throw away their hands.

I could be anywhere—Las Vegas, Atlantic City, Monte Carlo, Costa Rica. The muted jangle of the slots in the distance, the whisper of cards flying from the deck, the soft flutter of players shuffling their chips, the voices: *nut flush, kicker plays, aces up, good river, nice hand, bad beat, blinds please, reraise, cap it, ace high, check it, kick it, chop it, raise it, ship it* . . . I am in my element, safe inside the game. Is this how Jaymie feels when she's getting high? My time in the zone ends abruptly when I see a man walk by and think for a small part of a second that it is Buddy. It isn't. Just another wasted middle-aged gambler. Buddy is probably in Costa Rica running over a pot-limit holdem game. I push him out of my thoughts, but instead of getting my head back into the game, I find myself back with Hector Vega, hearing his voice.

"Peeky," he said, "I am rich now. The casino has brought me a lot of money. My family is rich. All my people."

We were sitting in the dark looking out over the desert, warmed by residual heat from the rock surrounding us. I was relieved that he had asked me no more questions about Buddy. Lying to Cisco had left me with a sick feeling.

"Gaming has been good for the Santa Cruz," I said.

Cisco made a noise with his lips. "You think the casino is this wonderful thing? We have land and money, sure. We have fire trucks and college funds and a hospital. But we are still red niggers, only now we are red niggers with money. Boy turns eighteen, gets his first quarterly, eighteen thousand dollars, he goes straight out and buys himself a seventy-thousand-dollar Cadillac Escalade on credit. He lives with his mother in a trailer and he drives an Escalade. My son-in-law Carlos—next time you see him look at his boots. Fifteen thousand dollars, Peeky. He is running my casino and he is wearing fifteen-thousand-dollar boots. Meanwhile, I have three grandchildren who are drug addicts, two running in a gang, one shot to death last week, a daughter dead from drink, and half my people have moved off the rez. The money saved us and it is our ruin. The money built a drug treatment center we didn't use to need. Tell me how this is a good thing, Peeky."

I said nothing.

"You know that our casino was originally financed by Magic Hand?" he said.

I nodded.

"They built it and brought in their slots and tables and their managers, and they gave some of our people jobs and money. It was a good deal. For seven years they have taken forty percent of the profits." He tapped off his cigar ash. "That's a lot of money. This is their last year, then they are supposed to leave, and the tribe takes over management."

"I thought Carlos Begay was already running things."

"Yes. My Navajo son-in-law. But who is running him? I wonder about these things, Peeky. Carlos is president, but he is surrounded by others. And now I am told—Carlos tells me this—that Johnson wants to renew his contract."

"Who is Johnson?"

"Bruce Johnson is Magic Hand. He is like a tarantula wasp. He stung us, laid his egg on us, and now we are being devoured. He wants us to renew with Magic Hand for five more years. You hear about the new white wine?"

I'd heard the joke, but I shook my head, letting him tell it.

"*We want a casino, too,*" Cisco whined, then broke into a creaky laugh.

I laughed, too, then asked, "Don't they have to leave when the contract expires?"

"It is not so simple. Do you know how many Santa Cruz are working at the casino now? Nineteen. Nineteen out of two hundred twenty employees. The rest are Mexican, Tohono O'odham, and white. Except for Carlos, all the managers are white, and most of them came out of Magic Hand. Johnson did not do what he promised. He did not hire and train my people. It was easy for him. You know why?"

"No."

"Because my people did not want to work. As soon as the quarterly payments kicked in, nobody wanted to work anymore. This was my fault, Peeky. I sold the soul of my people. Now Carlos wants us to renew the contract with Magic Hand, and increase the quarterly stipend to twenty-five thousand dollars. This is a very popular idea, as you can imagine."

"And what do *you* want?" It fascinated me how his manner of speaking had changed. Politically savvy, charismatic Hector Vega had replaced the cute, English-challenged Cisco.

"I want my people to work for their money. I want them back on the rez, and I want the rez to be a good place to live, to raise kids. I want to reduce the stipend, increase wages, build another school, and negotiate a supply of CAP water for irrigation. My people do not farm anymore. They say there is no water here, and they are right. Maybe if they had water they would farm."

"Farming is hard work."

"Very hard. And they won't do it unless they see the need. I have to show them."

"How?"

"Magic Hand has to go. It will be a difficult transition. Business will suffer. We will have to hire new management, new security. I want to make the stipend conditional on taking part in tribal ventures—the casino, public services, agriculture. It will get ugly, Peeky. Many will hate me."

"Then why do it?"

"For the future, Peeky." I felt his hand on my arm again. "You have a daughter. Would you turn away from your child in her time of need?"

"Of course not."

"I know this about you. To play poker with someone is to see into their heart. I know that you are a good woman, and I know that you can help me." He gave my arm a squeeze, then lifted his hand away.

"Help you how?" I didn't buy the bit about poker being the gateway to the soul, but it sounded as if Hector Vega was about to tell me what I was doing there.

For several seconds neither of us spoke.

"I have been asleep for several years," he said at last. "I have become little more than an invisible figurehead for my people. A ghost. I let them go too soon. The casino is being run by Bruce Johnson from Wisconsin and a Navaho wearing fifteen-thousand-dollar boots. The tribal council no longer hears me when I speak. I have no power. How can I deliver peace and happiness to my people if I have no power?"

"I don't believe that you are powerless."

"You are right, of course. Even a child has the power to scream." He drew on his cigar. "I am still a member of the council. But it is Carlos and his generation who now fill most of the seats. It will not be easy to regain control. I may have to do something remarkable to get their attention. You are right about power, Peeky. You know how you get power? It is like poker. First you convince them you are crazy, then you show them the goods."

"I just meant that you still have the respect of your people."

"Not the young ones. To the young ones I am a crippled old man, more dead than alive." Holding his cigar in his teeth, he reached down and moved his bad leg to a more comfortable position. "Did you know that you once worked for me?"

Somehow I was not surprised. "What did I do?"

"You helped my grandson."

"What was his name?"

"Andrew Ellis Tallis."

The name is familiar, but I can't place it.

"Little Smoke," Cisco said, reminding me.

"Oh." I remembered the case clearly. A Navajo kid named Charleston Eagle Pearson—he called himself Bird—was shot to death up on the Fort Apache reservation. It happened at a post-powwow gathering—what they call a "49"—that had turned into an all-night party. There were thirty witnesses to the shooting, every last one of them loaded on alcohol, meth, weed, crack, or all four. Most of them under eighteen. I talked to all of them and came up with thirty different versions of the shooting. The only thing all the witnesses agreed on was that Bird was stone-cold dead by the time the sun rose over the White Mountains. In such a case, it is not hard to come by reasonable doubt, which I provided for Little Smoke's defense team. He was acquitted.

"He was guilty, you know," I said to Cisco.

"Ayyyy . . . he's still got his troubles. But I appreciated what you did."

"I got a murderer out of jail."

"He is a good boy. He has not killed again."

"Good."

"You don't like working for the bad guys?"

"No."

"What about me? I've done some bad things."

"I'm not working for you yet. I don't even know what you want me to do."

"It is simple, Peeky." The tip of his cigar glowed. "I want you to be my prop."

He flicked his cigar out over the edge to join the dead goldfish.

Two red aces push Hector Vega from my thoughts and bring me back to Gila River. I raise, and get four callers. The flop comes ten, jack, queen. Two spades. I bet again, get two callers, then a raise from a bored-looking rock with one eyebrow. In love with my aces, I reraise. Call, call . . . the rock looks at me, shrugs faintly, and calls. The turn brings nine of spades. Three spades and four to a straight on the board. I check, the guy to my left bets, eyebrow man raises. I make a crying call, knowing I'm beat. I have two aces, sure, but any two spades, any king, any eight, any two pair beats me. The river is the trey of diamonds, a rag. Not that it matters. The eyebrow guy bets; I fold, the other guy calls. I start racking my chips, ashamed of the way I played.

I don't even bother to look when they show their hands.

Four a.m., I am lying on a king-size bed at the Holiday Inn in Chandler, light years from sleep. I need some of Jaymie's drugs right now, something to knock me out. I wish I had brought a nightgown. I think of the mess awaiting me at home. I think about money.

I dropped $260 at Gila River. Normally that would be no big

deal, but right now it represents more than ten percent of my bankroll. It was foolish. Irresponsible. I can't be throwing away my last few dollars like some sort of degenerate gambler.

I think about what Cisco wants me to do. He's either crazy like a fox, or as addled as he seems to want people to believe. Asking me to be his "prop" suggests the latter. In either case, he is using me.

The good news is, I could make some money. Enough money to get Jaymie into a treatment program.

The bad news is I could lose it all.

I watch the clock, counting silently, trying to predict the exact moment when the numbers will change.

A T EIGHT-THIRTY, after maybe two or three hours of sleep, I
call Eduardo. He sounds hung over, as usual, and has no
news to report. I put on last night's clothes and drive up to
Phoenix to spend money I don't have. I need everything; the task is
as overwhelming as it is rejuvenating. The two things should balance out, I figure. I spend four hours in as many stores, trying to
come up with five complete outfits, including underclothes and ac-
cessories. The idea is to get back to basics. I form a mental list:
black cocktail dress for all the times I get invited to swanky recep-
tions, which is never; one classic suit in navy blue; tropical woolen
skirts in beige and navy; a silk-and-wool jacket for all occasions;
one natural-color linen sundress; assorted cotton blouses in neutral
shades; basic black pumps . . .

It doesn't work. The very first item I buy is a short, tight, Ver-
sace knockoff made of some high-tech fabric that looks like the
hide of a sleek and elegant size-eight green dinosaur. I usually wear
a twelve, but this item picks up my eyes like you can't believe. At
Nordstrom's, I pick up a black leather skirt with western stitching
on the sides, a couple of silk blouses in electric blue and sea foam,
a linen jacket that is the exact color of last night's sunset, and two,
count 'em, two pairs of red high-heeled sandals, because I can't decide which I love more. I also check out a pair of Manolo heels like
the ones Gayle Vega was wearing. Six hundred bucks. Yikes. I pass.

By the time I'm done I've racked up $3,800 on my Visa, and I never did get that navy blue suit or those plain black pumps. Despite the hair ball of guilt in my gut—the money could have gone to save my wayward daughter—I feel much better now, thank you.

I arrive home with a backseat full of fashion and a Styrofoam clamshell of duck curry from Little Asia. My house is still a mess. Imagine that. I clear out my bedroom closet, throwing everything on the floor, then put away my new purchases. I take the duck curry out onto the patio and eat it out of the Styrofoam with a plastic fork. It could be spicier.

After eating, I phone the insurance adjuster and the locksmith and leave messages on two machines. I call my trash service and ask them to make a pickup. I've got a lot of junk. It didn't use to be junk, but now it is. Addiction Services Counselors should offer a similar service—one phone call, they send out a truck, pick up your addict, and haul her away.

I phone Eduardo. He picks up on the first ring.

"It's me again," I say.

"Peeky. You hear from her?"

"No."

"Me neither. I'm trying to track down Mannie, just in case he knows something."

Eduardo promises to keep looking. With a guilty twinge I recognize that a small part of me hopes it will be a few days before we find her. I have to get the rest of my life in order; I just don't have time to be a mom right now.

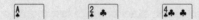

I want everything new. I want to start over. I don't want anything in my bedroom that has been defiled by unknown hands. I haul my mattress and box spring out to the driveway, and the garbage bags full of clothes, and the broken dresser.

I'm not up to bed-shopping, so I drive to Macy's and buy an air mattress, a set of sheets, a pair of goose-down pillows, and two cotton blankets. I inflate the mattress on my bedroom floor. It reminds me of my first apartment. Mattress on the floor, but it's all new and it's all mine. The locksmith calls back and says he can be there first thing in the morning. I tell him to bring a dead bolt strong enough to resist a battering ram. The insurance adjuster says he won't be able to make it until Friday. I close the door to the spare bedroom. That can wait. I clean the kitchen, throwing out everything in the refrigerator and most of the stuff in the cupboards, keeping only the unopened cans and the three bottles of Vouvray. My jaw is tight. The muscles around my eyes are locked in a hard squint. It feels good, this purge.

By dinnertime I have reclaimed the bedroom, the kitchen, the bathroom, and two closets. The pile of trash on my driveway is enormous. Much of it is still good, but I don't want it. Briefly, I consider sorting it out and donating the usable items to Goodwill, but the task is beyond me. Let the trash haulers deal with it.

I still can't bring myself to tackle the living room. Robert's ashes have put that project on indefinite hold.

I look at the clock. Almost seven, time to get ready for my new job. I check the image in the hall mirror. Not good. For the next hour I work on Peeky, turning her into someone who won't frighten animals or small children. I don't know what I'm in for tonight, but I want to make a good impression.

30

THE PARKING APRON in front of the Hector Vega residence is a study in mass consumption: a flashy new Cadillac, a Lexus, a Lincoln Navigator, and a bright yellow Hummer—about a quarter million bucks' worth of transportation that probably averages about ten miles per gallon. I park my little Miata between the Lincoln and the Hummer. It looks like a child's toy.

The door is answered by Cisco himself. He is wearing a black shirt with black embroidery and ebony snaps, black jeans, and black boots.

"Johnny Cash," I say. "The man in black."

He laughs. "Johnny was okay. I liked that Johnny Cash."

I follow him down the hall. He is walking faster than usual, and his hands are empty.

"No cane tonight?" I say.

"I'm having a good day," he says.

We enter the big room where Cisco and I ate dinner last night. Four men are seated around the poker table at the far end of the room. They look toward us as we approach, displaying varying degrees of surprise, puzzlement, and disdain. Clearly, I am not expected.

Dooley Braun is the most startled. His eyes go wide, his lips part, and a whorl of wrinkles appears in the center of his forehead. I wonder which car was Dooley's. Probably the Lincoln.

To Dooley's left sits a balding man with George Washington's chin and Karl Malden's nose. I recognize him as Alex Blackwell, U.S. congressman. Blackwell has held his congressional seat for more than thirty-five years, and was instrumental in obtaining federal recognition for the Santa Cruz. He is looking at me with frank, self-confident curiosity. This is a man who has built his fortune by understanding and manipulating people. I know which vehicle Blackwell drives. He wouldn't dare drive an import, and the Hummer is too inelegant. His car is the Cadillac.

Carlos Begay, sitting next to Blackwell, is openly hostile. His blocky but handsome features are set in a hard-eyed, knot-jawed look of anger and contempt. Definitely Hummer material. I wish I could see his boots, but his feet are tucked under the table.

The fourth man—by a process of elimination I put him in the Lexus—turns in his chair to see what everybody is looking at. I have never met this man, but I know from what Cisco has told me that he is Bruce Johnson, CEO of Magic Hand Gaming. His eyes grab me immediately, and a smile too sincere to be real spreads across his face.

"So this is our mystery guest," he says, standing up as so few men do these days. He crosses the room and takes my hand, gripping it just hard enough to show me that he is greeting me as an equal, but gently enough to acknowledge my gender.

"Bruce Johnson," he says. His eyes are the color of caramel just before it burns. He radiates the energy of an athletic thirty-year-old, but I can see from his skin that he is closing on sixty.

"Patty Kane," I say, and then I come very close to blushing. I don't know why I said that. I haven't introduced myself as "Patty" since high school. "Call me Peeky," I add hastily.

"I will, but only if you promise to *not* call me B.J."

"It's a deal."

Somehow, his smile finds another notch on the charm scale, and I have to look away to save myself. My eyes land on Alex Blackwell, who is also on his feet now, coming around the table.

"I don't believe we've met," he says, making it sound as if such a thing were nearly unimaginable. "I'm Alex Blackwell." His smile is good, too, but more fatherly, like something you'd expect from your local don. He doesn't shake my hand, he holds it.

Cisco says to me, "Peeky, you know Dooley and Carlos."

I nod to Dooley, and say, "Good evening, Mr. Begay," to Carlos. They both nod back, Carlos giving his head a perfunctory jerk while Dooley does his loopy bobblehead imitation.

"You must be the pro from Dover," Blackwell says, his smile becoming wolfish.

"I never knew what that meant," I say, taking back my hand.

"It means she's gonna kick our asses, boys," Johnson says. Everybody laughs, even me.

"Except Hector," says Blackwell. "Hector never gets his ass kicked, right, Hector?"

Cisco smiles. "You want to talk or play cards?"

"Shit, Hector, you know me. I like to talk more'n anything."

"Well, you just keep on talkin' then." Cisco pulls out a chair and sits down. "Rest of us, we'll chop up your money. Anybody wants drinks, you're on your own. Bar's over there." He points with his lips toward the near wall. Nobody goes for it.

"What're we playing tonight?" Johnson asks. "Three-six?"

"Fine with me," Blackwell says. "You okay with that, Carlos?"

"Whatever," Carlos says, looking unhappy.

"I just ask on account of last time you were complaining."

"I play whatever the fuck you want."

"Okay, okay." Blackwell looks at me and winks. "He's touchy."

I sit between Bruce Johnson and Carlos Begay, directly across from Dooley, who is having a hard time knowing where to rest his eyes. It has always amazed me that this nervous, expressive man was at one time a world-class poker player. He seems as readable as a traffic sign.

"I thought you didn't play anymore, Dooley," I say.

He shrugs, his shoulders rolling like water-filled balloons. "I play for fun."

Cisco gives us each a rack of black $100 Casino Santa Cruz poker chips, $10,000 for each of us. I take my chips from the rack and stack them on the felt in front of me. I've never played for black chips. Not that it's really mine—Cisco is bankrolling me in this game. Strictly speaking, I'm not acting as a prop. A prop is self-financed. Tonight I'm more like a shill, playing with house money. Only difference is, I get to keep what I win.

"No dealer tonight, Hector?" asks Blackwell.

"I thought we'd keep it private," says Cisco.

Blackwell raises his brow and rolls his eyes in my direction. Cisco just smiles. I try to pretend I'm comfortable horning in on this old boys' club.

Dooley shuffles the cards with a series of confident, efficient movements. He may not play much poker these days, but his card-handling skills have remained intact. Blackwell is unwrapping a thick cigar. Cisco's face relaxes into the same impenetrable, slightly bewildered expression he wears playing small stakes at the casino. Carlos Begay has adopted a contemptuous half-frown to let us know how little this game means to him. Bruce Johnson looks around the table, all eagerness and delight. He catches my eye and winks. I give him a dotty smile. We all have our act.

The game is holdem: two cards down, five community cards on the board, blind bets of $200 and $300 to the left of the dealer, best poker hand wins. I throw away my first half-dozen hands before the flop, trying to get a line on how these guys play. They are doing the same, starting out tight, getting the lay of the land.

Twenty minutes into it, with Carlos dealing, Cisco raises under the gun. Dooley and Blackwell fold, Carlos calls the $600 bet, Johnson and I fold. Carlos lays out the first three community cards: ace-jack-five. Cisco fires out another bet.

Even though I've played a lot of hours with Cisco, I'm pretty much in the dark here. If we were playing small-bet holdem I'd put him on a big ace, but shorthanded, high-limit poker is all about aggression. Cisco could be playing a lot of different hands—anything from pocket aces to seven-deuce off-suit.

Carlos calls.

The turn card is a rag: a four of hearts. Cisco bets $600. Carlos sits playing with his chips, frowning slightly. After about twenty seconds he shrugs as if to say, what the hell, it's only money, then pushes twelve black chips into the pot. It's the worst acting job I've seen since Prince quit making movies. The four must have hit him hard.

Cisco flashes his cards—ace, king—and mucks them.

"Good laydown," Dooley says.

Carlos shrugs and shows his hand. He has pocket fours, giving him a set—three fours. He seems disappointed that none of us are impressed.

My deal. I gather the cards and shuffle, happy to have something to do. The next few hands pass quickly, the small talk stays small, with Blackwell telling a few funny Washington, D.C., stories, Johnson topping him with a tale about how he almost came to own the Minnesota Timberwolves, and a poker anecdote from Dooley about playing no-limit holdem with the governor of Texas back in the 1970s.

Dooley, I learn, has more than one personality. The "normal" Dooley, the one I know from the casino, is uncertain, bashful, and a bit goofy. The other Dooley is a great white shark: calm, smiling, flat-eyed, patient, and deadly.

Carlos is the action at the table. He bets and raises with almost anything. I can see now why he was unhappy with the stakes—he is almost certain to lose. An hour into the game he has already bought in for a second rack.

Both Johnson and Blackwell play cautiously—too cautiously, in Blackwell's case. The congressman does not like to lose, and bets only when he is sure he has the best hand. It's tough to make a good hand pay off when you play that way—nobody will give you any action.

Johnson is somewhat more adventurous. On one hand he reraises my bet on the turn. I look at the cards on board—ace, trey, king, king—and fold my ace-nine. He shows me pocket queens. Oh well. Did he know I had the best hand when he reraised? I don't know if he was smart or lucky. I'm going to play it safe and assume smart. He's almost as tough to read as Cisco.

I notice a pattern with Carlos. After losing a big hand he shoves his chair back and stomps off. I get a glimpse of his fifteen-thousand-dollar boots, studded with chunks of turquoise and wrapped in a filigree of silver and gold. A few minutes later he returns, but instead of being calmed down by his short break, he seems even more on tilt. He bets and raises with just about anything he's dealt. Sometimes it works—a maniac can be tough to play against. He could have anything. When he hits a rush, his stacks rise at a furious rate, but he gives it away just as fast. As soon as I see this pattern I jump on it, and take down a couple of nice pots when Carlos overbets his hand.

Conversation at the poker table comes in sixty-second chunks. A joke must be completed between hands or it doesn't work. Same with anecdotes. Anytime you see someone trying to tell a five-minute story at the poker table, you know you've got yourself a sucker.

Conversational themes sometimes jump from hand to hand. For example, Blackwell folds a hand, turns to Dooley, and says, "Last week, up at Tucson National, four o'clock in the afternoon, I hit a ball maybe two hundred yards straight down the middle. We're driving up to it and, swear to God, y'all, a coyote comes loping out into the fairway and grabs the ball in his mouth and goes running off with it."

Dooley, still in the hand, says nothing. I'm not sure he heard a word Blackwell said, and neither is Blackwell, so he turns to me, looking for an audience. "Next time I go golfing I'm gonna pack a fucking gun. Pardon my fucking French."

Dooley wins a small pot; Carlos passes me the deal. I give myself a deuce, four. Easy fold. I flop a dangerous-looking board:

seven-nine-ten, all clubs. Johnson bets, Cisco, Dooley, and Blackwell all fold, Carlos calls.

Dooley says, "I use to have this coyote would walk into my house, right through the dog door, and eat the dog's food."

"What did your dog think about that?" Blackwell asks.

"He didn't like it much, but he was one a them Mexican dogs—a chee-wah-wah—so there wasn't much he could do about it except stay the hell out of the way. For a while I thought Pepper had developed a monster appetite. Didn't figure it out till one day I find this enormous turd on the kitchen floor."

Johnson, dealing the cards, says, "You know the Chihuahua is the only domestic dog native to the Americas?"

"Brucie knows everything," Cisco says to me. "Don't believe a word of it."

"It's true. The Aztecs used to eat them," Johnson says.

"They used to eat each other, what I hear," Blackwell says. "Hey, I got one. Two boys off the rez go to the big city for the first time. They see a hot-dog stand, so they decide to try one. After they get their wieners, one looks in his bun and says to the other, 'What part of the dog did you get?' "

Cisco laughs harder than anyone. "You gonna work that into your next campaign speech?"

"I save that one for friends. Raise."

"Call," says Carlos. The rest of us fold and watch Carlos lose two dozen black chips to Blackwell's pocket kings. "I should've won that one," Carlos growls, giving Blackwell a dark look.

"Hey, Hector," Blackwell says, "what's the difference between a poker player and a puppy?"

"I give up," says Cisco.

"After about six months, the puppy stops whining."

Carlos stands abruptly, walks to the window, and stares at his reflection.

Cisco says, "You hungry, Dools?"

"Course he is, Hector," says Blackwell, on a roll. "Look at the poor sod. He's in serious danger of falling below three hundred pounds."

Dooley smiles tolerantly and looks at Cisco. "You know me, Cis."

"Hey, Hector, can I call you Cis?" Blackwell asks.

"No," says Cisco, pushing back his chair. "What do you say we take a break? Maria has put out a nice spread for us."

While we were playing, a long table covered with food and drink appeared along the back wall. I am hungry and thirsty, but mostly I am in need of a bathroom, and a few moments alone with myself.

As soon as I am away from the game, and away from those men, my pores open up and my shoulders relax. This is not like any poker game I've been in before. The stakes are high, sure, but what's really getting to me is the undercurrent of testosterone-fueled hostility. These guys are at war.

I stare at my reflection and make a few minor adjustments. All I can do is keep my eyes and ears tuned, and play my best game. I'm down $2,100, but that can turn around in one or two hands. It's Cisco's money anyway.

That was the deal he offered me. My job back at the casino and a ten-thousand-dollar stake in what he called "the softest game in town." As if any game with Dooley Braun and Hector Vega at the table could be considered "soft." In return, I'm supposed to watch, listen, and inform. And make as much money off Johnson, Begay, and Blackwell as I can. Anything I win is mine to keep.

I am leaving the bathroom, about to turn out the light, when I notice a grainy black-and-white photo on the wall—several dozen men sitting at or standing behind a poker table supporting a large pile of cash. At the bottom of the photo is written "World Series of Poker." I look over the men and immediately pick out several of the old-time poker greats: Johnny Moss, Amarillo Slim, Jack Strauss, Puggy Pearson, and several others. I also see a younger, slimmer Dooley Braun delivering his sharklike grin from the front row. I'm guessing this is the World Series that Dooley won, but why would Cisco have hung it in his bathroom? Another face in the photo catches my eye. I look closer at the compact man in the far-right corner of the photo. He is wearing his long hair tied back with a bandanna, a thin cigar clutched between his teeth.

I knew Cisco learned to play poker somewhere, but I had no idea he had learned from the best.

31

WHEN I RETURN to the game room, it feels different. Blackwell and Johnson are standing by the windows talking and smiling way too hard. Cisco and Dooley are sitting at the card table, Dooley making his way through a platter of empanadas and flautas, Cisco sipping bottled water and talking. Dooley nods every few seconds, but I don't think he is listening.

Carlos is mixing a drink, cognac and Coke, his fourth. He's down the price of a new pair of boots. I guess at this point he figures a couple of drinks can't hurt. He might be right. He seems way too wound up and jittery. Maybe the alcohol will take some of the edge off.

Now that I can see them, I must admit his boots are spectacular. A squash-blossom pattern of turquoise is set into a matrix of silver and gold filigree. There must be a hundred chunks of polished turquoise on each boot. Even the heels are decorated with turquoise studs. Maybe if I win big tonight I'll order a pair for myself. I bet I could get them in a size six for under ten thousand.

"I like your boots," I say.

A muscle under his right eye is twitching madly. He makes a sound in his nose and drops his eyes to his feet, then looks up and away, as if I've evaporated.

Since Carlos is clearly not feeling talkative, I head for the dessert end of the buffet and pick out some fruits and small pastries. Blackwell sees me and turns abruptly away from Johnson.

"Hey, the pro from Dover," he says.

"What is that, anyway?"

"It's from *M*A*S*H*. Hawkeye says he's the pro from Dover."

"I thought Trapper John said it."

"In the movie, yeah, but in the book it was Hawkeye."

"Which Dover is he from? The one with the white cliffs or the one in Ohio?"

"New Hampshire, I think. There are a bunch of them, though, aren't there?"

"Well, *this* pro from Dover is losing," I say.

"That makes two of us. Four of us, actually. Hector and Dooley are cleaning our clocks. Maybe we oughta team up."

"Maybe they're from Dover."

Blackwell laughs. "Let me ask you something." He leans in close. "What are you doing here, anyway?" He is still smiling, but the question is put hard.

"Cisco invited me," I says.

"You call him Cisco, too?"

"That's the name he uses at the casino."

"Well, I've always known him as Hector. We go back a ways. I knew Hector when he was a Coyotero Apache. Hell, I knew him when he was living on gummint cheese and fry bread." Blackwell's lips curl into a parody of a smile. "You know him from the casino, then?"

"I work there. I'm a prop."

"A prop?" His eyebrows shoot up. "And you're playing stakes like these?"

"Just for a change of pace," I say.

A loud cackle grabs our attention. Cisco is laughing, slapping his knee, while Dooley is standing up brushing taco filling from his lap, his face red with embarrassment or anger—I suspect both.

"You know," Blackwell says, "I do believe old Hector has finally gone round the bend."

I win a few hands after the break, putting me up about four thousand. Carlos is playing worse than ever, pumping jerky, frenetic bets into the pot with hands a dog wouldn't play. His long fingers drum the table rail between hands. At each new deal he snatches up the cards hungrily, and what he sees writes itself across his normally impassive face.

Blackwell is a better player, but also more predictable. Whenever I'm in a pot with him he thinks he can run over me because I'm a girl. I let him bet me off a couple hands, then play back at him a few hands later with a raise when the turn puts a second jack on the board. Blackwell hesitates, then makes a weak call. I bet out when a rag hits on the river. Blackwell shrugs and pitches his cards into the muck. Just for fun, I show him my stone-cold bluff.

Carlos laughs and says, "She got you, Alex."

"I realize that," he says with a politician's grin.

Cisco is wearing his Mona Lisa smile. He has seen me make that play before. I don't bluff often, but when I do, I make it work. Blackwell and Carlos will be paying off my legitimate bets for the rest of the night. I might even get some action from Johnson, though so far he's been playing with a healthy dose of caution.

Cisco and Dooley, of course, are nobody's fools.

Blackwell keeps his game under control for about a dozen hands after my bluff, then Carlos wins a nice pot off him by hitting a long-shot draw. Something happens in Blackwell's head, an almost audible click. The next hand, Blackwell reraises Dooley, bets the ace-eight-six flop, bets again, and keeps betting when a deuce, and then another eight hits the board. Dooley calls him down. Blackwell flips up his queen-six off-suit.

"Sixes."

Dooley turns up his cards. "Nines."

It is one hell of a call on Dooley's part. As for Blackwell, it's official now: the man is on tilt.

Carlos and Blackwell are now in nearly every pot, shoving chips back and forth between their slowly eroding stacks, with Cisco, Dooley, Johnson, or me occasionally coming in to take a bite. Carlos busts out again when he flops top pair with jack-ten and runs smack into Dooley's pocket queens. He buys in for another rack.

Cisco, Dooley, and I are doing our own quiet dance, trying to stay out of each other's way as we take turns knocking off Carlos, Blackwell, and, less frequently, Johnson. The butchers are slaughtering the lambs, one chop at a time.

The biggest hand of the night goes down between Cisco and Dooley. I'm dealing. They raise each other three times preflop—Cisco finally just calls. I figure they've both got big pairs. I flop a deuce-four-seven of three different suits—rainbow rags. It looks like a safe flop to a big pocket pair. Cisco checks, Dooley bets, Cisco raises, Dooley reraises, Cisco thinks for thirty seconds, then calls. Now I put Dooley on pocket aces or kings, and I think Cisco is chasing. His check-raise and subsequent call surprise me. He must suspect that he's beat. But with nearly $5,000 in the pot, his $600 call is not so bad. He could catch a set and win three or four more bets.

Dooley's eyes are almost closed, his soft body is melting into his chair. Cisco's eyes are obscured by his thick glasses. His mouth is slightly open. They look like two old men sleeping.

Johnson, Blackwell, and Carlos Begay are watching intently. I turn an ace, putting two clubs on the board.

Cisco checks, Dooley bets, Cisco check-raises again! Now I'm completely lost. Cisco must have at least one ace, and the only card I can imagine him having *with* that ace, given the action so far, is *another* ace. So his check-raise and call on the flop had to be some weird version of a slow-play. But what the hell can Dooley have?

Dooley reraises, and Cisco instantly calls.

When I'm deep in a hand I can think about my own cards and the other player's cards, and I can think about what another player thinks I have, and what he thinks I think he has, and even what he thinks I think he thinks I have, but after that things get very hazy. I wonder how hazy things have gotten for these two.

"Card, Peeky," Blackwell says.

I turn up the river card, the ten of spades. Cisco checks. Dooley grunts and goes into a huddle, thick fingers riffling stacks of chips.

Cisco watches him for a few seconds, then says, "Don't bet it, Dools. I got king high and I'm gonna call you."

Dooley pushes out six black chips. "Call if you got to, Cis," he says.

Cisco flips up his hand, king-queen of diamonds, then calls the bet.

"King high, no pair," he says.

Dooley slowly deflates. I can almost hear the air hissing out of him.

"What the fuck are you doing to me, Cisco?" he says. "What are you fucking doing?"

"I called you, Dools," Cisco says.

Dooley smiles sadly and flicks his cards into the muck. He waddles off, hitching up his pants as he disappears down the hallway.

Blackwell says, "Hector, what in God's name just happened?"

Carlos is staring at the board shaking his head. "Man, I'd a made the nut straight," he says.

I gather the cards, square up the deck, and pass it to Johnson. "Your deal."

"Aren't we going to wait for Dooley?"

"Dools won't be back," says Cisco.

Blackwell, looking at the depleted stack in front of Dooley's empty seat, says, "Looks like he's down a few, Hector."

"He's good for it."

Carlos is staring hungrily at Cisco's enormous collection of chips. His eye is jumping; his lips are white with tension.

"Deal the cards," he says.

32

THE GAME BREAKS UP a little after three. Carlos bets his last eight chips on a pair of fours, loses to my queens and jacks, throws his hand faceup in the muck.

"Need another rack, Carlos?" Blackwell asks.

Carlos kicks back his chair and stalks off looking dark and dangerous.

"The man is irate," Blackwell says.

"He'll get over it," Cisco says.

Bruce Johnson, who caught a few good hands toward the end of the night, counts down his chips and cheerfully writes a check for $1,520.

Blackwell, who is down $8,000, says, "Put it on my tab, Hector."

Cisco shakes his head, smiling resignedly.

I have the feeling they've done this before. I'm up $12,800, half of what I need to put my daughter through treatment. We count up Dooley's remaining chips. He's down half a rack.

A few minutes later, Carlos returns carrying a tooled leather attaché case. His mood has shifted from dangerously pissed to goofy jollity. "You boys sure did kick my ass," he says with a laugh. It does not sound like something he would say, and his laugh has a hysterical edge to it. He pops open the case and brings out a sheaf of hundreds two inches thick—maybe fifty or sixty thousand.

Cisco says, "You're down three racks."

Carlos tosses the stack of bills onto the table in front of me. "Count it out, honey," he says.

"Whatever you say . . . sweetie pie."

He doesn't know what to do with that. I count off thirty thousand and hand the rest back to him. He frowns at the thin sheaf, shrugs, and says, "I guess I could've lost more."

I stay behind after Blackwell, Johnson, and Carlos leave. Cisco is sitting at the table racking chips. I pour myself a glass of red wine.

"You want something to drink?" I ask him.

"No thank you, Peeky." He looks up and smiles wearily. "You did okay."

"Not as good as you. What are you up? Thirty-some?"

"Ayyy, minus Alex's eight. I'll never see that."

I join him at the table and help him rack the chips.

"What do you think Dooley had that hand where you called him with king high?" I ask.

"Oh, he had a king-jack. Probably clubs."

"You can read him that good?"

"We've been playing together a long time."

"What was he doing in there with a king-jack? For that matter, how come you were pushing your king-queen so hard?"

"I don't know, Peeky. I really don't. Sometimes it just happens that way, you know? You got a read on the other guy, and you got a little something, and you run him down. I've seen you do it."

"Not like *that* you haven't."

He laughs. "So, Pee Key, what do you think of my partners in crime?"

I sit back and take a sip of wine. "You want me to just go down the list?"

Cisco nods.

"Okay, let's start with Bruce Johnson. Smart. Really smart. Charming as all get out. Likes to win. He'd rather win than breathe. If he knew how, he'd cheat. He just hasn't figured out a safe way to do it. Play with him long enough, he will. More likely, he'll claim the consolation prize."

"What's that?"

"You never heard that? You're the big winner and you walk out to your car and the guy you beat hits you over the head with a two-by-four and takes the money. He gets the consolation prize."

Cisco laughs. "Maybe twenty years ago. Nowadays he's too civilized."

"The two-by-four was metaphorical."

Cisco tightens his lips and nods.

"He's a beautiful man," I say. "He knows how to look at a woman."

"You got a little crush on him, Pee Key?"

"Just making a general observation. Did you see his leak?"

"He paid off too many bets."

"Right. He always started with good cards. Once he entered a pot he stuck around till the bitter end. Like that hand where he drew out on you with his ace-queen."

"He got lucky."

"Yeah. Point is, if he's got some chips in the pot, it's going to take some big guns to blow him out of it."

"Okay. How about Dools?"

"You know, I never saw him play before."

"He surprise you?" Cisco asks as he fills another rack.

"Yeah . . . not so much the way he played—you have to be pretty good to win the World Series—but it surprised me how angry he was. I never saw that in him before."

Cisco stops moving.

"Where'd you get that? From him going off that way?"

"No. It was more . . . I don't know. Women's intuition?"

"Hah."

"There was just something about him. You've all got a lot more money than he does. Money and power. A guy like Dooley . . . here he is working at your casino taking a paycheck. You still play at being equals, sitting around this card table, but Dooley knows it's a mirage. It burns in him."

Cisco nods, taking it in.

"As for the congressman, he's what-you-see-is-what-you-get."

"I've known Alex almost as long as Dools."

"He's not about money. It's something else with him."

"He wants our land," Cisco says. "It's a white man thing. First they take it all, then they give a little piece of it back, then they make us sell it back one piece at a time. Alex wants me to sell his friends two more sections so they can put up another development. I am not selling."

"It's more than just the land. It's whether you do what he wants you to do. He doesn't care how fast he gets where he's going as long as he's behind the wheel, you know? It's all about control."

"Sounds about right." Cisco sighs. "You don't much like my friends, do you?"

"With friends like those . . ."

"Yeah, yeah, I know. Okay. My Navajo son-in-law."

"Nice boots."

"I tell you how much they cost him?"

"Yeah. He lost two pair playing cards tonight. How many pairs of boots can he afford to throw away?"

"It's coming in pretty good for us. He has money."

"How did he end up running the casino?"

"I put him in."

"Why?"

Cisco shrugs. "I have no sons. Part of the deal we made with Johnson was that he put one of my people in charge before the contract expired. Carlos is family, and he had executive experience."

"He doesn't seem the executive type."

"He ran a trading post up at Window Rock selling dream catchers and sand paintings to the tourists."

"Oh." I take a moment to phrase my next observation, then

decide to simply say it. "He's not very stable. He might have a problem."

"You mean with the booze."

"Yes. Also, he does not respect you."

Cisco nods, his face hard.

"He thinks you're irrelevant—one of the reasons I say he's not very smart."

Cisco looks away, embarrassed.

"You asked me to be straight with you."

"Right now I am pretending you are somebody else."

I let him pretend for a few seconds, then say, "That's what you wanted to know, right?"

"I know Carlos is a problem. The lack of respect. Within the tribe, respect is power. Unfortunately, the younger members of the council listen to Carlos."

"It's more than just lack of respect. I think he resents you even more than Dooley does."

Cisco shakes his head slowly. "You are telling me things that I see but choose not to know. I have been playing the old fool for so long that I fear I have become him."

"An old fool would not hear what I'm saying." My wine has gone from my glass to my head. I twist the stem between my fingers and wait.

"So I can trust no one," he says.

"You can trust Blackwell and Johnson to look out for their own interests. Carlos is unpredictable—you saw how he played cards. As for Dooley . . . I'd keep him where you can see him."

"We go back a long ways, me and Dools. You know, I give him a piece of the action. He gets a tenth of a point of the card room gross."

"What's that, a couple hundred bucks a week?"

"Something like that."

"Pocket money."

"I suppose."

We sit there, each thinking our own thoughts. Cisco is an easy

man to be quiet with—my usual fill-the-silence-with-chatter impulse is muted. After a few minutes I say, "I have to tell you, I'm not
sure what I'm doing here. I'm not telling you anything you don't
know."

"You see from the outside. I am deep inside my family." He
meshes his fingers. "We are all tied together." He twists his fingers
into a knot. "I am caught inside. You see?"

I nod, thinking of Jaymie. "Families are confusing."

"You have a daughter."

"Yes. Jaymie."

He waits.

"She is having some troubles," I say. I hadn't intended to share
this with him.

"With the drugs, yes?"

"How do you know that?"

"People tell me things."

"Other Peekys?"

"Other kinds of people." He grins. "Like I told you before: I
checked you out."

"Oh." I imagine an army of Native American detectives hiding
in my bushes, then I think about Teresa Alvarez at Recovery Asso-
ciates. I see her face and something clicks.

"Teresa Alvarez?"

He nods and claps his hands. "Very good, Peeky! She is my
youngest daughter."

"So much for confidentiality," I say. Then something else hits
me. "Kind of a big coincidence, me ending up at your daughter's."

Cisco scratches his chin. "How did you find her?"

"A flyer I picked up at the card room."

"There you go," says Cisco.

"Oh. How did she know to mention my visit to you?"

"You told her you were a poker player. And that you worked at
the casino."

"She shouldn't have said anything."

"Yes, well, she probably feels very bad. But maybe it is a good thing, Peeky. Your daughter is welcome at Ridge Point, our chemical dependency program. We have many kinds of people there, not just Indians. It is state-of-the-art."

"Uh, thank you." The whole Jaymie thing settles on me, pressing me into the chair. "How much does it cost?"

"For you, it is what you can afford."

I am suddenly very empty and tired, and my eyes are wet.

"Thank you," I say.

"Peeky?"

"Yes?"

"Do you think it is possible that one of my close personal friends might have had something to do with the robbery?"

I sit up straight.

"Are you serious?" I ask.

Cisco looks old and tired. "Maybe I'm getting paranoid in my golden years." He stands, hands on the polished mesquite table rail, pushing himself erect. "But even crazy people have enemies. Tomorrow, Peeky. Tomorrow you come back to work. I have told Carlos to give you your job back. He has agreed to do this, to humor me. Come to work tomorrow and I will show you some things."

33

THE SKY IS BRIGHTENING over the Rincon Mountains by the time I get home. My living room is still a disaster area. I make a promise to myself to clean it up today. The pile of ashes by the fireplace is the scariest part of the mess. My traditional, semiromantic side tells me to buy a new urn and give Robert's "cremains" a new home. My pragmatic self says just vacuum him up. Robert was a pragmatist. He would've hoovered himself in an instant.

I am saved from having to make that decision by the arrival of the locksmith. It takes him twenty minutes to add a heavy-duty dead-bolt lock to the front door. I pay him, lock both locks when he leaves, stagger zombielike toward my bedroom, and fall face-first onto my new air mattress without bothering to undress. I spend about thirty seconds thinking I'll never be able to sleep, and then I am gone.

I awaken to the sound of the front door handle being jiggled. I open my eyes and sit up all in the same motion. Late morning sunlight is slicing through the miniblinds. The sound is gone. Did I dream it? I grab the .38 from the floor next to the mattress. I have never loved guns, but I feel Robert's hand in the taped-up grip, and I am made stronger. I move quietly from the bed to the open bedroom door and listen. Thank God I'm still dressed—it would be so much harder to confront an intruder in my nightgown.

I hear an airplane in the distance. The hum of the air conditioner. A car horn. I push my head out into the hallway and listen some more.

The sound comes from the back of the house this time. Metal on metal, the clack of a latch being released, the soft rumble of the patio door sliding open. My heart is pounding in my ears.

I can see down the short hallway to the kitchen doorway. I raise the gun and, holding it in both hands, my shoulder braced against the doorjamb, aim it at the exact point where I expect the intruder to appear.

I hear footsteps, rubber soles on Saltillo tile, then the fainter sound of feet on carpet. He's left the kitchen through the other door, straight into the living room.

I ease the bedroom door all the way open and step out into the hall. I hear a muffled curse from the living room, then a soft, scraping sound. I glide down the hall in my stocking feet, holding the gun straight out in front of me, using both hands. I peek into the living room.

At first I don't see him. I lower my gaze and find him on his hands and knees, jeans riding down his hips showing about two inches of ass crack. It looks like he's scrubbing the carpet. I step into the room, aiming at the crack.

What is he *doing*? For one full second I convince myself that this is some sort of weird nightmare. A man has broken into my house and he is on the floor, muttering to himself, sifting through my dead husband's ashes with his hands.

I take a shaky breath and yell something—I don't even think it's a word—as loud as I can.

He jerks as if he's been kicked, then slowly turns his head in my direction.

"Peeky?"

"Buddy. Jesus Christ."

He pushes himself up, palms grinding ash into the carpet.

"What the hell happened here?" he asks. Like it's my fault he's covered with cremains.

"What are you doing, Buddy?"

"You're pointing a gun at me, Peek."

"What's the difference? You're dead."

He raises his eyebrows and stares at me. I move the gun off him and point it at the ashes.

"What are you doing, Buddy?"

"Looking for a key."

"What key?"

"The key I left in that urn." He makes a surprised frown. "What happened?"

"I got robbed."

"Fuck. When? What day?"

"Sunday."

"Fuck." He stands up, brushing ashes from his knees. He looks old and tired. "Did they take anything?"

"Yeah, about forty grand."

"Oh man, they got your poke. Jesus, I'm sorry, Peek."

"Maybe you know who did it, Buddy." My voice is flat.

He shrugs. "You sure you haven't seen a key? A little thing." He holds his thumb and index finger about an inch and a half apart.

"I don't know what you're talking about."

"Shit. Maybe they got it. Maybe they think they got something but they got no idea what it's for or maybe they do and they don't know where it is. Now what the hell am I gonna do?" He's talking so fast I can hardly understand him.

"Did you kill that man, Buddy?"

"Who?" Blinking rapidly. "Woody? I'd kill that son of a bitch again if I could. You read in the papers what happened to Juan and Darrin? Woody. That night I went to meet him? Pulled a gun on me, but I was ready for him. I'm lucky to be alive."

"You're not alive," I say. "I identified your body."

"You did?" He grins, and the boy is back for a moment. "They bought it?"

"I think so."

"That's great." Suddenly cheerful. "Hey, you got a cup of coffee?"

"What's the key for, Buddy?"

"A storage locker down in Nogales. I stashed some money. Just got to move it across the border. A few hundred yards is all."

"Are you talking about the casino money?"

"Part of it. We whacked it up four ways, planned to get together later to make sure everybody got cut in fair. Me, I'm not greedy. I'm like you, Peek, I just want it to be fair for everybody. Not Woody. That's why I stashed the key here. Just in case. I didn't trust the son of a bitch, not after what he did to Darrin and Juan, so I dropped the key in your urn. I figured, you know, if things didn't go so good with Woody, at least he wouldn't get the money." He laughs, and I detect a note of hysteria. He follows me into the kitchen, his mouth going like a triphammer. "Christ, I've been going in a thousand directions the last few days. This isn't what I signed on for, suppose to be clean in-out in-out, nobody gets hurt, everybody fat and happy. Remind me not to get involved in any more armed robberies, would ya, Peek?"

"Buddy, are you high?"

"Couple a whites I got off Woody. Talk about your neighborhood speed freak, that guy was gonzo. Christ." He lights a cigarette. "I don't know what to do now. I'm too jazzed to think."

"Maybe if you gave the money back you'd calm down."

He gives me that look that's half mischievous boy, half kicked dog. "No can do, Peek. It's my nest egg. My golden parachute. My ace in the hole."

"How do you feel about decaf?" I say.

"Maybe with a shot of something in it?"

"You're drinking now, too?"

He shrugs, sits at the table, stands up, pats his pockets. "Got a match, Peek?"

"Your cigarette is lit, Buddy."

"Oh." He laughs. "Well fuck me with a totem pole. Hey, did you finally kill that plant your sister sent you?"

"Buddy, shut the fuck up, would you?"

He makes a zipper motion from one corner of his mouth to the other.

I set the gun on the counter and grind coffee beans. For a few minutes it's like old times, Buddy smoking, watching me make coffee after a long night, neither of us talking. Before, though, I wasn't making coffee for a robber and a murderer. Or at least I didn't know I was.

"What are you going to do, Buddy?" I meant the question to encompass the rest of his life, but his mind is on the money.

"I suppose I can just crack the lock. Go in there with a crowbar. Break into my own locker. What the hell, it's my stuff in there." He laughs. "Fucking ironic if I got busted for stealing my own money." He is interrupted by the same sound that woke me up ten minutes earlier: the rattle of the front doorknob.

"Expecting somebody?" he asks.

I set my coffee cup down. The doorbell rings. Buddy and I are looking at each other. Seconds pass. Whoever it is starts banging on the screen door.

"I suppose I should answer it. If I don't, they'll break in just like everybody else."

I go to the living room and peek past the blinds.

Jaymie.

I open the door.

"You changed the locks!" she says, accusing. Her hair is combed and her makeup is plastered on all the right parts of her face, but her eyes are red, and there is a slackness to her cheeks that makeup cannot hide.

"Where have you been?" I ask.

She pushes past me.

"God, what a mess! How come you haven't cleaned it up?"

"Are you okay?"

"I'm fine. Why?"

"Why? You disappeared, that's why."

"I've been staying with friends."

"What friends?"

"You don't know them. Got any ice cream?"

"Chunky Monkey?"

"Cool."

Ben & Jerry might be the only thing we have left in common. Jaymie follows me to the kitchen. The patio door is open. Buddy has disappeared; smoke from his cigarette still hangs in the air.

34

Y OU START SMOKING?" Jaymie asks, sniffing the air.

"No."

"Jesus, Mom, what's *that*?" She is looking at the .38 on the countertop.

"A gun," I say.

"Is it Feeb's?"

"It was your father's."

"Feeb's probably freakin' you took his gun away from him."

"Eduardo has it."

"Everybody I know is packing, even my mom. You guys are all psycho."

"I thought I heard somebody trying to break in."

"What if it was me?"

She's trying to put me on the defensive. And succeeding. I take out a carton of ice cream.

"How come you're all wrinkly?" she says. At first I think she's talking about my face, but she points at my blouse. "You sleep in your clothes?"

"I had a long night." But not much sleep. "You want coffee?"

She hesitates, but can't find anything wrong with the offer. "Okay."

Jaymie scoops Chunky Monkey into two bowls while I pour us each a cup of coffee. She lights a cigarette to go with her Chunky

Monkey. I get this weird déjà vu/twilight zone feeling like Buddy has morphed into Jaymie, and I'm doomed to play out the same cigarette and coffee scene over and over again.

"You should see your hair," Jaymie says.

I fight off the urge to run to a mirror.

"You should see your eyes," I say.

"I didn't sleep good last night," she says, her mouth full of ice cream, coffee, and mentholated smoke.

"Did you sleep at all?"

She shrugs, which I read as no.

I can't believe how hard this is. I take a breath and plunge. "Jaymie, I don't know what all you've been doing. I don't know if you're smoking crack or taking pills or what. But I think you need to get into a program."

"Program?" She laughs. "What have *you* been reading?"

"I'm serious, Jaymie. You need help."

"Mom, gimme a break. I'm fine. It's just— Everything's so *hard*. I need time to work things out."

"You're telling me you haven't been using drugs?"

"Yes! I mean no! It was just— Okay, I partied a few times. Eddie and I were going through a rough patch. I needed a break. Anyway, I'm done with all that." She gives me her full-faced wide-eyed little girl look. "I swear."

I want to believe her so much it hurts. I feel it in my ribs. But I force myself to say, "I don't believe you, Jaymie. I think you have a habit."

"You think I'm a junkie?" She laughs a little too loud.

"I don't think you can stop using without help."

"Well, I don't need *your* help, that's for sure. Little Miss Gamblaholic."

"We're talking about you. About the drugs. Crack, or whatever it is you've been taking."

"You wouldn't know the difference, would you? Look, lots of people like to get high now and then—it doesn't mean they're a bunch of depraved junkies. You'd be surprised who likes to smoke a pipe now and then. I see all kinds of people. Soccer moms, fire-men, politicians, even some of these gramma-grampa types from Green Valley. I half expect to see you doing it, Mom. You're the type. You wouldn't believe how many gamblers like to get high. I run into people from the casino all the time. Those casino Indians are into it big-time."

"Like who?"

"Like all of 'em. You'd be surprised." Her cigarette ash drops into her ice cream. "Oh, shit." She shoves the bowl aside and takes another drag. "Anyway, I'm not using now. If you don't want to be-lieve me, then you've got a problem, not me." She stares at me with her eyes turned up to full glare. "You want me to pee in a cup for you? Go get it analyzed? Is that what you want?"

I look away. I know what she is doing, turning it around on me again, but I don't know how to respond. This is not like poker. It feels more like four-dimensional chess played on a board the size of the universe.

"Why did you come here?" I ask.

"What, I can't come visit my mom?"

"Why come to me and not your husband?"

"Eddie?"

"You have another husband?"

"Eddie doesn't understand."

"Maybe he understands better than you think. Maybe he knows when you're lying to him. Maybe the reason you're here is because you know you can bullshit me."

Her face goes tight and I think she's going to start crying. In-stead, she starts looking around frantically.

"Don't you have any ashtrays?"

I snatch the cigarette from her hand and throw it in the sink.

"Shit, Mom, are you PMS'n or what?"

"No." Maybe I am, not that it matters.

"You could fool me." She looks at her nails. She looks at the cupboard above the refrigerator. She brushes a strand of hair back from her forehead. She looks at the door.

"Jaymie . . ."

"What?" Her eyes light on me, then flick away.

"You don't have to fix this alone."

"I'm not broken, Mom. I'm a human being. Christ, you're worse than Eddie."

"He wants to help. So do I."

Now she's giving me a controlled, measuring look. "You know what would help me right now?"

"What?"

"A place to crash. Just for a couple days."

"You should go home to your husband."

"I will. I will. But not right now."

"Where have you been staying?"

"Look, can we talk about all this later? I'm really— I just need to lie down for a while."

"Okay. But call your husband first." I toss her the cordless. "Let him know you're alive."

She massages the phone. "Okay."

I wait for her to dial the number.

She says, "A little privacy?"

I go to the bathroom and start the tub. The sound of running water helps. The guest bedroom is still a mess. I straighten up a little, put new sheets on the bed, then go back to the kitchen. Jaymie is holding the phone in her lap, looking miserable. I pour myself another cup of coffee.

"You talk to him?"

"I'm getting to it."

"He loves you, Jaymie."

"I know," she says. "Sometimes I wish he didn't."

The greatest therapeutic effect of a hot bath—assuming it's hot enough—is its capacity to suspend rational thought. I slide slowly beneath the surface, barely able to tolerate the heat. I can hear the mumble of Jaymie's voice from the kitchen. If Jaymie goes home to Eduardo, I think, it might be time to call Teresa Alvarez and set up an intervention. Teresa and I could just sort of drop in on them and . . . intervene. How would Jaymie react?

Not well, I think.

The whole process scares the crap out of me. How would I feel if Buddy and Jaymie and my sister and Eduardo all showed up at my door and said, "We've come to talk to you about how fucked up your life is, Peeky. We want you to check into the hospital for four weeks of brainwashing. . . ."

Ugh. I sink until my ears are submerged and close my eyes and let the hot water fever my brain. Fragments of thought come and go, making surrealistic connections: Jaymie raises Cisco three cacti, Johnson's smile beats aces up, naked boy shooting turquoise-encrusted gun, clown ashes in my living room.

I lay there until my heart starts pounding, warning me of hyperthermia. I sit up. How long have I been soaking? Ten minutes? An hour? My fingertips are wrinkled. Everything is fuchsia. I am a lobster.

I wrap myself in a towel and pad barefoot into the hall. The door to the guest bedroom is open. The bed is unused. Jaymie is not in the kitchen, either. If not for the empty ice cream carton and the sour smell of mentholated tobacco, her visit might have been a dream.

She has gone home to Eduardo, I tell myself. She called him, they talked, and she went home. Didn't she? I pick up the phone and hit the redial. On the second ring a male voice answers.

"Hello."

It is not Eduardo.

"Who am I speaking to?" I ask.

He hangs up.

The therapeutic effects of the bath unravel. I wonder whether Jaymie went through my cupboards searching for Cap'n Crunch. I wonder whether she noticed that the saguaro cookie jar is missing.

I see my purse on the countertop. I open it and pull out the wad of cash I won the night before. How much should I have? The $12,800 I won, plus about $1,500 I had in my purse before. I count it down.

Two thousand short.

I try to find a paring of comfort in the fact that she did not take it all.

35

I CALL EDUARDO at Sixth Street Motors and tell him about Jaymie's visit.

"You should have called me!"

"I'm calling you now."

"You say she took some money?"

"A couple thousand."

"That much? We won't see her for a week."

"I've been thinking about the intervention thing. You know, what Teresa Alvarez said about users who are forced into a program not doing so good. I can get her into this drug treatment place, Ridge Point, but she's going to have to make her own decision. I don't think we can make her do anything she isn't ready to do."

"You mean we do nothing?"

"Yes. No. I don't know. She stole money from me. That was the only reason she came to see me. She looked me straight in the face and lied to me."

"Maybe if we both sit down with her . . ."

"I don't think she'd hear a thing we said. I'm pretty mad at her right now, Eduardo."

"So what do you want to do?"

"I'd like to know she's safe. That's all. When she's ready to ask for help, then it'll be time to help her."

He doesn't speak for several seconds.

"I'll check out a couple places after work," he says.

"Call me on my cell if you find her."

I can't possibly feel much worse, so I tackle the living room. I start by sweeping up Robert's ashes as best I can. I dump him into an empty shoe box. It looks like something that would be good for my garden. Maybe he'd like that. Help the plants grow.

Part of me hopes Buddy will return. I didn't get a chance to grill him about who broke into my house. I'm sure he knows. I have other questions as well. Who else was involved in the robbery? Why did he go to meet Woody Stumpf if he thought Woody might try to kill him? But another part of me hopes I never see him again.

I figure about ten percent of Robert has settled deep into the carpet. The carpet will have to go—no way am I taking a daily stroll over my husband's cremains—but for now, I get out my old Electrolux to vacuum up what I can. Afternoon sunlight is slanting through the windows; the air is thick with dust motes. Robert motes. I am breathing him.

As I vacuum I realize that the one place the burglars didn't look when they tore my house apart was inside the vacuum cleaner. I make a mental note: vacuum cleaner bag—good place to hide money.

I'm shoving the nose of the Electrolux under the sofa when the machine emits a horrible squeal, the smell of burning rubber, then whimpers and dies. I pull the plug and sit on the cushionless sofa and start to cry. I am crying without knowing whether I am mourning Robert or Jaymie or Buddy or the vacuum cleaner or my own crappy life.

After a time, the tears stop and I feel better. I turn the vacuum on its side and see the problem immediately. Shreds of rubber belt are tangled around the rotary brush. I pull the remains of the belt clear and try turning the brush by hand.

It won't move the way it's supposed to. I twist it in the opposite direction and a chunk of metal drops out onto the carpet. Part of the vacuum cleaner? I pick it up. A bent and twisted key.

I look at it closely. The number 143 is stamped on the head. The other side says "Do Not Duplicate." The key is badly mangled. It doesn't really matter. Buddy will crack open his locker with a crowbar and be off to Mexico in no time.

I drop the key in my purse and look at the clock. Almost time to go to work. I wrap most of my remaining cash in tinfoil, label it "eggplant parmesan," and toss it in the back of the freezer. It's not as sneaky as hiding it in the vacuum cleaner, but it's a lot cleaner.

Also, Jaymie hates eggplant.

I am working on my face when the phone rings. I let the machine answer. It's Buddy. I listen to him talk a hundred miles an hour into the tape.

"Peeky, it's me. Sorry I had to take off like that. I'm skittish as hell. But listen, I'm down . . . you know, at my storage locker? This place is huge. There must be a thousand lockers here, and I can't remember which one is mine. The number's on the key! And I keep thinking. It seems weird to me that they'd go through your whole house and just take that one key. I mean, how would they know to look for it? They were looking for cash. So it doesn't make sense that they'd take the key even if they ran across it, so I'm thinking maybe it's still there, y'know? Like they knocked the urn over and the key flew behind the sofa cushions or something. Anyway, could you look around a little? Listen, I'll call you later, okay?"

He hangs up. I finish my face, push Buddy out of my mind, and go to work on my hair.

36

"Ayyy, Pee Key. Long time no see."

"Hi, Cisco. How you doing?"

"They let me win one now and then."

I laugh. Cisco is sitting at a $3–6 holdem table behind a nice pile of chips, about $400. The other players are not doing so well.

"Don't these folks know you're the pro from Dover?"

Cisco puts a finger to his lips. "Shhh!"

Nobody laughs.

"You gonna play with us, Pee Key?"

"Maybe later. I've got to go see Vergie and get myself officially reinstated."

"Okay, Pee Key."

As I walk through the Card Club toward Dooley's office I get a cautious smile from Richard, who is working the board, and a nod from Marisa, the floor person. They aren't calling security, so apparently the word has come down that I've been un-eighty-sixed. Martha Green, dealing Omaha at table five, gives me a smile and a wink.

I feel as though I've been gone for months.

Vergie Drucker is all business. By title she is Dooley Braun's executive assistant. In practice, she runs the Card Club operation. Vergie is not what you would call an expressive individual. Is she glad to see me back? Does she care? I can't tell. She has me fill out a new W-4, sign a confidentiality agreement and an employee pledge—both of which are just boilerplate designed to intimidate new employees—and she gives me a new time card.

"You want me to throw this away now, or wait till I get out the door?" I ask.

"Why don't you wait," says Vergie. She either has a very dry sense of humor, or no sense of humor at all. I've never been able to figure out which. She says, "You'll be taking Donny Keyes's hours, if that's all right with you."

I remember then that Donny got himself fired for going off on a slot machine.

"Who's got my old hours?"

"Sam Harris. New employee."

"You hear anything from Donny?"

"Not a peep since he got the boot," says Vergie. "He hasn't even been back to pick up his last paycheck. He's probably gone to Vegas. Isn't that where all you props go to die?"

Sense of humor, or no? I still don't know.

I never thought much about that "you can't go home again" stuff, but now I believe it. I'm playing in a shorthanded $6–12 holdem in the same old club with the same old faces, but it feels artificial and, after last night's $300–600 action, small. But I'm not here to play cards; I'm here as an extension of Hector Vega's influence. I am still not sure why, but I think it has something to do with Buddy and the robbery. One thing for sure: Hector Vega is not doing me favors for free.

Jaymie keeps popping up in my mind. I imagine myself walking the streets of Tucson calling her name. What more can I do? I take comfort in Cisco's offer to give her a bed at Ridge Point, then push Jaymie to a room in the back of my mind and try to focus on the cards.

At the moment, $6–12 holdem is the biggest game in the

house. That's unusual for a Thursday evening. I would have expected at least three red-chip games, and probably a pot-limit game
as well. Gene the Machine says all the higher limit players have
moved over to Casino Del Sol, the Pascua Yaqui casino.

"Them guys is superstitious as cats," he says.

I didn't know cats were superstitious, but I know what he
means. The robbery spooked them. Besides, it only takes one loose
player to move his action down the road, and the hyenas follow
him like wounded wildebeest.

The game soon fills up and I take a break. Martha is sitting
primly at the table in the employee lounge eating a cucumber and
carrot sandwich. She looks up at me, swallows delicately, and says,
"The prodigal returns."

I laugh. "Prodigal I'm not," I say. "Fired, I was."

"Ah well, biblical scholarship was never my strong suit. Love
the outfit."

I'm wearing a yellow linen top and a pair of metallic gold
slacks. It's the first time I've worn the slacks, and probably the last.
While they have the advantage of being impossible to wrinkle, they
also retain every BTU of body heat. I open my mouth to share this
bit of intelligence with Martha, then change my mind.

"Thank you," I say. "I feel like the Maize Queen."

"And a very fine Maize Queen you make. So, back from the
dead. How ever did you arrange that?"

"I guess someone decided they had made a mistake."

"Remarkable. I thought that ability had been bred out of the
male race entirely. I wonder if any of the others will be returning."

"Others?"

"Hanna, Rob Hall, Vang, J.C., Angela, and Greg. All made re-
dundant."

"Angela got fired? Isn't she Santa Cruz?"

"It was a virtual slaughter, dear. Saturday bloody Saturday.
Rumor is, they were copping chips—the dealers, that is."

"Were they?"

"I very much doubt it. Hanna and Rob are consummate professionals. Only J.C. is weak-minded enough to try something like that, and he's barely competent to shuffle a deck, let alone palm enough chips to make it worth his while. I think Vang got the ax because he's Vietnamese—you know, in the wake of Tran's incredible jackpot run. Whatever the truth, the rumors were enough to scare off our red-chip players."

"So that's why they left."

"Indeed. Another example of our leaders' brilliantly short-sighted approach to casino management: fire your best people and scare off your regulars. No dear, I fear it is all a vast conspiracy to give all our business to the Pascua Yaqui. It's quite mad."

"Have they been replaced?"

"The dealers? Not necessary, dear, what with the consequent drop in business." She looks into her lunch box. "Would you care for a sandwich? I've extra."

"No thank you. I'm cutting back on cucumbers this year."

I'm settling into a new $6–12 game when Cisco taps me on the shoulder. I shovel my chips into my purse and walk with him. He grabs my arm for support. His cane is hooked over his arm.

"Where are we going?" I ask.

"I want to show you my son-in-law's desk."

"Oh. Did you know they fired six dealers last week?"

Cisco nods.

"All the red-chip players are over at Casino del Sol," I say.

"You hear from your daughter?" he asks.

"She showed up in my kitchen this morning, stole some money from my purse, and left. I think she's got a serious problem, and I'm not sure there's a thing I can do about it."

"Don't forget, she is welcome at Ridge Point."

We enter the Slot Palace and wind our way through the labyrinth of clattering machines to the elevators at the back of the room. Cisco punches the button for the fourth floor.

"Right now I'd just like to know she's alive," I say. "So I can be mad at her."

"You feel guilty," Cisco says.

"I feel helpless. She's not ready to ask for help. If she doesn't want help, I don't think I can help her."

"It is a hard thing, to ask for help."

O UTSIDE CARLOS BEGAY'S OFFICE, a buxom Asian girl is
sitting behind an acrylic desk buffing her extraordinary
fingernails, bright scarlet decorated with metallic gold
dragons. She smiles and says, "Carlos and the others are expecting
you, Mr. Vega."

We enter the office through an oversize oak door that looks as
out of place as the receptionist's acrylic desk. The interior of Carlos's office is equally jarring. The walls are covered with artwork: a
six-by-eight-foot Navajo sand painting, a large oil painting of dogs
playing poker, a dream catcher six feet across, a painting of a re-
clining nude that probably came from behind the bar of a strip
club, and a garish landscape that might have depicted a sunset
over the Tucson Mountains. None of the art is particularly good,
in my view, and except for being mostly oversize and with a pre-
dominantly Native American/Southwestern slant, it doesn't go together well at all.

Carlos Begay is sitting behind a desk made of twelve-foot-long,
four-inch-thick lacquered mesquite planks supported by two
mesquite trunks that look as if they are growing right out of the
floor. The thing must weigh a thousand pounds.

"Nice desk," I say.

Carlos is wearing a dark suit, expensive-looking, over a pale yellow silk shirt with a bolo tie. The tie clasp is understated by Carlos's standards: a chunk of polished turquoise not quite as large as a walnut. He is also wearing the irritated, small-eyed look of a man whose valuable time is being wasted.

"What is she doing here?" he asks Cisco.

"My secretary," Cisco replies.

Blaise Hunt, looking rigid and attentive in his uniform, is planted solidly on a chair to the right of the desk. He gives me a reptilian blink.

Bruce Johnson has one slim hip resting against the front of the mesquite slab, hands in the pockets of a pair of soft khaki trousers, Bally loafers showing a wedge of tanned ankle, and a taupe, V-neck cashmere sweater so fine and thin I can see the shadow of his nipples. His understated outfit probably cost more than Carlos's suit. He gives me that boyish, confident Cheshire grin, teeth dazzling against his deeply tanned face. I fight back the urge to stroke him.

Standing off to one side is Gayle Vega, looking elegant as always. She is wearing a soft chocolate brown suit with delicate pin-striping. She nods, meeting my eyes, then looks away.

Cisco waddles over to one of the four vacant side chairs, grabs the back, and looks around. "We all here?" he says. "Okay then." He works his way around the chair and sits down. I take the seat next to him; Gayle sits on his other side.

"Hector and his women," Carlos says to Johnson, who does not respond.

Cisco says, "Sit down, Bruce. You make me feel like an old man."

"You're not old, Hector," Johnson says with a grin. "You're just getting broke in." He uncrosses his ankles, and folds himself into a chair.

"Okay then," Cisco says again.

We all wait expectantly. After a few seconds, Cisco says, "Carlos? You want to get things started?"

Carlos frowns. "This is your meeting."

"No, son-in-law, this is your meeting. You are in charge here, no?"

"You asked for this sit-down. What did you want to talk about?"

I notice that Carlos never refers to Cisco by name or by title.

Cisco says, "Are you asking me to take your place?"

"I'm asking you what you want to talk about."

"Do my words mean so little that you have forgotten our conversation this morning?"

Carlos almost, but not quite, rolls his eyes. "I haven't forgotten. You want to talk about the robbery."

"I want to know what we're doing, yes. And I think we should talk about the firings," Cisco says.

"The layoffs." Carlos gives me a hard look. I hit him back with my best smile.

"Where did our red-chip players go?" Cisco asks.

Carlos shrugs one shoulder. "We had a light week. After last Friday, it's only natural. Poker players come and go."

"Sometimes they just go."

Bruce Johnson blinks at this, holding his face in a near-smile. Blaise Hunt remains impassive.

Carlos, emoting great patience, sits forward, elbows on his desk, and folds his hands. "Hector . . ." he says.

Cisco's glasses seem to increase in opacity—he does not like his son-in-law calling him Hector.

Carlos continues, "Since I've been running this casino—and I *am* running it—our monthly gross has increased seventeen percent. Not one point of that increase has come from the card room. In this business, slots are the moneymakers. One slot player contributes more to our bottom line than any three poker players. A slot takes up a tenth the space of a poker table, and it requires one thirtieth the employees. I have numbers, if you want to look them over."

Cisco waits, giving Carlos nothing.

Carlos's voice becomes soft and unctuous. "I know you like to play cards, Father." He makes the more respectful form of address sound like an insult. "I like to play poker, too. But we are trying to run a business here." He looks over at Bruce Johnson. "Bruce, how many Indian casinos are there in Wisconsin?"

"Nineteen," Johnson says.

"How many of them offer live poker?"

Johnson shrugs. "Three, I believe. Just a few tables."

Carlos spreads his hands. "You see? But don't worry, Grandfather, I have no intention of shutting down the card room. I just don't see that losing a few players—temporarily, I might add—is something we need to worry about."

"Why did you lay off those six dealers?" Cisco asks.

"That was Dooley's decision."

"Dools hasn't made a decision on his own since he came to work here."

"After the robbery we had a falloff in business, so I suggested to Dooley that we needed to reduce our staff in the card room. We would also have fired Jenny Mai, but she and her cohorts seem to have left the area. As for your 'secretary' "—he gestures casually in my general direction—"Blaise felt he had sufficient reason to let her go, as you well know."

"We are not here to discuss that," Cisco says.

"It's your show, Father. Although why you should want to discuss any management issues at all with these two present"—his eyes touch on me and Gayle Vega—"I cannot imagine."

Cisco's neck grows a shade darker, something I have never before seen. Bruce Johnson is staring out the window, his smile grown wistful and distant. Carlos, with a disdainful pucker at the corner of his mouth, picks up a silver and turquoise letter opener from the desk and waggles it between his fingers.

Cisco says, "Are we so desperate for money that we lay off our dealers because of one soft week?"

"It's simply good business practice." Carlos looks at Bruce Johnson and shrugs as if to say, *You see what I have to deal with?* Johnson gives him nothing back.

Cisco says, "Bruce, Blaise, Gayle, Peeky, would you excuse us, please?"

The four of us get up and file out of the office into the reception area. The girl behind the acrylic desk is still working on her nails.

"I guess they're having themselves a little Indian powpow in there," Johnson says.

"You mean powwow?" I ask.

"I mean powpow. I've never seen old Hector quite so pissed off. I believe he's gonna tear Carlos a new one."

Blaise Hunt has found a place to stand from which he can keep an eye on the entire room. He holds himself apart from the conversation, but he is listening.

Johnson slips his hands into his pockets and says, "Only problem for Hector is, I don't believe he's got the council in his pocket anymore." He rocks back and forth on his heels, looking content.

"Whose pocket is Carlos in?" I ask.

Johnson laughs, then turns to Gayle.

"I hear you're the first Vega to turn lawyer."

Gayle nods.

"So, you here as an attorney, or as family?"

"My grandfather wants to show me how the casino business works."

"Well, what you saw in there is how the casino business works when it's not working. What's that old fox up to, anyway? He have an agenda, or is he just trying to keep Carlos on his toes?"

Gayle shrugs and turns her face away.

"For a lawyer you sure don't talk much." Johnson turns to me. "What about you?"

"I talk all the time."

"I mean, how come Hector's got you dogging his heels?"

"I guess today I'm his secretary."

I excuse myself and head down a short hall to the restroom,

where I regroup, regather, recomb, retouch. When I get back to the reception area Hunt, Johnson, and Gayle Vega are gone, the door to Carlos's office is closed, and Cisco is leaning on his cane waiting for me. He looks pale beneath his dark skin, and he says nothing as he takes my arm and leads me to the elevator.

38

M Y DAUGHTER'S HUSBAND shames me," Cisco says as the elevator doors close. "I thought that with you and Gayle there he would be more respectful. I must have my head screwed on ass-backward." He presses the button for the second floor. "How is it with your daughter, Peeky? Does she make you smaller?"

I think for a moment, trying to understand what he means. "Sometimes she makes me feel . . . inadequate."

"Yesss," Cisco says. "We will have to change that, no?"

"Bruce Johnson said you were going to tear Carlos a new one."

Cisco laughs. "I did that, I tore him a new one. But it won't take. Carlos will be back to who he is by sunset."

The doors open. We are just down the hall from Blaise Hunt's office.

"He is not all bad," Cisco says.

"Does he make your daughter happy?"

"Veronica was the only one who did not cry. She would just look at her mother with those big eyes. I think she is happy to be married to a man of importance. She loves her children."

"Does she know he's sleeping with his secretary?"

Cisco tilts, as if a strong wind has cut through the walls of the building and singled him out. I reach out to steady him.

"You think that?" he says.

"With those fingernails? She calls him Carlos."

"That's good, Peeky. I did not see it. But you are right. Carlos is still snagging." He shakes his head. "I wonder if Veronica knows?"

"If she ever comes down here to visit him, one look at those fingernails and she'll know. But as you say, he is a man of importance, and she loves her children. That might be enough for her."

We stand there in the empty hallway for a few seconds saying nothing, then Cisco squeezes my arm and says, "Come, Peeky. I want to show you some movies." We walk past Hunt's office to the end of the hall, where we enter a spacious, windowless room with a large-screen television set up at one end of a long conference table.

Blaise Hunt is standing on the far side of the room, his hands clasped behind his back. His eyes flicker across me but don't stick, as if I'm visual Teflon. Gayle Vega is sitting at the table. I have the feeling that there has not been much conversation in this room.

"All set, Mr. Vega," Hunt says with a clipped nod to Cisco.

Cisco smiles and pulls out a chair two seats to Gayle's left.

"Sit, Peeky."

I sit. Cisco takes the seat between us.

"Show us your movies, Blaise."

Hunt picks up a remote and turns on the television. "You want to see them in any particular order?'

"Start with the cage."

Hunt works the remote; a menu pops up on the TV screen. He selects Camera 32, 10:00–12:00, the day of the robbery. The screen fizzes and jumps, and we are looking at a wide-angle shot of the Card Club cashier cage from above and to the left. I was expecting a grainy black-and-white image, but this image is full color, and sharp enough to pick out the spots on a playing card.

"Go to the money," Cisco says.

Hunt fast-forwards. People zip in and out of the picture, cashing chips, reloading, or just passing by the cage. A digital clock at the corner of the screen ticks off the minutes. Hunt slows the tape at 10:37.

Two security guards enter the picture wheeling a metal cart. They stop outside the door leading into the cage. One of the guards says something to a girl in the cage—I think it's Camilla.

"Stop," Cisco says. Hunt freezes the picture. Cisco turns to me. "There was a lot of money in that cart. Do you know how much?"

"No."

"One million cash."

"Oh." The number hits me like a beanbag: it doesn't hurt, but I feel the size and weight of it. "I didn't think the card room did that well."

"It doesn't. We make most of our money on the slots, as my son-in-law delights in pointing out to me."

"Still, that's a lot of cash."

"It was from the display in the Slot Palace."

"Oh." The May Madness money. "From the plastic safe."

"Yes. Friday was the last day of the May Madness promotion. The money was being returned to the vault."

"Why bring it into the Card Club?"

"Because of the way the building is constructed—we hired one of Alex's developer buddies to design it. Blaise, you want to explain?"

Hunt clears his throat. "All the bingo and slots receipts have to enter the vault through the Card Club cage. The casino is like a pie cut in three unequal sections: slots, bingo, poker. The cashier cages are all in the middle, back to back, but they are not connected. Access to the basement counting room and vaults is through an elevator in the back of the Card Club cage. The money has to be wheeled from the slot and bingo cages through the casino to the Card Club. It is a poorly designed system."

"Why didn't you have more security if you had to move that much cash?"

"Policy," Hunt says. "If it was up to me, I'd have had six guys on it."

"We try to keep a friendly face here," Cisco says. "Large numbers of armed guards make people nervous. Also, when you move a lot of cash, you don't want to make a big deal about it, right, Blaise?"

"Normally, you don't want to attract a lot of attention," Hunt says.

"Run some more," Cisco says.

Camilla laughs and reaches under the counter.

"She's unlocking the door there," Hunt says. "Now you see them start to push the cart through into the cage. That was when they got the code orange. Here." He stops the tape. "The first guard, the younger one, is Marco Ruiz. The one on the left, Dave Garner, is receiving a code orange from the Slot Palace."

"What's a code orange?" I ask.

"That was when your friend Donny Keyes went postal on the slot machine," Hunt says.

"Show us that," Cisco says.

Hunt goes back to the menu, finds Camera 12, and brings up the clip. From above, a row of one-dollar slots, all of them being played. I recognize Donny Keyes at the slot on the near corner. He spins the reels, spins the reels, spins the reels, then, without apparent provocation, grabs the machine and starts rocking it. Other customers back away, out of the frame. At first the slot machine won't move, but Donny is a big guy. He manages to tip it onto its side. The first security guard shows up. Donny is kicking the machine, the toe of his shoe smashing through the glass over the reels. The guard grabs him by the arm but Donny flings him off and keeps kicking. Another guard enters the picture and leaps on Donny's back.

Hunt freezes the image at 10:37.

"Right about here, security made a code orange call for all available personnel to render aid."

"What happened to Donny?"

"He was escorted to his car and asked not to return. We haven't seen him since." Hunt goes back through the menu and returns us to Camera 32. "Here you see Garner and Ruiz pushing the cart into the cage. Garner is the senior. He stops moving when he

hears the code orange, then he directs Ruiz—see here? He sends
Ruiz off to the slot club to help them subdue Keyes."

The younger guard runs off, leaving the money cart with
Garner.

"Violation of protocol," Hunt says, freezing the image again.
"When you're moving money, you stay with it no matter what. I
had to fire Ruiz. Too bad. He was a good kid." Hunt's face is stiff as
oak.

"He was following his boss's orders," I say, automatically siding
with the terminated employee.

Hunt starts the tape again. Marco Ruiz disappears from view.
The other guard watches him go, then looks back across the card
room.

"Notice that he's not moving," says Hunt. "He is just standing
there with the cart halfway through the security door."

About five seconds later, the blue-haired, blue-gloved clown
enters the frame.

"Stop the tape," I say.

The image freezes.

"I can't watch this."

Both Hunt and Cisco are staring at me.

"Okay then," Cisco says. "Just tell us how you remember it."

"The clown shot all three of them. Dolores, Camilla, and that
guard, Dave Garner." Knowing his name makes it harder.

"In that order," Hunt says.

"Yes." I look over at Gayle. Her face appears composed, but her
eyes are filled with tears. Dolores was her cousin.

Cisco says, "Who would you have shot first?"

"I wouldn't have shot anybody," I say. But I see what he means.
Why did the clown shoot the two unarmed women first, then the
guard, who presumably posed the greater threat?

"Dave Garner stopped the cart halfway through the security
door," Hunt says. "He sent his partner off in violation of protocol,
and then he waited for the clown to arrive. The shooter saved

Garner for last because he knew Garner would stand there like a damned fool and wait for it."

"Then you think Garner was the inside man," I say.

"Garner and Darrin McConnell," Hunt says. "And your friend Donny."

"I don't know why you keep calling him my friend."

Hunt shrugs.

"It wasn't just them," says Cisco. "The timing was too perfect. They were either the luckiest robbers in history, or they had inside help."

"Three of them are dead," I say. "I think we can rule out lucky."

Hunt nods. "She's right," he says to Cisco. "The job was timed perfectly. They not only got the million off the cart, they also looted the cage for another two hundred eighty thousand. Neither Garner nor McConnell had been told in advance when the money would be moved."

"Who did know?" I ask.

"Just top management. Mr. Braun, Mr. Begay, Mr. Johnson. And me. We had a meeting on Thursday afternoon, where it was decided to move the cash to the vault at ten-thirty the following evening. By moving the money at an unannounced time—half a day before the official end of the promotion—we avoid being too predictable. No one else, not even Mr. Vega, was told when we would move the money. Even my security staff was not informed until an hour before the transfer."

"So you, Carlos, Dooley, and Johnson were the only ones at this meeting?"

Hunt nods.

"Why was Dooley there?" I ask.

Hunt looks at Cisco, who shrugs.

Hunt says, "The meeting was called to discuss the jackpot situation in the card room. Dooley and I knew that the recent run of bad beat jackpot payouts was no coincidence, and we thought we knew who was behind it."

"Tran Lui."

"Yes. The question was, with no indisputable proof, how should we handle the situation? Dooley wanted to fire Tran and all his friends on the spot." He looks pointedly at me. "But since ripping off the jackpot fund doesn't really cost the casino any money, Carlos and Bruce felt we should adopt a wait-and-see attitude. It just happened that with all of us sitting there in Carlos's office it seemed a good time to discuss moving the May Madness money back into the vault."

Nobody says anything for a few seconds, then Cisco clears his throat.

"Show us the other tape, Blaise," he says.

Blaise works the remote and finds Camera 8. We are looking straight down at a holdem table. He fast-forwards to 10:38. Three face cards are on the board. Nobody is betting. All the players—the dealer, too—have their heads turned toward the back of the room. Something happens—I assume it's the shooting at the cage—and they all jerk in unison. I recognize the dealer now by his slim wrists and thick black hair. Tran Lui.

"Stop the tape," I say.

Hunt freezes the image.

Cisco rests his hand on my arm and leans in close. "I need you to see this."

Hunt starts the tape again. A clown enters the picture from behind Tran. Orange hair, purple nose, yellow gloves. Buddy. He raises his hand, something in it, and touches Tran lightly on the side of the head. Tran jerks his head away, then slumps to the side. The clown leaves the frame. The collar of Tran's white shirt reddens. The red spills from his collar down over his shoulder. Bright red.

"Enough," says Cisco.

The image freezes. The right side of Tran's shirt has gone from white to scarlet, and my heart has turned to shit.

Cisco says, "Peeky?"

"What," I hear myself say.

"You know who that was?"

"Tran."

"No. The clown."

"Yes." I slump in my chair. I slump like Tran. I want to die. And then things are happening inside me and I stand up and start for the door, but there isn't time. I see a wastebasket but it is too late for that, too. I drop to my knees and clutch my belly and erupt. It rushes over my tongue and past my teeth like a long wet rope of hair and bile and filth. I am on my hands and knees, staring down with wet eyes at puke on carpet. It is the same carpet they used in the card room, faux mauve, a vomitous conglomeration of blue, green, red, brown, and pink, and all I can think is that this is the first time I've puked in public since I was three years old.

"Peeky?"

My stomach is a knot. I push myself up onto my knees and turn and look at Cisco. He is leaning toward me in his chair. The light is bouncing off his thick glasses.

"You okay, Peeky?"

Gayle Vega finds a tissue in her purse and brings it to me. I wipe my mouth.

"Why did you make me watch that?"

He sits back and says, "You did not know?"

I shake my head slowly.

"I had to be sure," he says. On the other side of the table, Blaise Hunt stares off through the walls.

"I need to wash my face."

Hunt directs me down the hall to a restroom. Gayle comes with me. I rinse my mouth and go to work on my face.

"That was certainly embarrassing," I say.

"It was understandable. You are emotionally involved with Buddy Balcomb."

"Yes. The emotion is loathing."

"It is as Grandfather says. It is the people we are close to who deceive us most."

When we return to the conference room Blaise Hunt is gone and Cisco is sitting alone. Gayle grabs her briefcase. "I have an appointment in downtown Tucson in twenty minutes. Are we finished here, Grandfather?"

"Yes, thank you, Gayle."

As soon as she is gone I say, "He's not dead you know." I can't bring myself to speak Buddy's name.

"We know that," Cisco says. "The police were able to identify the dead man by his fingerprints. A man named Stumpf."

"He told me he hadn't known anybody would be hurt." Buddy. I see him killing Tran, again, execution-style, a single, perfectly placed bullet behind the ear. One shot, like he knew it would be enough. As if he had done it before.

"I'm sorry I lied to you," I say.

"A woman who lies for her man . . ." He shrugs. "That is not so terrible a thing."

"I never knew . . . I never thought Buddy could do something like that." I take a deep breath. "It's not like it was the first time I ever fell for some asshole."

"So I got a chance with you?"

A laugh explodes from my lips. I quickly stifle it, blushing, thinking I may have offended him horribly. After all, we're only thirty or forty years apart. Cisco sees my discomfiture and breaks into his own creaky laugh, and then we are both laughing.

"Pee Kee," Cisco says, gasping, "you funny." He holds out a hand. "Come."

I take his hand and climb to my feet, wiping away tears with the back of my hand. He guides me out of the conference room, leaving the soiled carpet behind. In the elevator the scene on the security camera replays itself in my head. I shake it off and force myself to say, "Do you really think one of your management team was involved in the robbery?"

"Peeky . . ." Shaking his head. "I do not know. It could be somebody said something, and it was repeated. An indiscretion. What do you think?"

"I think that if Carlos or Johnson were in any way involved, you might like it."

"You are very astute, Peeky. The council meets on Friday. We will make our decision then about whether to renew our contract with Magic Hand. With Carlos on the council, I do not have the support I need. Discrediting either Johnson or Carlos might do the trick, but I do not seriously think my son-in-law had anything to do with the robbery, at least not intentionally. As for Johnson, Casino Santa Cruz is making him thirty million a year. Why would he risk losing that?" The elevator doors open on the casino floor. We move slowly through the banks of slots toward the front entrance.

"How about Dooley?"

Cisco shrugs. "He has always played by the rules. To Dooley a cheater is the lowest form of life on the planet."

"Do you trust Blaise Hunt?"

"He has never given me reason not to."

"Except that one of his men was apparently involved in the robbery."

"So was one of Dooley's men. So was one of yours."

"Good point." We maneuver around a large woman in an oversize wheelchair who is playing three slots at once. "That doesn't give us much to go on."

"No."

"But any one of them could have let something slip. Maybe Darrin McConnell overheard an offhand remark from Dooley about the cash being moved."

"Vergie is close-lipped as an oyster."

"True."

We walk through front foyer and out of the building. My air-conditioned body shrinks from the wall of late afternoon heat. I feel it first in my lips, then my cheeks, then my legs. Beyond the edge of the canopy, the parking lot is a band of unbearable brightness, sun crashing off a thousand shining reflective surfaces. I find my sunglasses and slide them onto my face. I look at Cisco. Behind those thick eyeglasses, his eyes have disappeared in a whorl of wrinkles.

Several vehicles have crowded beneath the canopy: a taxi, three hotel shuttle buses, and a couple of SUVs. My attention is drawn to one of the SUVs, a black Cadillac Escalade with tinted windows, gold-plated wheels, and matching trim. Black vehicles are rare in Arizona. Leave one parked in the Tucson sun for a few hours and you'll know why.

A copper-skinned young man with hard good looks and a long black ponytail gets out of the black SUV, opens the passenger-side door, and starts pitching cans and paper bags over the backseat into the cargo area. He looks like a younger version of the Hector Vega in that 1970s news photo, except for the scrawl of tattoos on his neck and arms.

Cisco says to me, "Let's take a ride, okay?"

THE INSIDE OF THE SUV is trashed. Empty soda cans rattle across the floor, muffled by several thousand calories worth of crumpled Whataburger bags. The leather upholstery exudes the faint odor of marijuana beneath a stronger reek of cigarettes.

The driver does not ask where we are going, and neither do I. I am feeling so numb I hardly care. We drive into Three Points, then take the Ajo Highway east toward Tucson. Cisco leaves me alone with my thoughts for the first few miles.

The Ajo Highway is the ugly route into town. It is a transition zone between the three reservations—Santa Cruz, Tohono O'odham, and Pascua Yaqui—and the cheap corner of Tucson. The highway itself is a minimally maintained two-lane lined with marginal businesses that become denser as we go along. Residences are scattered on either side—mostly inexpensive block houses, mobile homes, and ratty-looking apartment complexes. The foothills are covered with rocky scree pegged with unhealthy-looking saguaros and scraggly creosote bush. The best cacti were looted back in the seventies and eighties, and are now serving time as decorative landscaping in Scottsdale, Fountain City, and other carefully imagined Phoenix and Tucson suburbs.

McDonald's, Carl's Jr., Starbucks, and the rest of the chains are only beginning to make inroads here. Most of the money has gone to the northwest and southeast. Nobody with any serious cash wants to work or live next to the rez. I wonder how many centuries it will take to change that.

As if reading my thoughts, Cisco says, "Alex says the only way land value can go up out this way is to build a stockade."

"Stockade?"

"He wants to put in one of those planned communities with walls high enough no Indian can climb over them. Says he's going to call it Fort Whitefolk."

I think he's joking but I'm not sure.

"Alex owns a lot of land out here. I let him buy a few chunks back in the early years. What Alex likes to call 'tit for tat.' "

"He got you your federal recognition," I say.

"Yes. We paid a big price, though. Still paying."

"Are you going to tell me where we're headed?"

"You'll see. Peeky, how long did you know Buddy?"

The shift in subject takes me several long seconds to absorb and respond.

"A little over a year," I say. My voice comes out flat.

"You saw him after the robbery?"

"Twice. No, three times. He was going to . . . he said he had to go away. He said Woody Stumpf forced him to help rob the casino. Blackmailed him. Told him nobody would get hurt. He said he had to leave the country. Mexico, or maybe Costa Rica. They play a lot of poker in Costa Rica."

"Did he say anything about the others?"

"Just Woody Stumpf. Later, after they were already dead, he mentioned Darrin McConnell and that other man, Juan Allones. But somebody broke into my house and went through everything I own. I think somebody thought Buddy had used my place to stash the money from the robbery, but all they got was *my* money. Forty thousand dollars."

"They went through everything?"

"Every room. Every closet. Cut open my sofa cushions, my mattress, looked everywhere."

"You lose anything else?"

"My gun."

"You said you saw Buddy three times."

"Yes. Once right after the robbery. He was waiting for me at home. Then, the next night, he came to say good-bye. He said he was going to meet Woody."

"The third time?"

"This morning, just for a few minutes."

"So he was still in town this morning. What did he want?"

"I don't know. Just to say good-bye, I guess." Why don't I tell him about the key? Maybe it makes me feel more secure to have some small bit of information to call my own. "He was pretty skittish. Jaymie showed up, and Buddy took off, I don't know where."

"You tell me if you did?"

"I think so," I say. We cross the freeway and head into South Tucson, turning left on Fourth Avenue. A few blocks later we pass Mi Nidito, one of the oldest and most popular Mexican restaurants in Tucson. I haven't eaten there in years.

Cisco grasps my forearm with that warm, dry wrinkled hand. "If you see him again, you tell him to give me a call."

I think Buddy is about as likely to call Hector Vega as he is to cold-call a raise with a seven-deuce. "I hope I never see him again," I say.

We make a left, then a right. We are in residential South Tucson, a neighborhood of small bungalows, mostly well kept, but with a few houses badly in need of a bulldozer.

"It is not about the money," Cisco says. "I just want to know who he was working with. I am too old now to care about the money."

"It's always about the money," I say.

We pull over to the curb behind an oversize white pickup truck with dualies, a light bar, and a huge chrome-plated rear bumper displaying stickers that read "Powered By Fry Bread" and "Caution: I Brake for Orgasms." A young man is sitting on a jump seat in the pickup bed drinking a Zima. Our driver rolls down his window. The Zima drinker hops down from the pickup and strolls over. He is wearing sunglasses, a black tank top, and a Casino Santa Cruz baseball cap.

"Ayyy, Smoke," he says, leaning his thick, heavily tattooed forearms on the driver's side door. He pushes his shades up onto his forehead and peers in at us with bloodshot eyes. "Mr. Vega, how you doing?" The yeasty odor of malt beverage fills the cab.

"I'm good, Richie. How 'bout you? Staying out of trouble?"

"You know me, Mr. V. Peace out."

Cisco shakes his head, smiling. "Which house is it?" he asks.

Richie turns his head slightly and points with his lips. "With the cactus."

The house is a typical-looking double bungalow with the skeletal stump of a long-dead saguaro jutting from an otherwise barren front yard.

"Is she in there now?" Cisco asks.

"Yah. She went out this morning but she been back, I dunno, a while."

"Thanks, Richie."

"You want us to stick around some?"

"Maybe."

"Okay, Mr. V." He punches our driver in the shoulder. "How *you* doin', brah?"

"Richie?" Cisco says. "How about you give us a minute, okay?"

"Sure, no problem, man." He straightens and swaggers back to the pickup.

Cisco turns to me. "Your daughter is in there."

"Jaymie?"

He nods. "You said you'd like to know where she was."

"What kind of place is it? Who lives there?"

"Bunch a peoples," says our driver. "Some Mexicans, and some dudes from Benson. Peoples come and go."

I stare at the dead cactus, at the curtained windows. No sign of life. I try to imagine what is going on inside. Is it like the place in

Redington Pass? Nice and clean? Young, healthy crack addicts reading magazines and doing laundry?

"You want to see her?" Cisco asks.

"I guess so."

Cisco says, "Go get her, Andrew."

Andrew? I suddenly recognize our driver as Andrew Tallis, aka Little Smoke, the kid I helped beat a murder rap six years ago. One of Cisco's grandsons. Smoke gets out and confers with Richie, who reaches into the pickup cab, grabs something from behind the seat, and puts it in his waistband under his shirt. I think it's a gun, but I can't be sure. They saunter across the street to the bungalow, climb onto the open porch, and knock on the door. It is answered by a short, thin man wearing a white T-shirt. They talk for a few seconds, then the man disappears back into the house, leaving the door ajar. Richie lights a cigarette, looks over at us, lifts his sunglasses and winks. A minute or two later, Jaymie appears in the doorway looking sleepy and disheveled. They exchange a few words. Jaymie looks over at the SUV. She can't see me through the tinted windows. Richie hangs his cigarette from his lips and reaches for her arm. She bats his hand away and backs into the house. Smoke grabs her before she can close the door and pulls her out onto the porch. She swings at him with her free arm but is intercepted by Richie. I can hear her cursing at them as they walk her across the street, one on each arm. I roll down the window.

Jaymie looks awful. I can hardly believe this is the same girl who was in my kitchen not twelve hours ago. Her makeup is crusty, her eyes are red, and her hair is badly in need of a brush. She is wearing a wrinkled men's dress shirt, a pair of nylon gym shorts, and flip-flops.

"What the hell is this," she says. "You *kidnapping* me?"

"I would if I thought it would help," I say.

"Like you give a shit."

At the moment, I'm not sure that I do. She looks like a stranger to me.

"Let her go," I say.

Richie and Smoke look to Cisco for confirmation. Cisco nods, and they release her.

Jaymie shakes her arms violently, shedding the memory of their grip. She backs into the middle of the street.

"Christ. My own mother hires a bunch of gangbangers to kidnap her own daughter. You think *I'm* fucked up? Look in the mirror."

"I want my money back, Jaymie."

"What money?"

"The money you took from me this morning."

Her mouth tightens, then she shrugs, reaches into the waistband of her gym shorts, unclips a beaded coin purse and tosses it at me. I catch it. I unzip the purse and pull out a folded wad of bills. A quick riffle makes it look like about a thousand.

"Where's the rest?"

"I owed Fozzie. That's all I got left. You happy?"

I am not happy, I am tired and sad. "When you're ready to clean yourself up, call me," I say. "I can get you into a program."

"When you're ready to quit sticking your nose in my business, maybe I will." She whirls and walks back to the house, her gait rubbery and uncertain, as if the street is surfaced with gelatin. The door is locked. She bangs on it and shouts.

"Fozzie! Open the door, Fozzie!"

"Fozzie don't want her around no more," says Richie.

Jaymie kicks the door. "Goddammit, Fozzie, you son of a bitch!"

"He say she's a pain in the ass."

"What do you want to do, Peeky?" Cisco asks.

Jaymie gives the door a final kick, then comes back across the street, limping now. She ignores me and walks up to Richie.

"Give me a goddamn smoke, okay?"

Richie unrolls a pack of Marlboros from his sleeve and offers it to her.

"You need a ride someplace?" I ask.

I don't exist.

"Got a light?" she asks Richie.

Richie produces a disposable butane lighter in a handworked silver and turquoise sleeve. Jaymie leans into it, holding her hair back with one hand, and sucks flame into the tip of her cigarette.

"Thanks." She turns away and starts walking toward Sixth Avenue, walking on planet Jell-O, favoring her bruised toes. No makeup, no purse, nothing but a cigarette, a pair of gym shorts, and a shirt that doesn't belong to her.

"Peeky?"

"What?"

"What do you want us to do?"

I look at Cisco, at the glare from his thick glasses, and I see Hector Vega. Why did he bring me here? So that I would be beholden to him? Does he still think I'm his Judas? His way to get to Buddy?

"Peeky? Are you okay?"

I open my eyes. Cisco, Smoke, and Richie are all staring at me.

"Take me home," I say.

40

THERE WAS A TIME IN MY LIFE—it seems like years ago, but it has been only a few days—when coming home was a comfort. The familiar smells and spaces of my little adobe home once embraced me. Now I am a stranger here.

I can still see the pale shadow of ashes on the living room carpet. I need a new vacuum cleaner. Maybe one of those British machines that are supposed to be so good. Maybe when I replace the carpet I'll get one. The answering machine is blinking. Four messages. I press the button.

"Peeky? It's me." Buddy. "Peeky? You there?" Sounds of breathing, traffic in the background, the disconnection click.

Second message: "Peeky?" Three seconds pass, a muttered curse, disconnect.

The third and fourth messages are hangups. I'm glad I wasn't there to take the calls, glad he doesn't have my cell-phone number. I move from room to room, expecting anything, looking in every corner to make sure no one is there. No Buddy, no Jaymie, no mysterious strangers. I check the freezer. My "eggplant parmesan" is intact. I serve myself a bowl of ice cream and pour a glass of wine. The ice cream is too cold on my teeth. The wine tastes harsh and astringent. I wish I smoked. If I smoked, a cigarette might make me feel better. It seemed to work for Jaymie.

I know I did the right thing. The only person who can help

Jaymie out of the hole she's dug for herself is Jaymie. Jaymie the stranger. I see her walking away in her flip-flops, cigarette in hand, going who knows where. Someone else's daughter. I cling to that, giving myself time to recover.

It has been a lousy day. I close my eyes and clamp my jaw and push them away, all of them—the not-my-boyfriend, the not-my-daughter, all of them. I put them in a box and I lock it.

It works for about five minutes, then they come back.

Busy, I need to stay busy. I putter around the house for a while, cleaning. I take a shower, change into fresh clothes, put on a new face. All the while they are circling, just out of mindsight: Cisco, Buddy, Jaymie . . . I can't do it. I open the freezer, unwrap the package marked eggplant parmesan, and shove the entire wad of frozen bills into my purse. I'll drive up the Gila River and see if I can find a good game, give my head a rest. I let myself out the front door, then stop.

Where the hell is my car? Damn. It's still parked at Casino Santa Cruz. What was I thinking, having Cisco's grandson drive me straight home? I go back inside. Take a cab? I hate cabs. Besides, getting one here in Tucson might take an hour.

I pick up the phone and call Eduardo.

"I can't believe you didn't call me right away." Eduardo looks at me, his whole body turning, and the truck heads for the curb.

"Look out!" I shout.

He straightens the wheel just before we hop the curb. "How come you don't call me?"

"I've had kind of a rotten day." I say, my fingers white on the armrest. "Besides, I did call you."

"I been going crazy, man." He smells like beer. "Where was this place?"

"South Tucson, just off Sixth, on Thirty-first. A place with a big dead cactus in front."

"I know that place. Bunch a *pinche putos*. I didn't think Jaymie would get that low."

"I don't think she's there anymore. They kicked her out. Last time I saw her she was walking toward Sixth. Look, Eduardo, I think we just have to let her go. She has to figure some things out on her own."

"I think maybe I figure some things out for her, okay?" He speeds up, hitting sixty miles per hour on Campbell Avenue.

"You better slow down, Eduardo."

He lets up on the gas, slowing down to maybe fifty-five.

"I think I know where she went," he says. "There is a place right by there where I find her once before, a guy I know. Look, I take you to your car, then I'm gonna go get her."

"Maybe you should think about it some."

"I am sick of thinking. I am going crazy."

"Slow down, Eduardo. You want another DUI?"

That slows him down to forty-five, only fifteen miles per hour over the limit.

"I'm okay," he says. "I only had eight or nine little Coronitas."

"That makes you illegal."

"No, no. Twelve is my limit."

"Pull over, Eduardo."

"What? Why?"

"Pull over."

He pulls over, scowling, scraping the curb with the front wheel.

"Okay, what? You gonna tell me I'm drunk?"

"I'm driving," I say.

He shoulders open his door muttering something under his breath in Spanish that I translate roughly as "goddamn pushy white bitch." Since I'm not all that sure of my Mexican slang, I let it go. We switch places. Eduardo is in the passenger seat pouting. Not actually pouting, but close enough. I get a flash of how he was at age five when he didn't get first swing at the piñata.

"Okay," I say. I put the truck in gear, but I'm not sure where to go. I could stick with the original plan and go over to the casino to get my car, but that would mean letting Eduardo drive off on his own. Not good. I could turn around and drive back home, but that would still leave Eduardo with his truck. Or we could go back to Eduardo's, but that would leave me stuck at his place. I take a good look at him. I've seen him drunker. Maybe a burrito will sober him up.

I say, "How about we head down to the Crossroads?"

The Crossroads is a South Tucson institution—a drive-in, eat-in restaurant with low prices, a huge menu, casual service, and wildly uneven quality. I've had some of my best-ever Mexican meals there, and some meals so poorly prepared that a rez dog wouldn't eat them. You take your chances; it's all part of the ambience.

We go inside and take one of the cracked vinyl booths. Eduardo orders a beef chimichanga served enchilada style. That'll either sober him up or kill him. I order three carne asada tacos, one of their more reliable items. We don't talk much while we are waiting for our food. Eduardo sips Coca-Cola from a tall red plastic tumbler while I nibble on chips and salsa.

"I'm sorry I didn't call you right away," I say.

He grunts.

I say, "Look, if we find her and drag her out of another crack house she'll just take off again."

"What about, you know, do an intervention?"

"If she goes home, either yours or mine, by her own will, we might be able to talk her into getting help. But we can't just kidnap her."

"I know that," Eduardo says. "But I got to do something. Maybe I say something to her and it gets through, you know?"

I know exactly how he feels.

Our food arrives. It looks good today. Eduardo's chimi is an

enormous deep-fried log covered with red enchilada sauce and
melted cheese. My tacos are beautiful—three overlapping tortillas,
no larger than my palm, each with a few choice bits of grilled steak
and a fluff of finely shredded cabbage. On a separate plate are six
bowl-shaped slices of tiny Mexican limes. I squeeze a lime slice
over one of the tacos, fold the tortilla over the meat and cabbage,
and bite into it. As soon as the salty beef and tangy lime hits my
tongue I realize that I've eaten almost nothing all day but a few
spoonfuls of ice cream. I devour all three tacos in about five minutes and wish I'd ordered three more.

I sit back and watch Eduardo demolish his chimichanga and
think about Jaymie. Nine hours ago she was in my kitchen drinking my coffee and stealing my money. It feels like weeks. Something she said this morning sticks in my mind. Something I should
ask her about.

Eduardo has finished his chimi and is finishing off the basket
of chips.

"Pretty good, huh?" I say.

He nods, shoving the last tortilla chip into his mouth.

"How are you feeling?" I ask.

"Okay." He looks better. "I got a little headache, you know?"

"You still want to go look for Jaymie?"

"I got to know if she's okay. You know, it is just a few blocks
from here, the place I think she is at. People where she stays sometimes."

"Okay, but I'm driving, okay?"

He shrugs.

"And there'll be no hauling her off against her will if we find
her. We just talk to her, okay?"

"Sure. I mean, you are right about that, Peeky. Just talk."

"I mean it, Eduardo."

He holds up his hands. "I just want to see her, that's all. My
wife."

41

THE HOUSE IS ON THE WEST SIDE of Sixth Avenue. The front lawn is a mat of dead grass decorated with a few empty beer cans. The front porch is shaded by a long, low tile roof and screened by a network of vines. It would be a nice place to sit on a summer evening if it wasn't piled with broken furniture, empty beer cartons, and dead potted plants.

"What makes you think she's here?" I ask.

"I know these people, Leon and his old lady. They use to be friends, only now they're all messed up." He points at the fading bruises on his face. "Leon and me, we got into it, last time I was here."

"Oh. Great."

Eduardo knocks on the door.

"Maybe nobody's home," I say after about half a minute.

Eduardo knocks again, harder. The door opens a few inches, stopping at a chain. A tall, bug-eyed, goateed man looks out at us.

"The fuck you want?" he says.

"You know what I want, Leon. Is she here?"

"Just a sec." He closes the door, then opens it a few seconds later. "She ain't here." He closes the door and we hear the click of a lock. Eduardo starts banging on the door with the side of his fist. "Goddammit, Leon, open up!" The veins on his neck are bulging and his face is the color of new brick.

"Maybe we ought to go," I say.

"The hell with that." He reaches under his shirt and pulls something out of his belt. The .44 Magnum I took off that kid up in Redington Pass.

"Eduardo, don't!"

I throw an arm across my face as he empties two rounds into the door latch. The sound is painfully loud in this confined space. Eduardo kicks the door with his boot heel but it holds. He fires another round into the lock, then slams his shoulder into the door. The door gives way and he is inside. I follow him, my ears ringing.

Three people are sitting bolt-upright on a leather sofa, wide-eyed and open-mouthed: Leon, a dark-skinned woman with a tight cap of graying hair, and Jaymie, looking small at the far end of the sofa. I am reminded of the three bears. On the oak coffee table in front of them is an overflowing ceramic ashtray the size of a dinner plate, a bamboo bong, two small glass pipes, and a *Martha Stewart Living* magazine. The faint odor of hot plastic hangs in the air. The only sound is the rattling of a swamp cooler from the next room.

Eduardo, breathing heavily, points the gun at Leon.

"Eduardo, don't," I say.

Eduardo's nostrils are flared and his knuckles are white on the grip. I place my hand lightly on his arm, using Cisco's little trick. I can feel his muscles straining against the weight of my hand—a weight that is purely psychological.

"Easy," I say. "Let's talk now."

Eduardo's arm slowly sinks. I let my hand slide down to his wrist and gently remove the .44 from his grasp. His momentum has left him, he seems shocked to be standing there.

"Jesus, Eddie," Jaymie says. "What's the matter with you?"

Eduardo gives her a hard, hurt glare.

Jaymie says, "You coulda killed somebody."

Leon says, "You fucked up my door, dude."

"Screw you," Eduardo says. It's all he can come up with. I know how he feels—instant adrenaline hangover.

Jaymie lights a cigarette, crosses her arms, and leans back into the sofa cushions.

"We just wanted to make sure you were okay," I say to Jaymie. She snorts. "Why wouldn't I be okay? Because some beaner asshole might shoot the door down and kidnap me?"

I look at the pipes on the coffee table, then back at Jaymie. Is she high? Of course she's high. When was the last time I saw her straight?

"We're not here to kidnap you. I just want to talk," I say.

Eduardo and Leon are watching each other warily. I'm glad I have the gun.

"About what?" She gives Eduardo a sideways look.

"About you getting your crackhead ass into treatment!" Eduardo says.

"Screw you."

Eduardo starts toward her. I cock the gun. It's only a click, but it works. Everyone stops moving and looks at me

"Eduardo, let me handle this," I say. To my surprise, it seems to work. He backs up a few steps.

I push aside the ashtray and magazine, sit on the coffee table in front of her, and rest the .44 on my lap. Jaymie is squinting at me suspiciously, using her cigarette to create a veil of smoke between us.

"I wanted to ask you about something you said this morning."

Eduardo says, "You coulda just opened the door, Leon."

"She didn't want to see you, man."

"Shut up," I say. They do.

The gray-haired woman sitting beside Jaymie picks up the magazine and starts reading as if we are not there.

"You were talking about people from the casino using drugs," I say to Jaymie.

She rolls her eyes. "Is that all you think about? Your precious casino?"

"No. Sometimes I think about you. But there's not much I can do for you right now, is there?" I pick up the glass pipe from the coffee table. It looks like a stretched-out lightbulb with a blackened bowl at the fat end. "Is this a crack pipe?"

She shrugs.

"Jaymie, I'm not here to make you do anything you don't want to do. We're not here to bust anybody."

"You sure busted my goddamn door," Leon says.

I stay focused on Jaymie. "I just need some information. Then we'll leave."

Leon says to Eduardo, "How come you always gotta be such an asshole, Eddie?"

"Me? You're the one turned into a goddamn crack fiend."

"Hey, don't you think I got feelings?"

The woman reading the magazine laughs through her nose.

"What does it look like?" I ask Jaymie.

She says, "What does *what* look like?"

"Crack."

She compresses her lips into a flat smile and looks away.

"I just want to know. I'm not going to do anything."

Jaymie gives me a measuring look, then slips her hand between the sofa cushions and comes out with a small, clear, blue-tinted plastic bag. Inside are some chunks of a hard, waxy-looking substance. I open the bag and take a closer look. White, irregular rocks, tinged with yellow. I thought it would look more . . . dangerous.

"I thought it came in little glass tubes."

The dark woman says, without looking up from her magazine, "Ricky switched to baggies."

"Who's Ricky?"

The woman doesn't answer.

Jaymie says, "The guy that kicked me out this morning."

"I thought that was Fozzie."

"Ricky Fazzaro," she mutters.

"Oh. This morning you said some 'casino Indians' were using crack. Who were you talking about?"

She is giving me a very peculiar look. "I don't know. They come around in their big cars."

"You talking about those rez dudes?" Leon says, looking over at us.

"Yes."

"Buncha psychos. Fuckin' gangbangers. Even Ricky don't like dealin' with 'em."

"Why is that?"

"'Cause they don't give a shit about anybody but their own ass."

Coming from a crack dealer this should be funny, but I'm not laughing.

"Fuckers come banging on my door all times of night, disturbing the neighbors and shit, treat me like their gofer dog. Fuck 'em. I don't need it, y'know?" He gives me his best tough-guy look, then suddenly laughs. "Course, none of 'em ever shot down my fucking door."

"So these are younger guys?"

"Yeah, mostly, but we even get some of these rez mamas, and older guys, too. Like the Hummer dude. See him all the time. Dude just pulls up in his big yellow Hummer and leans on his fuckin' horn, King Shit, too important to, like, get out and knock on the door. Sometimes I just let him sit out there and honk."

It looks like my long-shot draw just came in.

"Sometimes he comes up," says the gray-haired woman, still reading. I wonder if she's somebody's grandmother.

"Yeah, if I ignore him long enough," Leon says.

"He has nice boots," says the woman.

"Yeah." Leon laughs. "He has really nice boots."

"He come around pretty often?"

"Couple times a week, maybe."

I think for a moment. "Jaymie?"

"What? I'm not going with you."

"I need you to do something for me."

"THAT WAS GOOD," I say.

Eduardo looks surprised. "What was good about it?"

I turn the truck west on Ajo, heading toward the casino. I say, "Well, nobody got hurt. Jaymie is okay. They don't seem like such bad people. Not like that bunch out on Redington Pass."

"Leon is a complete asshole. I still think we should've grabbed her out of there."

"It wouldn't have helped." I am feeling weirdly optimistic. "Jaymie has to make her own decisions."

"How can she do that? She is all messed up in the head."

"Did you see the expression on her face when we left? She couldn't believe we were leaving her. Part of her wanted to come with us."

"You know what I should have done? I should have shot Leon."

"You can't do much for Jaymie if you're in jail."

"Maybe I wouldn't miss her so much."

"You did good, Eduardo. The next step is up to her. Look, she doesn't have any money. How long do you think they'll let her stay there?"

Eduardo lifts a foot to the dashboard and cups a hand over his forehead.

"I got a headache."

"Good," I say. "That means you're sobering up. By the time we get to my car you'll be able to drive yourself home."

I am sitting in my Miata outside Casino Santa Cruz. It's dark out, but the day's heat is still radiating off the surface of the parking lot. I can feel perspiration beading on my forehead. I am thinking how cool it is inside the casino.

For the first time in days, I feel I've been dealt a playable hand. I don't know what the game is, but I know I've got a mitt full of cards. I've learned that Hector Vega's son-in-law is a crackhead. That's got to be worth something. I've got the key to a storage bay that might contain some of the stolen casino money. I've got my wheels back. My daughter is no longer missing—she's staying with a crack dealer, but at least I know where she is. And I've got a gut feeling that whatever happens next, I will be the one pulling strings for a change. Bottom line, I'm feeling lucky.

Which is exactly why I should go home and get some sleep instead of walking into the casino. Feeling lucky is one of the worst things that can happen to a poker player.

Robert once told me that a cop is at his sharpest when he is "a little bit tired and a little bit hungry." At the moment I am both, but I don't think Robert meant it literally. I think he meant that you should not hit the streets brimming with cocky energy, feeling as though the masses owe you respect. A cop sated with his own power and glory is close to a dead man walking.

Same thing applies at the poker table, only instead of a disconnect between citizen and cop, it is about losing one's ability to play the table. It happens to every poker player. You're playing game X, but everybody else is playing games Y and Z.

Most holdem players will play an ace-ten offsuit from any position. Not me. It's a trouble hand, and it's not my style. I'd rather wait for something better. But every now and then, when I'm hitting a lot of hands and the other players are running scared—in other words, when I'm on a heater—I'll raise with that ace-ten and make money doing it.

In holdem, only about 50 of the 1,320 possible two-card combinations are what you might call premium hands. The majority of hands—900 or so, depending on your style of play—are unplayable garbage. Premium hands and garbage hands are relatively easy to play. The cards say raise or the cards say fold, and that is what you do.

It is the remaining 300-odd hands that present a challenge. Those are the hands that might or might not be playable, depending on one's position, bankroll, risk tolerance, and table image. The player also needs to consider the quality of the opposition, the culture of the particular game, the house rake, who is winning, who is losing, and what happened the previous hand. These are the types of hands—ace-nine, jack-ten, jack-queen, six-six, ten-eight suited—that start to look playable when one is "feeling lucky."

It is a busy Wednesday night in the Card Club. I stop in the entryway and scan the room. Some of the red-chip players must have returned—I see what looks like a pot-limit game on table 20.

I don't see Cisco. That's good. I'm not ready for him yet.

I walk up to the board and greet Richard. He seems startled to see me.

"Peeky! I didn't know you were working!"

"I'm just here to play. What have you got for me?"

He looks at the board where the active games are listed. "Fifteen-thirty and six-twelve holdem. I've got two seats open in a four-eight Omaha game."

"How about that five-ten pot-limit game?" I ask.

He raises his eyebrows at that. I don't usually play pot-limit. "It's four-handed right now," he says. "The usual bunch of stones, plus Johnny K. They busted Lemon out a couple hours ago. Of course Mutter's gone, they can't drain any more yolk outta his nest egg. Haven't seen Buddy since last week." He shrugs. "It's not a great game, Peeky."

"That's what I figured." But I am feeling lucky, and I've got close to $15,000 in my purse.

The dealer, a gray-haired, ponytailed man named Doug, says, "Evening, Peeky."

"Hi, Doug. You got some big cards for me tonight?"

"Anything for you, dear."

Yassir is having a good session; he actually smiles at me when I sit down. Al Rafowitz, hiding behind his Ray-Bans as usual, has just won a small pot, and is stacking chips resignedly. I'm guessing he's a loser on the night. Next to Al, an aggressive young turk named Johnny K. is sitting behind about $20,000 in chips. Big night for Johnny. Lars, a crotchety old stone who plays so tight you can hear him squeak when he reaches for his chips, is hunched over his usual modest stack. Three stones and a maniac. Tough game.

Five-ten pot-limit is a big game by my usual standards—potentially bigger than the $300–600 game I played at Hector Vega's place. But like I say, I feel lucky, so I buy a rack of green and a rack of black—$12,500 total. Let 'em know I'm serious.

Since I am feeling lucky, I know I have to keep an eye on myself. I manage to watch a few rounds without getting involved in a hand. Pot-limit holdem is the most sophisticated, intricate, and challenging form of poker I know—more complex than limit holdem, and more delicate than no-limit. Played correctly, it requires patience, aggression, mathematical aptitude, people-reading skills, salesmanship, and an iron gut.

I remember one night Buddy, no slouch at pot-limit, was lying next to me in bed reading a *Discover* article about the king cobra. He kept interrupting my own reading to deliver a series of king cobra factoids: one of the most deadly snakes . . . world's largest venomous snake . . . up to eighteen feet long . . . the only snake to build a nest and protect its eggs . . . eats snakes, including other cobras . . . excellent eyesight . . . highly aggressive . . . highly intelligent . . . highly dangerous . . . "Sounds like it'd make a good pot-limit player," he said.

I throw away an ace-queen when Yassir raises; a few hands later I dump pocket queens in the face of a reraise from Al. I wait; I watch. It's not hard to play tight when you're getting mediocre hands. The only pot I go after, I'm in the small blind. Al, Johnny, and Yassir limp in. I just call with an ace-king. Lars checks the big blind. The flop comes two rags with an ace. I bet the size of the pot and they fold like dominoes. Maybe I should've checked—I don't claim to be an expert at pot-limit.

A few hands later I sense a presence behind me. Doug looks up and his mouth falls open.

"Mind if I join y'all?" Dooley says, pulling out the chair to my right.

Everybody at the table tries to conceal their surprise. To my knowledge, Dooley has never sat in on a game in his own card room. I guess there's a first time for everything.

He settles his bulk into the chair and looks around. "How y'all doin'? What I got to buy in for here?" He pulls a wad of money out of his pocket—typical gambler's roll, about three inches in diameter, wrapped in a thick blue rubber band. "Five thousand enough, or do I got to risk more a my hard-earned money?" He looks at Johnny's stack. "How deep are you, son?"

"'Bout twenty," Johnny says.

"Okay then." Dooley hands his roll to a chip-runner who has appeared at his elbow. "I think I got about twenty. Change it up, honey."

The runner starts to count out the bills, but Dooley shoos her off. "Go do that at the cage, sweetheart. My say-so." He turns to the dealer. "Let's look at some cards, Douglas."

Almost as startling as his presence at the table is Dooley's confident and breezy manner. How many personalities does this guy have?

With Dooley in the game, I tighten up my play even further, and watch the deal go four times around the table without seeing a flop. Johnny K. is doing most of the betting, with Dooley a close second. No large pots develop, with most hands being conceded on the flop.

At one point Dooley looks at me and says, "You still here, Peeky? Thought you'd left."

"Tonight I only play pocket aces," I say, which is close to the truth.

"You hear from Buddy lately?" he asks.

I'm not sure how to answer that. Dooley must know that Buddy was one of the robbers. At least I think he knows—I'm really not sure who's in the loop. I decide to tell him what I told Cisco.

"He stopped by my house this morning."

"Really!"

"Just for a moment. I don't know where he is."

"Why'd he come by?" He smiles and stares at me, unblinking.

"Well, you know, we've been seeing each other. I guess he just wanted to visit."

Doug pitches us some fresh cards.

Dooley looks at his and mucks them. I do the same.

"I can understand him wanting to see you," Dooley says with a fixed smile. His eyes have taken on a flat, hooded look. "He want anything else?"

"He only stayed a couple of minutes," I say. I wish I was wearing my sunglasses. I feel like this man can see straight through my pupils into my soul.

"You see him again, y'all let me know. I'd sure like to talk to him."

"I hear that a lot."

"He's a popular fella. Y'know, me and Buddy go back a ways. Knew him when he was playing up in Phoenix."

"Is that a fact." Is that why he's sitting in this game? To grill me about Buddy?

Two more cards have appeared in front of me. Two black aces. Damn, now I have to play a hand.

Johnny K., first to act, says, "Raise." He matches the ten-dollar big blind and raises the size of the pot, making it $35 to go.

Dooley says, "I know people are looking for him is all. Thought maybe I could take some of the heat off."

Yassir scowls at his cards, shuffles his chips for a few seconds, and reraises to $100, calling the $35 and raising $65, to make a total pot of $150. Betting in pot-limit holdem can be ferocious.

"Just want to talk to him is all," Dooley says.

"Let's play cards, Dooley."

"Sorry." Dooley folds; I kick it all the way up to $350. Lars and Al both fold. Johnny K. calls, as does Yassir. There is $1,065 in the pot after only one round of betting.

Dooley leans into me and says, "You have him give me a call."

"Okay," I say, just to shut him up. The flop comes ace-king-seven, with the ace and seven both hearts. I love it. I flopped top set. At the moment, I have the nuts.

Johnny K. checks. I smell a check-raise coming, and that's okay with me. I put him on an ace-king, or maybe pocket kings. Something huge. It doesn't matter. Whatever he has, I have better.

Yassir stares glumly at his cards, fiddles with his chips, knuckles his left nostril, performs several additional ritual motions, then checks. He smells it, too.

Dooley says, "You hear what I'm saying, Peeky? I just want to talk to him."

"Bet," I say, blocking out Dooley's voice. I push out a stack of fifteen $100 chips, overbetting the pot by about $400 in hopes Johnny will see it as a sign of weakness. In pot limit, a raise is normally limited by the size of the pot, but at Casino Santa Cruz a player can overbet the pot at any time. His opponent can call the entire bet, or ask the dealer to count down the pot and limit the bet. In effect, the players have the option to agree to make the betting no-limit at any time.

Johnny does not ask for a count. He pounces, just like I thought he would, shoving all his chips forward. He wants to win it right now. He knows his big cards are still vulnerable.

Yassir makes a wet sound with his lips. I'd almost forgotten he was in the hand. He shakes his head and fires his cards into the muck.

I have about $10,000 left in front of me. I wish I had more.

"I call," I say.

Johnny flips up his cards. Pocket kings, a heart, and a spade. He didn't really want me to call, but he still thinks he's a big favorite. I show him my aces, his worst nightmare: set over set. Johnny looks as if he's taken a medicine ball to the solar plexus. He sags in his chair, knowing he's a huge dog to the hand. Only the case king or runner-runner hearts can save him.

"Ain't over yet," says Dooley.

Doug burns a card and turns the ten of hearts, giving Johnny a flush draw to his king of hearts. He burns another card, pauses for a moment—some dealers just can't resist—then rolls over the deuce of hearts.

With a shout, Johnny jumps straight up out of his chair and punches the sky. I am staring speechless at my set of aces, now just so much toilet paper.

"Ace high flush," says Doug, pushing forward the ace-seven-ten-deuce of hearts to go with Johnny's king of hearts. He folds my beautiful black aces into the muck.

I feel Dooley's eyes drilling into me.

Johnny is saying, "Oh my God, oh my fucking God," as Doug pushes him the pot.

Yassir, who hates with Syrian passion to see the odds so defiled, says, "That was ugly."

43

I AM IN THE RESTROOM staring at a woman with hollow cheeks and bloodless skin, forty-four going on sixty. Her eye makeup has gone crusty. Her lips look like two pale worms locked in a death grip. Her lifeless hair is the exact color of Clairol Natural Light Auburn. It looks about as natural as a maraschino cherry. What color is it really? She has no idea; it's been too many years.

I don't remember how I got here. One moment I am watching the dealer push a $30,000 pot to Johnny K., and the next instant I am staring at this wreck of a woman in the mirror. Did I black out? Is this what happens to alcoholics? I put my hands under the faucet and let the cool water run over my wrists.

Thoughts batter my skull, trying to get in or out. I grab hold of one that is telling me I had the best hand. My play was correct, and in the big poker game measured by the years of my life, I'm ahead of the game.

I still have a couple thousand dollars in my purse. Technically, I'm not busted.

Somehow that doesn't make me feel much better.

The water running over my hands is warmer now. I carefully wash my face using the horrible pink soaplike liquid from the wall dispenser. I pat my face dry with paper towels, then get out my makeup kit and get down to work.

But I am still playing that hand. I know I should let it go. He had a long-shot draw and he caught. As poker pro Puggy Pearson once said, "I'll tell you 'bout luck. I believe in it, sure, even though I know there ain't no such thing."

My plan is to head straight out of the casino, get in my car, and crawl back to my den to lick my wounds. I almost make it, but Richard spots me on my way out.

"Peeky! Hang on a sec." He leaves his station beneath the board and trots after me. "I thought you'd left. Mr. Johnson is looking for you."

"Mr. Johnson? Bruce Johnson?"

"He asked me to send you up to see him."

"I was just going home."

Richard shrugs. "I'm just supposed to give you the message. If you want, I'll say I never saw you."

It's tempting, but I'm too much the good little girl to ignore such a summons. Also, I'm curious.

A guard is waiting for me at the elevator. He escorts me to the top floor, but instead of guiding me to an office, he leads me into a stairwell. We climb a short flight of stairs. He opens a metal door leading out onto the roof. It's like opening an oven door—the roof has been sucking up sunlight all day long, now it's sending the heat back into the sky. The guard points and I see, at the far end of the expanse, what looks like a brightly lit floating oasis.

"Over there," the guard says. As soon as I step out onto the roof he closes the door. A warm breeze ruffles the edge of my dress. I feel heat waves from the roof climbing my legs. I walk across the dead white surface toward the oasis. It feels as though I'm walking on slightly sticky rubber. Good thing I'm not wearing heels. As I get closer, I see that the oasis is a sort of raised-bed garden about forty feet long. It is surrounded by a thick hedge. The light is coming from two overhead halogen lamps, the kind that light up freeways at night.

I find a break in the hedge and climb four shallow steel steps. The light is intense, nearly as bright as high noon in Tucson, but bluer, and without the heat. I shade my eyes with my hand and try to make sense out of what I'm seeing.

It's not the roof garden I expected, but a rectangular patch of bright green Astroturf surrounded on three sides by a hedge of rosemary. The fourth side simply ends at the edge of the roof, looking out over the unlit desert side of the casino complex, nothing but blackness beyond.

Two palm trees set into enormous clay pots rise above a small bench and a portable bar. In the daytime they would provide some shade; now the gray trunks rise above the lights into the dark.

Bruce Johnson's slim figure is posed near the edge, holding a golf club, casting a double shadow. Several golf balls are scattered on the turf. Johnson's attention is focused on one particular ball balanced on a tee. I stop and wait for him to make his shot. He brings his club slowly back, then resettles it behind the ball. He shifts his weight from one foot to the other, planting himself solidly. He has given no sign that he is aware of me, but I'm sure he knows he's being watched. The club comes back in a smooth, decisive motion, and he strikes, putting his entire body into it. I think of a rattlesnake.

With a sharp crack, the ball disappears into the black.

"Good shot," I say.

He turns and smiles. He is wearing sunglasses with green teardrop-shaped lenses.

"I send a guy out once a week to gather the balls. Three hundred yards is nothing from up here. Do you golf?"

I shake my head.

"It's a terrible thing, golf." He walks over to the bench and leans the driver against the back. "Worse than drugs. And more expensive." He props a hip against the corner of the bench and crosses his arms. His movements are languid and loose-jointed. Maybe he does yoga or something. "It's addictive because nothing satisfies like hitting a perfect drive. And there are no perfect drives."

"Not even a hole-in-one?"

"No one expects to hit a hole-in-one. Perfection requires the satisfaction of expectation. Anybody can hit a hole-in-one by accident."

"I wouldn't know."

"Sure you would," he said. "You gamble, right?"

"I don't gamble. I play poker." I think of those runner-runner hearts.

"Fair enough. And what is poker about?"

Big question. I don't have a pat answer. "How do you mean?"

"What is the essence of the game? Why do you play it?"

"It's my job."

"But you'd play even if it wasn't your job, right?"

"I suppose."

"Why?"

"For fun. For relaxation."

"I've heard that same excuse from golfers and drug addicts. I heard you just took a bad beat."

"News really travels around here."

He laughs. "Was it fun?"

"It comes and it goes. No big deal."

"You want to sit down?"

I sit.

"Something to drink?"

"No, thank you."

"Do you want to know why I play golf? Let me tell you. I do it to make that little white ball do what I want it to do." He pauses to let that sink in. It doesn't sink very far. "Of course, the ball does whatever the hell it wants to do. Most of the time. Sound familiar?"

I give him a blank face, even though I think I know where he's going.

Johnson bends at the waist—his body folds like a book—and comes up with a golf ball. He holds it between his fingers like a gem. "It's all about control, Peeky. That's what it is. The reason I'm in business, the reason I play golf, and the reason you play poker . . . it's all about convincing ourselves that we are in the driver's seat." He tosses the golf ball into the air and catches it. "You have Hector's ear," he says. The ball goes up, the ball comes down. "How does that make you feel?"

"It doesn't make me feel like I have any kind of control, if that's what you're getting at."

"It's not." He twists and hurls the ball out over the edge. I am reminded of Cisco casting dead goldfish from his pool. "Do you know who is running this casino?"

"Carlos Begay, I suppose. He's the president."

"That's right. But at the moment, Carlos is relying heavily upon my guidance. Control, Peeky. It's not about money or titles. It's about control. As I'm sure you have observed, Carlos is . . . erratic. I had hoped to leave here two months ago, but so long as Carlos is nominally in charge, I can't. I have to protect my interests."

"I thought your interests were about to expire."

"Our work contract expires in October, yes, but Magic Hand will continue to receive substantial payments for another two years. It's important to me that this venture continue to turn a profit. Casino Santa Cruz is perilously positioned here. Both the Tohono O'odham and the Pascua Yaqui casinos are closer to Tucson. A few stupid moves—like firing all those dealers—and we lose players. At the moment our gross revenues are on the order of forty million a year. If that dropped to twenty million we might well be looking at a net loss. It could easily happen."

I don't buy his numbers, but I nod. "Why are you telling me this?"

"I want you to understand why it is important that the Santa Cruz renew their contract with Magic Hand. Without professional

management, this place will devolve into another marginally prof-
itable bingo hall and slot club. It's in everybody's best interest for us
to continue on here. Carlos can keep his title, and we'll continue to
hire and train any Santa Cruz who show a desire to work, but
we, Magic Hand, need to be guiding the ball."

"Yes, but why are you telling *me* this?"

"Hector wants me out. You have Hector's ear."

"You overestimate my influence."

"Perhaps," he says with a liquid shrug. "In any case, he is making a mistake you may be able to help him to correct."

"I think right now he's preoccupied with finding out who was
behind the robbery."

"Really?" Johnson's eyebrows come together. "I'd almost forgotten about that."

"That's because your granddaughter wasn't killed."

"Touché." He picks up another ball and starts tossing it from
one hand to the other.

"You're on the list of suspects, y'know."

"I am?" The ball-tossing stops. "Why?"

"Because you knew when the promotional money was being
moved from the Slot Palace to the vault."

"I did?"

"You and Hunt and Carlos and Dooley."

"So I'm a suspect?" He laughs. "Do you have any idea how
much money I've made here over the past five years? Why would I
risk that for pocket change?"

"You might have passed the information to someone else. Un-
intentionally." I give him a second. "Did you?"

"Not that I recall." He closes his eyes for a moment, then opens
them and gives me his best smile. "No, I'm quite sure I didn't."

A♠   2♣   4♣♣

Home again. No car out front, no one searching for a key in the
living room, no one eating my Chunky Monkey. Nothing but half

a bottle of Vouvray in the fridge and an inflatable mattress on my bedroom floor and a blinking light on the answering machine. I take out the half bottle of Vouvray and pour myself a glass. I take a sip. It tastes of acid and yeast, and I am overwhelmed by a sense of sadness and tragedy. I press the button on the answering machine and listen to three hangup calls. Buddy or Jaymie? I suspect the former.

I return to the kitchen and attempt an elegant pose at the Formica table. I should be in a tragic painting, staring off beyond the canvas, hand forever closed around the stem of a glass filled with cheap French wine.

ACES. I HAVE FOUR ACES. No, I have five aces. How many
aces are in this deck? And what is that horrible relentless
ringing? I open my eyes. I am awake now. But the ringing
continues. I search blearily for the time, but my clock is broken—
instead of the time it is showing three vertical dashes. Stop the goddamn ringing. I bring my palm down on the clock, fingers pressing
every protuberance, to no effect. Still ringing. I sit up. It's the
phone. I grab the receiver from its blinking base.

"Hello?" The display on the clock changes, now it reads 1:12.
Not broken after all.

"It's me."

It takes me a second. "Jaymie?"

"Yeah. I got what you wanted, okay?"

"You did? Okay, um, good. Can I come by in the morning?"

"I'm not at Leon's anymore. Look, I need a ride. Can you pick
me up at the Crossroads?"

It takes me half an hour to get cleaned up, dressed, and out the
door. It's cooled off outside, all the way down into the eighties.
As I back out of my driveway, top down, I hear the sound of a
car engine starting. A pair of headlights comes on a half block

down the street. I take off, make a left, kill my headlights, double back down the alley, pull into a neighbor's carport, and wait. Nothing. I wait for five minutes, then put up the top and drive back down the alley to the cross street. I turn left and head for South Tucson, checking my rearview mirror every few seconds.

Probably just a coincidence, but as Cisco has pointed out, even the paranoid have enemies.

Jaymie is sitting on the sidewalk in front of the Crossroads drive-in restaurant with the neck of a Corona trailing from her right hand and a cigarette burning in her left. She peers suspiciously into the Miata. I roll down the window and wave. She drains the last of her beer and flicks her cigarette into the gutter, then picks up a purse-size black object by its handle—it's not a purse—and lurches to her feet.

"Took you long enough," she says as she gets into the car. "I've been kicked out of more places in the past twenty-four hours than Courtney Love."

"You got kicked out of the Crossroads?"

"They were closing."

"Oh." I let a few seconds tick by. "So?" I ask.

"Here." She dumps the black thing into my lap. It's a camcorder. "It's Leon's. I don't give a shit if you give it back to him."

"I just wanted some photos," I say.

"Yeah, well I didn't have a *camera,* Mom."

"Okay." I turn the camcorder in my hands. I've never used one. I don't know what to do with it. She grabs it back.

"Can we just get out of here?"

"Where do you want to go?"

"I don't care."

I put the car in gear and roll away from the curb. "So Leon kicked you out?"

"Yeah. I think he was afraid you and Eddie were gonna come

back. And then your friend with the boots shows up, and Leon gets all, like, they're out to get me. When I left he was duct-taping the curtains to the windows."

"Why would he do that?"

"So the bogeyman can't peek in. He gets that way." She starts energetically picking her teeth with her fingernail.

"Are you hungry? Have you eaten?"

Jaymie doesn't say anything for half a block, then gives an exaggerated shrug.

"I could use a cup of coffee."

I find a Waffle House on the other side of the freeway. Jaymie insists she's not hungry, but when the waitress shows up she orders scrambled eggs, potatoes, a toasted bagel, and bowl of Frosted Flakes to go with her coffee. I order a blueberry waffle. Jaymie lights a cigarette. I fiddle with the camcorder, trying to decode the symbols labeling the buttons. Jaymie is watching me through slitted eyes.

"Here." She grabs the camcorder from me and flips out a small display screen. "You can watch it here. This button is fast-forward, this is reverse, this is play." She backs up the tape, frowning, squinting, cigarette pinched between her thin lips. Twenty-three going on sixty. "When I heard your friend outside honking, I started it up and set it on the end table with a bunch of other junk and just let it run." She points out a piece of black electrical tape on the front of the camera. "I stuck a piece of tape over the record light so he wouldn't know it was running."

"Good one," I say, impressed.

"Here." She turns the camcorder around so the display is facing me and pushes it across the table.

I peer into the tiny screen. All I see is a dark, empty sofa viewed from one end. I hear a clunking sound, and what might be a door opening.

"The light was lousy, of course, so the picture's kind of dark. But you can hear him talking. I'll turn it up." She adjusts the volume slide, and I hear a distant, tinny version of Leon's voice.

Thought I told you to cut out the goddamn honking. My neighbors get pissed. Well, shit, don't just stand out there. Come on in.

The next voice sounds like it could be Carlos.

What the hell happened to your door?

It broke.

The voices get louder.

What do you need?

Got an ounce?

Got eight bills?

What do you think?

Have a seat. I'll be right back.

A figure dressed in black plops down on the sofa. He turns his head toward the camera—I can make out his features now. He is smiling in a way I've never seen before, but it is unquestionably Carlos.

Hey there, Mama, how you doing?

Jaymie's voice comes on.

I'm okay. You're getting an ounce, huh?

What the fuck.

I hear you.

Carlos pulls something from his pocket and turns it over and over in his hands. I think it's a pipe.

Want a taste?

Jaymie stops the tape.

"That the guy?"

"Oh, yeah."

"The whole tape is full of him. After Leon got back with the ounce he just sat there doing hits and talking shit for like an hour. Driving Leon nuts. He can't stand the guy. That what you wanted?"

"Even better." I smile at her. "Thank you."

"You're welcome."

Our food arrives, and we both dig in, grateful for the distrac-

tion. Ten minutes later I am left with only a few deflated blueber-
ries on my plate. Jaymie has been moving her food around without
getting much of it into her mouth.

"Now what?" I ask. "You want me to drop you off someplace?"
Which crack house, I almost add.

Jaymie mumbles something into her plate.

"What's that?" I lean forward.

"I said, 'I was hoping I could stay with you.' "

45

CISCO IS WATCHING THE VIDEO; I am watching Cisco.

Ahhhhh . . . fug. Carlos's hand falls to his lap.

"What is that?" Cisco asks.

"A glass pipe. He's smoking crack cocaine," I say.

Another hand reaches into the frame and takes the pipe from Carlos's hand.

Okay?

"That's Leon, the dealer."

Carlos touches his face and stares at his hand.

Got a beer?

Now he wants a beer. Christ.

"How did you get this?" Cisco asks.

Get him a beer.

Get him a beer yourself.

"That's my daughter," I say.

Cisco grunts and hunches his shoulders.

Christ, I'll get my own goddamn beer.

Carlos gets up off the couch.

"She made the tape for me."

"Turn it off."

I stop the recording. "It goes on for a while."

We are sitting at the yellow table in Hector Vega's card room. Cisco is wearing a long black bathrobe. He is gripping a gold-and-red Casino Santa Cruz promotional mug in both hands, staring off through the wide window, across the desert, toward Tucson. Sunlight lances into the room at a steep late-morning angle. The sweet-sour smell of black coffee clouds the air between us.

"We show each other the worst movies," he says.

"I'm sorry."

"This is the man my daughter married."

"That night we played cards here? Remember he kept getting up to go to the bathroom? I'm pretty sure he was smoking crack that night."

Cisco nods. "I knew there was something. I did not think it was this." Wrinkled, knuckly hands massage the gold-and-red mug as if he is trying to reshape it. The corners of his mouth tuck in and he turns his bright black eyes on me. "Tell me what you believe, Peeky." He releases the mug and makes a fist with his right hand and presses it to his chest. "Here."

"Do you mean about Carlos?"

He nods.

"I think he has a serious substance abuse problem. And messed-up people do messed-up things. Woody Stumpf had a drug problem, too."

"You know this?"

"Buddy told me. So that could be a connection between Carlos and Woody, but I don't know . . . there are a lot of people out there getting high, that doesn't mean they all know each other."

Cisco's head falls forward into a nod, and stays down. I would think he has fallen asleep, but the fingers of his left hand are still active on the mug.

"Father?" Maria has appeared with a coffeepot. Cisco's head snaps up and he smiles, holding out his mug.

"Thank you, Maria."

"Are you hungry?"

"No, thank you."

"You should eat," she says.

"Soon. Right now we need to talk, Peeky and I."

Maria nods, frowning, and gives me a brittle look. I'm not sure, but I think I've just been cursed. She turns abruptly and stalks out of the room. Cisco watches her go with a mild smile, then turns back to me.

"Your daughter. How is she doing?"

"At the moment she's asleep on my bed. At least, she was when I left her."

"Good."

"I saw Bruce Johnson yesterday."

His head comes up. "Was he smoking crack, too?"

"I was at the casino, and he asked to talk to me. He—"

"He asked you to convince me to renew his contract," Cisco says, interrupting me.

"Yes."

"Because my son-in-law is an incompetent crackhead." I can taste the bitterness in his voice.

"I don't think he knows Carlos is using."

Cisco sips his tea, staring out the window.

"I don't know if this helps, but I don't think Carlos's abilities have anything to do with how things have been going."

Cisco shakes his head. "It doesn't matter. We are all but extinct."

"Bruce Johnson has been sandbagging Carlos from day one."

Cisco's face is locked into a grim smile. I don't know if he is listening to me.

I say, "Johnson mentioned firing all those poker dealers as an example of Carlos's lousy judgment. But I wonder who planted the idea in Carlos's head in the first place."

Cisco is shaking his head slowly, but I do not think it is in response to anything I've said. He is listening to some other voice. Still, I keep talking.

"He's working Carlos from both ends—undermining him as an executive, and bribing him with promises at the same time. You told me before that Johnson favors increasing the quarterly stipend. I'm sure he's offering Carlos more money as well. And Carlos must know on some level that he can't handle the job. Keeping Johnson around gives him an in-house mentor. From his point of view it's win-win."

"Win-win?" Cisco looks as if he just ate a bad oyster. "This is politics, Peeky. You know what is win-win? It is when somebody gets fucked worse. This videotape, it is our what do you call it—our nuclear option. I thought I wanted to know these things about Carlos. Now I see that it only makes things worse. He is my daughter's husband, and I put him in charge of gaming operations. I was the one. I use Carlos's drug use to bring him down, and do you think the council will turn to me for guidance? No. Magic Hand will be ready to step in for another seven years, and that is exactly what will happen. I say fuck 'em. They can have it."

"What about the congressman? Does he have any influence with the council?"

"Alex? He won't make a move until he knows who the winners are." Cisco stands abruptly and shuffles across the room to the bar. "Care for a drink?"

"Just water, please."

"Okay." He pours a generous three fingers of bourbon into two rocks glasses, adds a couple of ice cubes to each, and shuffles back to the table holding a drink in each hand.

He sits down and pushes one of the glasses toward me.

"Funny-looking water," I say.

"Ancient Indian ritual," he says.

"I didn't think you drank."

"Special occasions only."

"What's special?"

"I 'specially need a drink," he says with a creaky laugh.

With nothing whatsoever to celebrate, we click glasses and drink.

"How would you feel about addressing the tribal council tomorrow?" Cisco asks. He has just poured himself a second drink. His cheeks are flushed.

"And tell them what?"

"I bring you in as an investigator making a report. You show them your movie."

"Now you want to show it? I thought you said it was a nuclear option."

He shrugs. "Stir things up. It can't hurt."

"Are you sure?"

"No!" He takes a large swallow of his bourbon. "What the hell, I am just this old man who does not want their quarterly payments increased. This old man who wants their sons and grandsons to work with their hands in the dirt. Not a popular idea with these Escalade-driving young turks. If it takes an atom bomb to get their attention, then I say *ka-boom*."

"I thought the council was this old boys' club. How will they feel about a white woman coming in and smearing one of their own?"

Cisco laughs. "They won't like it much! Especially when you tell them about Johnson making Carlos his boy."

"How many are on the council?"

"Six, plus Carlos."

"How many of them support you?"

"The two fossils. The younger ones, they think it is a good thing to have a white man doing their work for them. They think it is clever."

"I been here since the beginning. Without me, the Santa Cruz don't exist. I'm like Adam. Hell, I'm like the Creator." He slams his hand on the tabletop. "They try and give that son of a bitch Johnson another contract, they'll find out what I'm made of. Bunch of pussies." He rattles the ice in his glass. *"Uno mas?"*

"No thanks." I'm still working on my first drink, and feeling its effects.

Cisco maneuvers his way back to the bar and sloshes another three ounces of Maker's Mark into his glass.

"Without me, they are all dogshit. I made this fucking tribe."

"Fuck it, I'll run the goddamn casino myself. You, too. You can have Hunt's job. What the hell, you're like family already. I ever tell you that?" He grabs my hand and leans over the table and stares into my face. His eyes are brimming. "I swear to God, Peeky, I love you like a daughter."

That's when I realize how profoundly drunk he is. And I still haven't finished my first drink.

I think Maria wants to kill me.

"You get out!" she shrieks.

Cisco is slumped in his chair, glasses crooked on his lumpy nose, a bead of drool gathering at the corner of his mouth.

"Don't you want me to help get him to bed?"

"You are a white witch. Get out! Witch!"

"Look, I didn't know . . . I didn't do anything."

She grabs the camcorder and hurls it at me. Somehow I manage to catch it.

"Get out!"

When I don't move fast enough she grabs a pool cue from the rack on the wall and comes after me.

I get out.

46

I FEEL SMALL IN MY MIATA, trucks and SUVs roaring by on either side. I can feel the midday heat radiating right through the fabric above my head as icy air swirls around my feet. I keep telling myself that I did nothing wrong.

Somehow it doesn't make me feel much better. Watching Cisco drink—it took him all of twenty minutes to reach oblivion—has left me feeling physically ill. I'm woozy from the whiskey, too, even though I never finished that first drink. I've never had much tolerance for hard liquor.

I creep along at five miles per hour under the speed limit, driving like the alcoholic old lady I might one day become. Everybody I know is hooked on something. Ticking off names in my head, I fail to come up with the name of one person in my life who isn't a drunk, a drug addict, or gambleholic. Yesterday I would have cited Cisco as a shining beacon, but now I know better. I feel lost and betrayed. I wish I was a box turtle. With a single act of will, I could close myself off from the world and wait for rain. Instead, I am toddling along half drunk in my little red ragtop.

Poor Cisco. I hope he's okay.

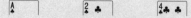

Eduardo's pickup is parked in front of my house. I pull into my driveway and brace myself for whatever scene I'm about to walk in on. I let myself in the front door. The living room looks okay. No blood on the walls.

"Anybody home?" I call out.

Nothing. I walk down the short hallway to the kitchen. Looking through the patio doors, I see them sitting outside. Eduardo is drinking a Corona. Jaymie has a glass of wine, probably the last of my Vouvray. They are talking. For about two seconds I consider backing off and letting them have their time together.

To hell with that. I pull the door open and go out to join them.

You would think that everything was okay. You would think that Jaymie had not run away repeatedly, that she hadn't stolen my money to smoke crack and hang out with a bunch of low-life drug dealers. You would think that Eduardo was an easygoing guy who would never drink too much or get into fights. You would never dream that I was a professional gambler whose boyfriend was a cold-blooded killer.

We keep it light. Eduardo runs up to the Safeway to get some food for a cookout. While he is gone, Jaymie and I busy ourselves in the kitchen making potato salad. I tell her about Cisco getting blotto and somehow turn it into a funny story. She tells me about the time she and Eduardo went to the Grand Canyon, and how he discovered that he was afraid of heights. We say nothing about the future. We do not talk about money, or drugs, or where she is going to sleep. Maybe tomorrow I will call Teresa Alvarez and set up a meeting, just the four of us, but not today.

Jaymie says, "Oh, I forgot, Buddy called. He wanted to know if you had found a key or something?"

"Did he say where he was?"

"Yeah. Nogales. Why is he in Nogales?"

"It's a long story."

Eduardo returns with charcoal, steaks, corn, and a case of Coronitas. We laugh at him because he bought enough meat to feed a platoon. He grumbles good-naturedly, something about the value of leftovers, and loads the grill with charcoal. We all have a Coronita. I rarely drink beer, but those little seven-ounce bottles are just too cute to pass up.

It is almost dark by the time we sit down to eat. The meat is overcooked, the corn is tough, and the potato salad is missing something, I don't know what. Maybe onion or salt. But we are all starving, and it goes down fast. Jaymie keeps saying, "Isn't this fun?"

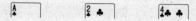

It is nine forty-five. Jaymie and Eduardo are giggling over some memory—I haven't followed their conversation for the past twenty minutes. I announce that I am going to bed.

"So soon?" Jaymie says. But she doesn't try to talk me into staying up. I push myself through my nightly ritual, scrubbing my teeth and face and applying overpriced mystery creams to my aging tissues. My head hurts. I decide I am hungover. One large whiskey and two Coronitas. And six hours with my daughter and her husband, talking about nothing at all.

47

THE DOORBELL DRAGS ME FROM SLEEP. The clock reads 11:23, and it's dark out. Jaymie and Eduardo have left. I've been asleep less than an hour. It rings again. I throw off the covers and put on my robe and slippers and shuffle to the living room. I turn on the light and peek past the curtains. It takes me a couple seconds to recognize the tall, slouching figure on my front step. Donny Keyes.

Without thinking too hard about it, I open the door. Donny doesn't scare me. He's a big old hound dog. Even if he did beat up a slot machine. Even if he did it to provide a distraction for the casino robbers. To me, he's just another prop.

"Peeky," he says. His face is all doom and gloom, but that's normal for Donny. A lot of props get to looking that way. Or maybe it's that people who look that way become props. He waits for my response.

I don't say anything. Let's see what he comes out with.

"How you doing?" he asks, finally.

"I'm okay."

"I, um, I'm, um, I'm looking for Buddy," he says, kicking the welcome mat with his toe. Reminds me of this eight-year-old boy who used to come around looking for Jaymie to play with him.

"Everybody's looking for Buddy," I say.

"He here?"

"No, and I don't know where he is." I look past Donny and see his faded blue Cadillac parked at the curb. Eduardo's truck is gone.

"I hear you had a problem with a slot machine," I say.

Donny rolls his shoulders. "Fuckin' slots." He smiles abashedly. "Hey!" His eyebrows shoot up as if he has suddenly discovered the answer to a vexing problem. "Mind if I come in for a minute?"

Normally I would have asked him in already, but I keep looking at that blue Cadillac. I wonder if Mandy Krause is looking out her window this time.

"Why?" I ask.

"I, um, I gotta use your bathroom." There is an animal opacity to his eyes.

"I'm sorry, Donny, this is a bad time for me." I try to close the door but his thick fingers wrap the edge and force it open. His hand shoots out and clamps onto my upper arm. He pushes me back into the house. Kicking the door shut behind him, he slams me against the wall. My head cracks plaster; the wall mirror jumps off its hook, hits the tile floor, tips face forward, and shatters.

"I know he was here, Peeky." He is pressing me against the wall with his body. His breath is all cinnamon and funk. I hear his feet grinding bits of broken mirror into the tiles. His face is enormous, the pores on his nose are craters.

"Get off me, Donny." I get my hands between us and try to push him away. He is a mountain. I curl my fingers and dig into his chest with my nails. He pushes himself back, still gripping my arm, and flings me across the room. I land on the living room carpet, the exact spot where Robert's ashes were scattered.

Donny is standing over me. Now he is holding something in his hand. A small handgun. A LadySmith.

"Is that my gun?"

"I didn't come here to hurt you, Peeky."

"Too late," I say, sitting up, rubbing a bruised hip.

"I need to talk to Buddy."

"Too late," I say again. "He's come and gone. Forever, I hope."

Donny stares down at me, blinking slowly.

I say, "What are you after? The money from the casino? Buddy's gone and so is the money. You know what you should do, Donny? Get the fuck out of Tucson and never look back. The Santa Cruz know everything." I decide to take a shot. "They know you were behind the robbery."

"Me?" Donny laughs. "All I did was bust up a slot machine."

"Maybe, but do you think Blaise Hunt is going to let you slide just because he can't get you in court?"

Donny's eyes narrow and his face hardens. "Where is Buddy, Peeky?"

"Are you deaf? I don't *know*. You want me to guess? Mexico. Argentina. Antarctica. Assturkistan."

"Where is the money?"

"I don't know that either."

He looks at me for a long time. Two props staring at each other.

I say, "Look, I want nothing to do with any of you. If you got a problem with Buddy, it's got nothing to do with me. And by the way, you owe me about sixty grand for the B and E. I had to throw away everything you put your grubby paws on."

"Don't fuck with me, Peeky."

"I wouldn't dream of it."

His lower eyelid twitches. He raises the gun and points it at me. Donny must have decided going in that he would become Mr. Heartless-cyborg-robot-man, like a guy who has decided to bet his hand to the end no matter what.

"Are you going to shoot me with my own gun?"

"Do you *want* me to shoot you?"

"What do you think?"

"I need that money, Peek."

"There's my purse." I point at the tile table near the front door. "There's a couple thousand in there, that's it. Take it and get the hell out of my house." I must be nuts. The man is pointing a gun at me. I should be trying to calm him down. I should tell him that Buddy is in Vegas, or Yuma, or Nogales—someplace he might believe. I should tell him anything to make him stop pointing that thing at me. The problem is, part of me doesn't care if he shoots.

But most of me does. I do not like the way he is looking at me.

The doorbell rings. Donny freezes up for a second, glaring at me as if I've somehow set him up. "You expecting anybody?"

I shrug my shoulders. I hope it's the cops. About a hundred of them, in riot gear.

Donny goes to the window and looks past the curtains.

"Some Indian kid," he says in a low voice, looking at me.

The doorbell rings again.

"Wait for him to go away," Donny says.

We wait in silence for a minute, then two.

"Hey, anybody home?"

Donny jumps. The voice is coming from the back of the house. I hear soft footsteps, then see Smoke come in through the kitchen.

"Whoa! Hey!" Smoke says, his eyes on the gun in Donny's hand. Donny brings the gun up, pointing it at Smoke. "Easy!" says Smoke, holding up his palms.

Donny's eyes shift from Smoke to the front door, then back again. "Who the fuck are you?" he asks.

"Who the fuck are *you*?" Smoke says.

Donny waves the gun toward me. "Get over there."

"The fuck you gonna do, shoot me?"

"I might."

Smoke shrugs one shoulder and takes a few sideways steps in my direction, keeping his front toward Donny. From where I'm sitting I can see the taped-up butt of Robert's revolver sticking out of the back of his belt. Great. Now I'm being robbed by two people. With my own guns.

The doorbell rings again.

"He ain't going away, old man," says Smoke. "You gonna shoot us all?"

"Shut up." Donny moves a few steps toward the kitchen.

"That's right, old man. Time to go bye-bye." Smoke's right hand moves back a few inches.

Donny edges into the short hallway, looking back and forth from the kitchen to Smoke. For the moment, neither of them are paying any attention to the middle-aged woman sitting on the floor. I am rigid, not breathing, waiting for the end of the world. I don't know what I want to happen. Smoke scares me just as bad as Donny.

Then, like a rubber band breaking, Donny takes off through the kitchen. Smoke has the gun in his hand, but he doesn't go after him.

"What a pussy," he says. He opens the front door and lets Richie in.

"Was it the guy?" Richie asks Smoke.

"I don't know." They both look at me.

"His name is Donny Keyes," I say. "I think he was one of the men involved in the card room robbery."

"Sheee . . . my little cuz got killed in that. I shoulda shot the fucker."

I climb to my feet. "I thought you were the one about to get shot."

"By that pussy?" Smoke laughed. "Not hardly. Dude ran like a fuckin' girl." Smoke looks at me. "No offense."

Richie laughs, then sees the gun in Smoke's hand. "Where'd you get that?"

"On the kitchen counter. Good thing, too. Dude was packin'." He looks at me again. "You okay?"

Maybe they didn't come here to rob me after all.

"What are you doing here?" I ask.

"Ol' Hector asked us to keep an eye on you. Good thing, ay? Hey, Richie, you wanna go out back, make sure that dude's not hangin' over the fence or somethin'?"

"You the one with the gun, bro."

"Pussy," says Smoke with a flat grin. He goes out through the kitchen while Richie opens the curtains and looks out the front window at Donny's car.

"Nice car. I bet he'll be back for it—whoa, there he is!" Richie is shouting. "Smoke! Dude! He's out front!" He yanks open the front door. Donny is sprinting from the side of the house toward his car. Smoke comes charging back through the kitchen and living room and hits the open front door running. Donny is in his car; the engine starts and he squeals off. Smoke is ten feet behind the car, running flat out, holding the gun out in front of him in one hand. As the Cadillac pulls away Smoke fires three times. The Cadillac fishtails around the corner and is gone.

"Sheee*it*!" Smoke staggers to a stop and slaps the gun against his thigh so hard I think for a moment he's shot himself. He stomps his foot and walks stiff-legged back to where Richie and I are waiting on the front step. Across the street, I see Mandy looking out of her window.

"Think you hit him?" Richie asks.

Smoke shakes his head and says, "We best get our asses outta here. Go get my whip, dude." He tosses him a set of keys.

Richie snatches the keys out of the air and trots off down the sidewalk. A familiar-looking black Escalade is parked down the block.

Smoke hands me Robert's revolver. "You shouldn't leave these things lyin' around."

Speechless, I take the gun. He looks at the Escalade backing up the street toward us. "Listen, we can't stick around after, you know——" He mimes shooting a gun.

I nod.

"You gonna be okay though, right?"

"I'll be fine," I say.

The Escalade is at the curb with Richie at the wheel. Smoke starts toward it, then stops and looks back at me. "I mean, Hector, he be really pissed off otherwise."

"It's okay," I say. "Really."

48

THE LOCKSMITH SCOWLS AT THE KEY, turning it in his thick
fingers. "What did you do to it?"

"I vacuumed it."

"Chewed it up pretty good." Giving me an accusing look, as if
I've mistreated something precious. His shop, not much larger than
a garden shed, smells of oil and metal.

"Can you fix it?"

"Nope. Try to straighten this out, it'll snap right off if you try to
use it."

I wait for more.

"Could try and hammer it back in shape, then make a copy, I
suppose. That is, if I wanted to get myself in trouble. You see what
this says?" He points at the head of the key and reads it for me.
"*Do not duplicate.*" He gives me the smug look of a bureaucrat
denying an application. "Not supposed to copy these. Against the
law."

"Oh dear," I say, wondering whether there really is such a law.
I look out the window. Eduardo is sitting in the passenger seat of
my Miata sipping a Starbucks triple latte, looking miserable. He's
paying the price for drinking most of a case of Coronitas.

After Smoke and Richie left last night, I got in my car and
drove over to Eduardo and Jaymie's apartment. There was no way
I could have slept at home alone. After three minutes of pressing

on the buzzer, Jaymie opened the door. I started to explain to her what had happened, but she wasn't taking it in.

"Can I use your sofa bed?" I asked.

"Whatever." She staggered off to bed.

I headed for the spare bedroom and the Iron Bar of Agony. There would be plenty of time in the morning to tell her about my late-night visit from Donny Keyes. But when I woke up, Jaymie was gone—and so was Eduardo's pickup truck.

The locksmith says, "Course, if I made a copy and kept the original, that wouldn't be so bad. Might work. Only I could still get in trouble."

"Would you be willing to do that?"

He purses his lips and slowly shakes his head, but I notice he is still holding the key in his hand. I open my purse and take out two twenties and set them on the countertop. He looks down at the money and I see the pink tip of his tongue dart out to taste his lips.

"What was that about?" Eduardo is wearing the darkest pair of sunglasses I have ever seen. They must make them specially for hangover victims.

"I had a copy of a key made. It cost me forty bucks."

"Seems kind of steep."

"It's a valuable key."

He shakes his head. "Now where we going?"

"My place." I put the Miata in gear and pull away from the curb. It's another hot day; they're talking a hundred ten degrees.

"You don't want to go back to Leon's, see if maybe she is there?"

"I'm not going to chase her anymore, Eduardo. And neither should you."

"She took my truck!"

"You'll get it back. Eventually."

"Yeah, I don't know about that," he says, slumping lower in his seat. I notice something pushing out the belly of his loose, oversize *guayabera*.

"I thought we agree you'd leave that at home," I say.

"Leave what?" he says, pouting like a hungover eight-year-old.

I reach over and poke the .44 Magnum through his shirt. "That."

He reaches down and shoves the gun deeper into his waistband. That can't be comfortable.

"Now you can pretend it's not there," he says.

Just as well. I don't actually mind that he is armed.

I take out my cell phone, punch the redial button, and brace myself. I've called Cisco twice today already. Both times Maria answered. Both times she hung up as soon as she heard my voice.

This time, no one answers at all.

"No luck?" Eduardo asks.

"Nope."

"Too bad," he says. Not that he cares. Eduardo is thinking about only two things right now: his wife, and the pain behind his eyes.

I say, "Do you ever look at your life and say, 'This isn't working out. I'm starting over.' You ever do that?"

Eduardo looks at me. "You mean like reincarnation?"

"Only without the part where you actually die. I mean just close up shop, buy a fake I.D., and get a job at a Wal-Mart in Des Moines. Call yourself Christine Johnson, buy a house in the burbs, grow yourself a big butt, and let your hair go gray."

"You mean have a sex change?"

"No. I'm talking about me. You'd move to Boca Raton and call yourself Chico Gonzales."

Eduardo sips his Starbucks. "I never thought about that," he says. "Where's Boca Raton?"

"Florida."

He nods. "I could see that. Get a job on a boat or something."

A card stuck in my front door requests that I contact the Tucson Police Department. Apparently they showed up after the shooting incident, found no bodies, no property damage, nobody home. Given the number of nuisance calls the cops get from Mandy, there will be no follow-up. I crumple the card and let myself into the house. Eduardo, still with a death grip on the remains of his triple latte, shuffles in behind me.

Everything looks pretty much the same as I left it: shards of broken mirror on the floor, empty bottles on the kitchen counter, dishes in the sink.

"What happened to your mirror?" Eduardo asks.

"I had a little scuffle here last night, remember? The reason I had to come and stay at your place?"

"Oh. Yeah."

The answering machine is blinking; I press the button.

"Peeky, this is Gayle Vega. Could you call me please?" She rattles off a phone number; it sounds like a cell phone exchange. I dial the number immediately. Gayle picks up on the second ring.

"Gayle, this is Peeky."

"Peeky, I'm glad you called."

"I've been trying to reach your grandfather, but Maria keeps hanging up on me."

"Yes, she is . . . upset with you. She holds you responsible for Grandfather's lapse."

"You mean his drinking."

"Yes."

"Is he okay?"

"He's fine, but he's not here."

"Is he at the casino?"

"No."

"Do you know when he'll be back? Is there a way I could reach him?"

"I'm afraid not. He's up on the San Carlos. He did not say when he would be returning."

"This is important."

"I'm sure it is. My grandfather's health is also important. He needs to make himself pure again."

"Oh. I didn't know, you know. We were just sitting there talking and he poured himself a drink and the next thing I knew he was gonzo."

"I am not blaming you."

"Please tell Maria how sorry I am."

"I will do that."

"I was doing some work for him. I have some information he's going to need for the council meeting tonight."

"Yes, this is why I called. Grandfather will not be able to attend the meeting, but it is important to him that his views be expressed. He asked me to represent him, and he suggested that you might wish to be there as well."

"I could do that. They will be making a decision as to whether or not to renew the contract with Magic Hand, right?"

"That is my understanding. Grandfather said you had a film clip?"

"He called it his 'nuclear option.' "

"Perhaps the time has come to exercise that option."

"Your grandfather once told me that power is like poker. First you convince them you are crazy, then you show them the goods."

"That sounds like Grandfather. Is this film clip 'the goods'?"

"I have something else in mind."

"I'll just be a couple of minutes," I tell Eduardo, who has been standing listening to my side of the conversation with uncomprehending apathy. I go to my bedroom and change into khaki shorts, tennis shoes, and a white sleeveless top. Boring, but comfortable. I don't think I can accessorize my way out of this outfit, so I don't bother. There is a time for looking good, and a time for action. They do not always run concurrently.

I hear the clink of glass from the kitchen. Eduardo cleaning up from last night? I am surprised. I give myself five minutes to work on my face. The results are less than impressive, but I'm good to go if you don't get too close. Eduardo doesn't count. He's family. Besides, I don't think his eyes are working so good this morning.

I find him in the kitchen chasing his latte with a Coronita.

"I thought we finished those off last night."

"One left," he says. He's looking a bit more alert.

"Let's go."

49

E XPLAIN TO ME AGAIN what I am doing here," Eduardo says.
"Moral support," I say.
"I don't like Nogales much."

We are driving south on I-19. The speed limit signs now read in both miles and kilometers per hour. Mexico, dead ahead.

"I thought you grew up there."

"On the U.S. side, yeah. I got out as soon as I could. In Nogales everybody thinks I am Mexican. I am three generations American."

"Same as me." My grandparents on my mother's side came over from Poland back in the thirties.

"You are white. It is different."

I don't argue. I know what he means. Nogales is a border-straddling town—two towns, really—with each side competing for most ugly. Personally, I think the U.S. side wins by a nose. The Sonora, Mexico, side, with its hundreds of tiny shops, bars, restaurants, shantytown housing, and enormous population, is far more textured and interesting. I probably think that because I'm American. The streets of Nogales, Sonora, are teeming with tourists from Tucson, Phoenix, and Green Valley gawking at the beggars and buying their serapes, OxyContin, tequila, and counterfeit Cuban cigars. The U.S. side is full of Mexicans shopping the American stores for blue jeans and toaster ovens. I guess it's all about what you can't get at home.

But no matter which side of the border you're on, it's better to be white. To the shopkeepers and restaurateurs and cops and border guards, dark skin looks like poverty and drug smuggling and wetback labor. Light skin looks like money. Guess who gets treated better? I don't blame Eduardo. I wouldn't want to look Mexican in Nogales either.

"Don't worry about it. We won't be here long."

A few miles later he says, "I gotta find a bathroom."

I pull into a Circle K on the north end of Nogales. Eduardo goes searching for a restroom while I look through the battered Yellow Pages hanging from the pay phone on the outside wall. The phone is missing its handset, and about a quarter of the phonebook pages have been ripped out, but the section on "Storage—Household and Commercial" is intact. Following the example of those before me, I rip the needed pages from the phone book.

I am in my car looking through the list, circling likely prospects. Buddy said that his locker was "a few hundred yards" from the border. I narrow it down to self-storage places within one mile of the border crossing.

"I found three," I say when Eduardo returns.

"Good," he says. "Are you going to tell me what we are looking for now?"

I hold up the key. "Number one forty-three."

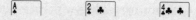

The second place we visit, AAA-ABC Mini Storage, is a half acre of long, low, flat-topped cinder-block buildings, each of them with about twenty garage doors set along the length. There are nine of these buildings inside a small compound surrounded by chain-link fencing. The fence is topped with a coil of razor wire.

There is no attendant on duty. The outer gate is locked. I try using the key. At first it won't fit into the lock. I am about to give up and go on to the next storage place, but I remember that the locksmith warned me that the new key might be "a mite sticky." I wiggle it back and forth a few times and it pops in. One twist to the right and the gate swings open.

Up until this moment I have been an ice queen, as cool as if I were playing a hand of holdem. Now my heart speeds up and my hand is shaking as I jiggle the key trying to get it out of the lock. It takes only a few seconds, but it seems like minutes.

"Leave the gate open," I say to Eduardo. I don't want to deal with that lock again.

We are the only ones in the storage compound.

"I don't like this place," says Eduardo, echoing my eerie last-two-humans-on-earth feeling.

"Then let's get it done and get out of here."

We find number 143 halfway down the fourth building from the left. Except for a small stenciled number, every bay is identical. I can see how Buddy forgot which one is his. The door lock accepts the key easily. I give it a twist. Eduardo grasps the handle and rolls up the overhead door.

The storage locker is about eight feet wide by twelve feet deep. At first I think it is empty. Then I see a bright green nylon backpack leaning against one wall.

"That it?" Eduardo asks.

"I don't know." I step into the bay and lift the pack. It isn't heavy. I bring it outside into the daylight.

"You gonna look in it?"

I'm shaking so hard I have trouble grabbing the zipper, but I do. I bend over and open the pack and find myself staring into the eyeholes of a rubber clown mask.

"I hope that's what I think it is."

I look at Eduardo, confused by the change in his voice. He is not looking at me. He is turning to look at something behind him. Every muscle in my body contracts.

"Because if it's not, I'm gonna be real upset with y'all."

Eduardo moves slightly. I see Donny Keyes's morose face. My eyes jump to his left hand. My own gun, pointing at me. I am still confused—that was not Donny's voice I heard.

Then I see him. Standing behind Donny, about ten feet back. Looking the way he might look holding the mortal nuts after all the money has run into the pot, a broad white smile stretching his face, as if it's all over but the counting.

"Dooley," I say.

Dooley, hands in his pockets, rolls his round shoulders in a parody of an abashed shrug.

Donny says, "You only got one Injun with you this time, huh Peeky?"

"I'm not an Indian," Eduardo says. "I'm American."

Dooley laughs. "Ol' Hector might want to argue you that point, son. He says if you ain't Indian, you ain't American."

I am thinking that Eduardo might want to argue using the .44 he has tucked under his shirt. I hope he waits for the right moment. If there is a right moment.

Dooley nods at the backpack and says, "Ship it, Peeky."

I lift the backpack by a shoulder strap and toss it underhanded toward his feet.

Dooley nudges it with his toe. "Let's have a look," he says to Donny. He holds out his hand. "Give me the gun."

Donny hesitates, then hands my LadySmith to Dooley. I can tell from the way Dooley holds the gun that he knows his way around firearms. I hope Eduardo sees that, too.

"See what we got here," says Dooley.

Donny squats beside the backpack and pulls out the clown mask. He opens the pack wide and comes out with a red T-shirt, a pair of yellow rubber gloves, and a small canvas tote bag. He unzips the tote bag and stares into it.

"Please tell me it's full of money," says Dooley, keeping his eyes and the gun on me and Eduardo.

"Jackpot," says Donny. He looks up, smiling happily.

Dooley swings his arm toward Donny. The gun jumps; Donny's head snaps back, followed by his body. I hear the shot echoing through the aisles of storage bays, and then the sound of Donny's ruined skull hitting the asphalt with a soggy crunch. His legs jerk a couple of times, then he is still.

Dooley has the gun back on me and Eduardo. I look into the end of the barrel and a fatalistic calm settles upon me and within me. The cards have been dealt. I live or I die.

But I'm still kicking, so I attempt a desperate bluff. "They all know, Dooley. Hunt, Cisco, Carlos. They know it was you. It won't help you to kill us."

Dooley shrugs. "What makes you think I want to kill you?"

"I don't think you do."

"You don't?" His smile returns.

"There's no point. Your only chance now is to run. You can be over the border in ten minutes."

"What if I don't believe you? Maybe nobody knows a thing."

"I'm not lying."

"Then what are you and your boyfriend—"

"I'm not her boyfriend," Eduardo says.

"Oh, right, I forgot." Looking at me. "Your boyfriend is that backstabbing sumbitch Buddy Balcomb. Y'know, I actually trusted him. That's the only reason I brought him in on this opportunity."

"Some opportunity," I say, looking down at Donny's body.

"Donny was unstable. I couldn't count on him. I've been real disappointed in you, too, Peeky. Ever since you took off that jackpot."

"What do you mean?" The longer I can keep him talking, the longer we live.

"You helped that shitheel dink Tran and his crew rip off a jackpot, Peeky. Don't you know that's *wrong*?"

"I had nothing to do with that jackpot business. Besides, how is that worse than murder and robbery?"

Dooley's face slams shut. He points the gun at Eduardo. "Put him inside," he says, gesturing with the tip of the gun barrel.

I look back at Eduardo. He isn't getting it.

"He wants you to move Donny into the storage bay," I say.

"I think he's dead," Eduardo says.

"He damn well better be," Dooley says. "Now drag him inside."

"He's *dead*." Eduardo sounds terrified. I don't blame him.

"Do it now." Dooley cocks the revolver. The sound of the hammer clicking back into place helps Eduardo to overcome his phobia. He grabs Donny by the ankles and drags him into the storage bay. Donny's shirt rides up under his armpits, showing his long, white, hairy belly. His ruined head leaves a wet red stripe on the asphalt.

"Now close the door," he says.

Eduardo starts to pull down the overhead door.

"From the inside," Dooley says.

"I got claustrophobia."

"Do it." Dooley aims the gun at Eduardo's chest.

Eduardo lowers the door. At the point where we can see only his legs from the shins down, two things happen at once. First, I see the gun in Dooley's hand jerk up. At the same moment the garage door explodes from within; shards of particleboard come flying out at us. Dooley's gun is jumping in his hand. Multiple gunshots come so close together I hear it as the roar of a jackhammer. Dooley staggers back and falls, and I see the red and blue bottoms of Eduardo's K-Swiss sneakers through the open ten inches of garage door.

I am backing away, one step at a time, thinking I might survive after all. The calm acceptance I had been feeling evaporates: with hope comes fear.

"Fuck." Dooley is gripping his left leg, his face contorted. I keep backing away, willing him to forget about me. I don't know if Eduardo is dead, but if he's not, his only chance is if I can get away and call an ambulance.

"Bitch."

I stop. Dooley is sitting up, aiming the gun at me.

"You knew he had a gun!" He says it as if I have broken some rule.

I say nothing.

"Come here."

I could run. There is a good fifteen yards between us. He'd probably miss me if he shot. Hitting a running target with a hand-gun is no sure thing. The odds would be in my favor. But turning your back on a man with a gun is not so easy either. I walk toward him.

"It's your goddamn fault I had to shoot him," Dooley says.

I don't bother to answer that. Dooley was dropping the hammer even before he knew Eduardo was armed.

"Get the bag," he says.

I pick up the tote bag. Now that I am dead again, I have recaptured my sense of calm.

"Help me up."

The inside of his left leg is soaked with blood from just below the crotch down to his ankle. He's leaking but not spurting. From the tear in his pants it looks like the big slug ripped off a good chunk of muscle but missed the femoral artery. It must hurt like hell.

"Are you going to shoot me, too?" I ask.

He gives me a wet-eyed, hard-jawed look: his poker face pasted over severe pain.

"I'm not gonna shoot you," he says. "I want you to drive." He stands up using one leg, not an easy feat for a guy his size. "I can use you right now, Peeky. Don't make the mistake of thinking I *need* you."

"Okay." I step into him; he drapes one arm over my shoulder. With the other he presses the gun barrel against my ribs.

"Let's go," he says, shifting more of his weight onto me.

It's a long three-legged walk to the gate. Dooley's breath is loud in my left ear. He stinks of fear sweat. Or maybe it's me. After a few clumsy yards we get into a rhythm and quickly make it back to the gate.

Dooley's Lincoln SUV is parked next to my Miata.

"Where do you want to go?"

"Over the rainbow, Dorothy." I think maybe he is getting deliri-ous, but I take his meaning. He wants to cross into Mexico.

"How? You can't walk across."

"We'll drive. Get in," he says, guiding me toward the driver's side of the SUV. I climb up into the driver's seat. It's huge.

"Put the bag on the backseat."

I lift the tote bag over the seat back and drop it.

Dooley makes his way one-legged around the front of the vehicle, leaning on the hood for support, his eyes never leaving me. Again, there is a moment when I might have made a run for it, but I can't make myself do it. He opens the passenger door and somehow gets himself up onto the seat, soiling the tan leather with a smear of fresh blood.

"There's a blanket in back. Get it."

I lean over the seat and find a light wool blanket folded on the backseat. Dooley spreads it over his lap, then hands me the keys.

"Let's go."

I start the engine. Dooley opens the glove compartment and comes out with an amber prescription bottle. He shakes three oblong tablets into his palm and swallows them dry.

"You really want to do this? We should get you to a doctor."

"I can wait."

"What if they ask us to get out at the border? They see you bleeding all over the place, they're going to have questions."

"Just go," says Dooley.

50

Trucks and cars are backed up twenty deep at the border crossing.

"This is good," Dooley says. "They're busy."

"Either that or they're on some sort of alert, checking out every vehicle." I am mentally rehearsing. My plan, such as it is, is to create some sort of scene at the crossing. Hysterical kidnap victim, for example. Anything to get them to take a closer look at Dooley.

Dooley says, "I know what you're thinking, Peeky."

"You do?"

"It'll probably work. You put on a show for those Mexican border guards, I'm screwed. I'll be kicked back across the border so fast I won't have time to stop bleeding." His mouth tightens into a grim smile as he stares down the line of cars in front of us. "Not that it'll matter. I'll be stone-cold dead." He turns his head toward me. "And so will you." He looks deathly pale. I'm thinking the border guards will take one look at him and order us both out of the vehicle.

"It doesn't have to go that way."

"You're right. You could be a good little wifey, and we slide through slick as shit through a goose. I drop you off at some little *taverna*. Couple margaritas, then you walk back across the border. And I live out my days as a rich gringo."

"Even if I behave perfectly the border cops might just decide to take a closer look at us."

"That would be what you call a bad beat." His face is looking looser. Those pills he took—probably some sort of pain meds—must be kicking in. "But you take your chances. You know? Christ, I know you know. Trying to outfox the foxes. Sucking up to old Cisco and all the time planning on grabbing the loot for your pretty li'l self."

I'm not sure what to say. If I tell him he's right, will that make him more or less likely to kill me? I think about the ease with which he executed Donny Keyes. No, it won't help to have him think me a crook.

"I wasn't planning to keep the money," I say.

Dooley giggles. "I almost believe you, Peeky. You had me fooled on that jackpot scam at first, too. I actually thought you just stumbled into it. I shoulda known. Shoulda known. You were in it from the start, you and Tran. Now you and Buddy. Got it all figured out now."

"I had nothing to do with taking off that jackpot."

"Yeah, uh-huh. Tell me that again and I'll shoot you right here."

I half believe him. Better change the subject.

"So, how did you happen to turn up at the ministorage?"

Dooley reaches up and taps the rearview mirror. "Know what this is for? Y'all oughta use it now and then."

"You followed me all the way from Tucson?"

"Little red dot," he says. "Picked you up right out of your neighborhood. Little red dot on the highway."

On top of my fear, I am embarrassed. I'm supposed to be this hyper-observant person. I notice things. But even though I checked my mirror repeatedly on the drive to Nogales, I never noticed the white SUV. Too damn many white SUVs in Tucson. I was stuck watching for a baby blue Cadillac.

I pull ahead. Only four cars in front of us now. The line is moving quickly; most of the vehicles are simply waved through. Crossing the border is usually no big deal in Nogales—the serious vehicle inspection takes place on the highway outside of town.

"Half expected to find ol' Buddy waiting for us back there."

Dooley is looking very relaxed. "Or were you gonna rip him off, too?"

"I wasn't ripping anybody off. You must be confusing me with yourself."

Dooley blinks rapidly, trying to process that. Then he laughs.

"Shit, darlin', I never rip anybody off. I outplay 'em." His face is rubbery and moist.

"And if that doesn't work, you kill them."

Dooley erupts into deranged laughter. There is a moment when I might snatch the gun, but it passes before I can make myself act. He realizes he's let his guard down, his face tightens, the tip of the gun barrel digs painfully into my side. Beads of sweat ooze from his cheeks and forehead.

"I really will shoot you," he says. "Anything goes wrong, I shoot you. You believe me, don't you?"

"Yes," I say. And I do.

The two cars in front of us are waved through. I pull forward and stop. A uniformed young man with an automatic rifle slung over his shoulder peers in at us. I give him the best smile I can.

He waves us through.

A♠   2♣   4♣♣

You can feel the energy the moment you cross over. Nogales, Arizona, is a sleepy town of twenty thousand. The most popular tourist attraction is the local Wal-Mart. But Nogales, Sonora, is a thriving, vibrant, impoverished, growing metropolis. The streets are crowded with shoppers, vendors, hustlers, beggars, and gawkers. Thirty years ago the two Nogaleses mirrored each other in size, but with the advent of the *maquiladoras*—U.S.-owned factories on the Mexican side of the fence—the population of Nogales, Sonora, has exploded to nearly four hundred thousand.

"Turn right," Dooley says.

I make a right onto a narrow, shop-lined street. We weave our way past a donkey cart, a fruit vendor, and four men carrying a legless piano. "Just keep going." He rolls down his window. "Hot as hell in here."

I don't point out to him that the air-conditioning is blasting inside the SUV, while it's in the low nineties outside. We cut through the shopping district, past Avenues Obregon and Hidalgo, and ascend a steep hill into a residential area. The street narrows. The mirrors brush against walls of oleander on both sides.

"I thought you were going to drop me at a *taverna,*" I say. We are in a neighborhood of narrow, twisting hilly streets lined with older houses, the Nogales upper-middle class, people making five or six thousand dollars a year.

Dooley does not reply. His face is the color of beef fat, slick with perspiration. He is breathing rapidly through slack lips.

"You okay?" I stop and put the SUV in park. "Dooley?"

His eyes are closed. Slowly, I grasp his wrist and push the gun away from my side, then remove it from his slack fingers and tuck it between my legs. I lift one of his eyelids. His pupils are huge.

Now what? My first thought is to get the hell out of the truck and walk away. My second thought is to take the tote bag full of money with me. Also, I need to get Eduardo some help, assuming he's not beyond it already. I'm fumbling with the seat-belt release when I hear a familiar voice.

"So what happened to him?"

My entire body goes rigid and a squeal erupts from my throat.

"Didn't mean to scare you, Peek."

I draw a shaky breath and swallow.

"Buddy," I say.

51

People are looking for you," I say.

"Is that so?" He rests one forearm on the the open passenger window, leans into the cab, and looks at Dooley's slack face. "Is he awake? Hey, Dooley!" He snaps his fingers under Dooley's nose. No response.

"He got shot."

"You shoot him?"

"Eduardo did. Listen, Buddy, I have to make a call."

"Call who?"

"Eduardo is hurt. Dooley shot him. He might still be alive. I need to get him an ambulance." I dig in my purse for my cell phone. Buddy watches me, tense as a cat. I turn on the phone and dial 911. The operator answers in English, to my relief. I don't know why I was expecting Spanish—the woman on the other end is probably in Muncie, Indiana. Or New Delhi. I quickly give her the information. Buddy is watching me, now with a bemused expression.

"You're a good woman, Peeky," he says after I disconnect. "Thinking of Eduardo at a time like this."

"What time is that?"

He shrugs. "You know. Tote bag full of money, man half dead on the seat next to you, foreign country. Me. Funny. You don't seem all that glad to see me."

"Where'd you come from, Buddy?"

"Where's the gun, Peeky?"

"What gun?" I squeeze my thighs together.

"Dooley had a gun. I saw him put you in the car."

"How . . . oh. You saw us at the storage place."

"Yeah. I was waiting up the road for the guy who runs the place, some old half-crazy juicer I've been trying to get hold of to find out which goddamn bay I rented. The guy owns like twelve of these self-storage places. Makes a ton of money on 'em. Anyway I finally get the geezer on the phone and he says he's coming down to Nogales this morning, and I'm supposed to meet him. Only he doesn't show up of course, so I'm up at the Circle K trying to call him every five minutes and watching the road just in case he drives by and what do I see but you in your little red car."

"Have you been taking uppers, Buddy?"

"Am I talking too much?"

"You seem a little tense."

"Unlike Raggedy Andy here." He lifts Dooley's right arm and lets it flop back down. "Anyway . . . where was I? Oh yeah. I saw you and figured out what you were doing here. Figured I'd let you go ahead and get the bag for me. Only then this piece a shit shows up . . . by the way, where's Donny?"

"Donny's dead."

"Huh. I figured. Heard some shooting. So then I see you and Dooley coming out, and Dooley's not looking so good. I'm standing like ten yards away from you behind a palo verde. Could've stepped in then, but I got this idea y'all might be heading 'cross the border, which was where I wanted to go anyway, and I thought I might just as well let you take the money across for me. Figured I could catch up with you here."

"You were behind us?"

"Second car back. Where's the gun, Peek?"

"Dooley tossed it. He was afraid to bring it across the border."

He shakes his head. "Peeky . . . I can't believe you're trying to put one over on ol' Buddy."

I stare back at him. Is this really the man I used to sleep with? He is watching me with a flat smile and flatter eyes, snakelike. A look he might use to intimidate an opponent at a poker game: I got your ass.

"Tell me something, Buddy."

His smile tightens.

"Why did you shoot Tran?"

His smile wavers. "You saw that, huh?"

I nod.

He shrugs and prods the insensible Dooley with a forefinger. "Ask your old boss here. He was the one wanted it done."

"Why?"

"He probably would've had me do you, too, only he knew I wouldn't. It was that jackpot."

"You killed Tran because he scammed a jackpot?"

"Dooley was really pissed off about those jackpots getting hit."

"Why? It wasn't his money."

"Dools just doesn't like cheaters." He laughs. "He had no problem setting up the casino job, but he won't abide a card cheat. Funny, isn't it?"

I don't think it's funny at all. But at least I've got him off the subject of the gun between my legs.

"I suppose you want the money," I say. "It's in the back."

"I know that."

"So take it."

"And then what, Peeky?"

"And then you leave. Go wherever the hell you want. And I go back home and try to forget about all this."

Dooley's rapid breathing has slowed.

"You sure? You don't want to come with me? Live like a queen in paradise?"

As if there were any doubt before, now I *know* he's deranged.

"I don't think so," I say. I can't hear Dooley breathing anymore. I wonder if he's dead.

Buddy brings up his left hand and shows me a small semi-auto, looks like the same .32 he used to kill Tran. He is not exactly pointing it at me, but it's close.

"I need you to give me that gun, Peeky. I know you got it."

"Why? You think I'd shoot you? Just take the money and go." I don't want to give up that gun.

"C'mon, Peek." He shifts his gun a few degrees—now it's pointing at my knees.

Would he really shoot me? I'm not sure. I relax my thighs and slowly pick up my gun by its barrel and start to hand it to him. Buddy is smiling and reaching for it with his right hand. His left hand, holding the .32, is resting on the bottom edge of the window.

That's when Dooley makes his move. His right hand clamps Buddy's left wrist and slams it against the window post. The gun fires, shattering the plastic cowling around the steering column. Dooley pulls Buddy half into the cab through the window, wrapping his arm around Buddy's neck and pounding his fist into him. I can't see the gun. I still have my gun, but I'm more interested in getting out of the SUV than I am in shooting anybody. Dooley twists his body, pulling Buddy through the window into the SUV— Buddy's head is almost in my lap. Both men are pounding at each other in the cramped space. Dooley's face has gone from white to bright pink. I shoulder the door open and stumble out into a hedge of oleander. I have my gun up, pointing it into the SUV. Part of me just wants to fire into the tangle of bodies. I hear the stifled thud of another gunshot, and for a second I think it was me. Dooley has Buddy bent backward over the center console, his head jammed under the steering wheel. I still can't see who has Buddy's gun. Another gunshot, this time so muffled that I know the gun has to be sandwiched between their bodies. Both men jerk, and then they are still, Dooley's torso sagging over Buddy, motionless as a spent lover.

I stand half buried in the oleander hedge with my gun in both hands, covering them both. Seconds pass. I hear the soft rumble of the engine at idle. I think I can see a shallow, rhythmic, heaving motion in Dooley's body. Is it Dooley breathing, or Buddy moving beneath him?

A lake of blood rises on the tan leather seat as I wait for one of them to move. Seconds pass.

"Dooley?" I say.

He doesn't respond. I prod his shoulder with the tip of my gun barrel. "Dooley?" Nothing. Blood is running over the bolster and soaking into the carpet.

"Peeky . . ."

I shift a few inches to the side so I can see beneath the steering wheel. Buddy's face is tipped back, eyes open, staring at me.

"Get him off me." Buddy's voice is weak, as if he can't get enough air into his lungs. "I can't move."

"Are you shot?" I ask.

"I don't know."

"Good-bye, Buddy," I say.

I move toward the rear of the vehicle, oleander dragging across my back. I open the back door and grab the tote bag.

"Peeky?"

Buddy's aging Buick is parked a few yards behind the SUV. Two kids maybe ten years old are peering into the windows.

"Hey!" I shout.

They melt into the oleander hedge. I run to the car and tug on the door. It's locked. Briefly, I consider returning to Dooley's car to get the key off Buddy. Instead, I find a piece of brick by the side of the road and use it to smash the window.

The interior of the car reeks of cigarettes and male perspiration. I rifle through it quickly and finally find a folded and duct-taped paper grocery bag jammed under the front seat.

I tear through the duct tape, open the bag, and look inside. More money, probably what Buddy took off Woody Stumpf the night he killed him.

"Too bad, Buddy," I say into the bag. "You got greedy."

52

WHILE STANDING IN LINE at the border checkpoint I get to know the young couple behind me. Between them, they are carrying four shopping bags containing, among other things, two bottles of tequila, a patchwork leather handbag, four serapes, a bottle of Mexican vanilla, and the ugliest metal lampshade I have ever laid eyes on. The male half of the couple, a pudgy, thirtyish fellow with cheeks lit up by several margaritas, smells like a cheap cigar. The woman, who also enjoyed her margaritas, wants to tell me all about how the ugly lampshade is going to add rustic charm to her Southwestern-style living room. I smile and do my best to enjoy their recounting of their Nogales adventure.

As soon as I can get it in, I mention that I need a lift into Tucson.

I can't go back to the self-storage place. With two gunshot victims, the police will be far too interested in the owner of a certain red Miata. Eduardo is either dead or in the hospital—there's nothing I can do for him now.

"Sure, you can ride up with me and Andy," says the woman.

Andy eagerly nods his agreement, then says, "Assuming we don't get busted by Dirty Harry up here."

Dirty Harry is a neat young man in a uniform who looks about as much like Clint Eastwood as I do. But in this context, he's just as scary. I wonder how many phony Cuban cigars Andy has concealed on his person.

Worrying about the future helps keep my mind off my immediate problem, which is walking through customs carrying a handgun and a million bucks in stolen cash. I suppose I could have ditched the LadySmith. I probably should have. But it was a gift from my husband, and I want it. I take deep breaths to calm myself and pretend I'm running a garden-variety bluff: go ahead, call me; see what I got.

"We've only got this little rental car, so it'll be crowded," the wife is saying.

"I'm sure it will be fine."

"It's a Ford Focus," says Andy.

"My name's Amelia," says the wife, "but I like to be called Amy."

"It's got plenty a pep, though," says Andy.

"I really appreciate this." With an idiotic grin I nod my way through the conversation, and suddenly I am at the front of the line. The customs agent gives me a practiced X-ray-vision look and says, "U.S. citizen?"

I nod and try to smile, but his X-ray eyes are already on the couple behind me, and he is waving me through.

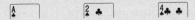

The Santa Cruz Nation's tribal headquarters got a lot of publicity when it was erected in the late nineties. Designed by a hot young architect who claimed to be one quarter Native American but who later turned out to be Korean, the building was supposed to evoke racial memories of an ancient Hohokam platform mound. The architectural reviews were, to put it mildly, mixed.

I've seen pictures, but this is my first real look at it.

The building is an elliptical structure about the size of a football field. The bottom two thirds has steeply sloped earthen walls, like the Hohokam mounds up near Phoenix. The flat top of the mound is crowned by a jagged twenty-foot-tall palisade of stripped and pointed logs. The logs, I remember reading, are from Douglas firs harvested in the White Mountains. They were stripped and pointed by hand using Native American labor. The overall look is that of a forbidding, impregnable fortress. Not pretty, but it makes an impression.

"It looks like a giant with a flattop," says Andy. "Like he's sticking the top of his head up out of the ground."

"That's not very nice," says Amy. "I'm sure they did the best they could with what money they had."

"I'm not saying I don't like it," Andy says. "I'm just saying, *sheesh!*"

I get out of the car, thank them, and give them directions back to Tucson. They refuse my offer to pay for gas, and leave me with a phony smile locked on my face. I work my jaw muscles as I follow the walkway from the parking lot toward the building.

As I get closer I can see that the walls are not actually made of packed earth, but of some modern aggregate made to look like dirt. And there are windows—small, variously shaped openings camouflaged by some sort of reflection-damping screening. The palisade, too, is interrupted by dozens of vertical windows, like archer's slits.

I follow the walk to a break in the fake earthen wall, follow a zigzag into a covered courtyard, and push through a pair of double glass doors into a broad, softly lit foyer with a low ceiling. The floor is an elaborate mosaic depicting, I think, a Hohokam canal system. The building was rumored to have cost fifteen million dollars. I'd be willing to bet it cost a lot more.

Gayle Vega, wearing a perfectly tailored suit the precise color of Hershey's semisweet chocolate, rises from a leather sofa at the far end of the canal system. Her heels click out an impatient rhythm as she crosses the mosaic.

"I didn't think you were coming," she says.

"I ran into a couple of problems."

She looks at the backpack. "Is that it?"

I nod. She gives me a critical once-over. I look awful and I know it, especially compared with her crisp, professional good looks.

"I could use a mirror," I say.

Gayle nods. "We've got a few minutes."

Five minutes later I emerge from the restroom, a new woman. Maybe not new, exactly. More like refurbished. I'm hoping I've worked my face into something that won't cause dogs to bark or young children to burst into tears.

"You look great," Gayle says as we walk down a long, curving hallway. "Only the bag doesn't go with your lipstick."

"I know. I'm a fashion disaster."

"Well, wait till you see these guys. John Bluewolf, your sponsor, hasn't changed his shirt since the last millennium. You'll know which one he is, the other council members give him lots of space. Dohasen Hant will be the other old one. Adrian Dreadwater is the one who agreed to invite you to address the council, but only because his aunt is my godmother. He'll be the one wearing the do-rag. Looks like Geronimo. They were right there with my grandfather when he got the tribe recognized. They have no love for Magic Hand, but they don't say much, and they don't like change. Grandfather has been doing their talking for them for the past thirty years."

"But they vote, right?"

"There's no voting per se, just a lot of talk. The final decision on formal matters is made by the chief or, in this case, the senior clan leader. Tonight that would be John Bluewolf."

"Then if John Bluewolf wants Magic Hand out, there's no problem. Right?"

"Wrong." We stop outside a door made of rough-hewn wooden planks overlaid with saguaro ribs. Above the door is a stone lintel decorated with petroglyphs. "The chief makes his decision based on what the other council members have to say. He would be unlikely to decide against a majority."

"So essentially, it comes down to a vote."

"I guess you could look at it that way. The other families are represented by Tom Tendoy, Bob Yotimo, and Adrian. They are younger and less traditional, and usually go with Carlos. You know where he stands."

"So there are five of them?"

"Seven, with Carlos. Although he isn't a council member or a family representative, as president of the casino he is given a voice in council on casino-related matters. If Grandfather were here, there would be seven."

"And you are representing him."

"Not exactly. I'm passing his wishes on to the council, but my voice won't carry his weight."

"Have you heard from him?"

"No, and I don't expect to. Right about now he's probably sitting in a sweat lodge pushing the bad spirits out through his pores."

I can't tell if she's joking. "Do you think he's going to be okay?"

"Oh yes, absolutely. This isn't the first time he's taken the cure. Basically, he'll hide out up there until he thinks it's safe to go home again. My aunt Maria is something of a terror, as you saw."

"I saw. So what's the routine here?"

"When we go in, they will probably be discussing some other matter. They'll either finish their discussion, or they'll stop talking as soon as you walk in. Three things you should remember. Don't say anything until you are invited to speak. Address the eldest man in the room first—that'll be John Bluetooth. And don't stand with your back to anyone. It's considered rude. Are you ready?"

I sling the tote bag over my shoulder. "As I'll ever be."

The council chamber is much smaller than I expected. Three shallow, carpeted steps descend into a circular pit, the center of which is about twelve feet in diameter. The recessed lighting is low and the air is hazy with burnt tobacco. The steps continue around the room, forming three tiers of seating. Six men are seated around the circle on the bottom tier. I see Carlos on the far side of the room. The shriveled one in the ragged buckskin shirt sitting by himself must be John Bluetooth. A couple of the men give me a curious glance, but no one formally acknowledges my presence.

One of them, a heavyset man wearing a black leather vest over a blue chambray shirt, is speaking in a low voice. At first I think he is holding forth on a weighty matter affecting the future of the tribe. Then I hear what he is saying.

". . . they're going to start him this fall, and the kid's only a junior, you know? I mean, the kid is amazing. Already three inches taller than me, and a solid two-twenty. Seems like yesterday I was showing him how to tie his shoes."

"He's a good kid," says the man sitting to his left. He is dressed in light green trousers and a yellow polo shirt, ready for the golf course. "My second son played with him last year. He's up at ASU now. Wide receiver. Hands like glue."

"We should probably talk about enhancing our scholarship program for athletes, you know?" says the first man.

An older man, probably Dohasen Hant, leans forward and says in a loud voice, "They already go to school free. What do you want?"

"Athletes have special needs," says the first man, speaking slowly and loudly. "They need tutors, Dohasen. Like we never had."

"Tutors?" Dohasen Hant shakes his head and crosses his arms. "Jim Thorpe had no tutor."

It's been a long day with no sleep and too many people getting shot. I'm dead tired, my feet are killing me, and these guys are talking football.

"Excuse me," I say, breaking the first rule.

They all look at me.

"I just need a minute," I say, breaking the second rule by addressing them as a group. I walk into the center of the circle and turn my back to Carlos. Might as well break all the rules.

"I have something you all might be interested in." I upend the tote bag and dump a million dollars in cash onto the floor of the council chamber.

For a few seconds no one says a word. Then John Bluetooth clears his throat with a sequence of phlegmy gurgles.

"You just gonna have to clean that up now, young lady," he says. His eyes are pale with cataracts.

"You don't want it?"

"It's money, John," says Dohasen Hant.

"It's the money stolen from the casino last week," I say.

They are all leaning forward staring at the pile of cash.

"Who are you?" asks Dohasen Hant.

"My name is Patty Kane. I work for Mr. Vega."

"Where did you find this money?"

"I took it from the people who stole it."

"And who was that?" Carlos asks.

I turn to face him. "I'll tell you all about it," I say. "But first I'd like to show you a movie." I hold up the camcorder containing the recording Jaymie made. "Is there a TV here I can plug this thing into?"

53

I AM SITTING BESIDE EDUARDO, holding his limp hand, when I hear a sudden intake of breath. I turn and see Jaymie standing in the doorway, her hand covering her mouth.

"He's going to be okay," I say quickly.

She takes a few tentative steps toward the bed, her eyes going from Eduardo's bandaged head to his pale, slack face to the tubes feeding into his arm to the machines monitoring his vital signs. She stops a few feet from the bed.

"What happened?"

"He was shot, Jaymie. But he's going to be okay."

"Did he . . . did he shoot himself?"

"No!"

She blinks, and tears spill down her cheeks.

"Why would you think that?" I ask.

She shakes her head. "Because of me," she says.

I move from sorrow and tenderness to shock and anger; my body shudders under the transition.

"It's not always about you, Jaymie," I say.

Jaymie blinks confusedly, looking from Eduardo to me, from me to Eduardo. Then she moves to the bedside and reaches out and puts her hand on his face.

The next day I go back to work.

Everything seems normal. No one seems to know anything about what has happened, and I don't want to talk about it. Manuel moves me from game to game. I win some, lose some, finish my shift and drive back to the hospital. Jaymie is asleep in a chair. Her face is free of makeup and she looks all of sixteen. Eduardo is awake.

"Hey," he says, trying for a smile.

"How are you doing?" I ask.

Jaymie stirs but does not awaken.

"Headache," Eduardo says. "The police were here." He sips from a box of apple juice with a straw.

"Oh. What did you tell them?"

"I don't remember. They say I got shot in the head and the hip. I'm lucky to be alive. I guess I got a thick skull."

"It helped that the bullets went through a door before they got to you."

"Is that what happened? Last thing I remember is I was dragging that guy into the storage bay."

"Then you two started shooting at each other."

"I shot? Did I hit him?"

"You hit him."

"Good. Is he dead?"

"Yes. I'm really sorry I got you into it, Eduardo."

"That's okay. I'm glad I shot him." He points with his straw at Jaymie. "Hey, maybe we should do that intervention now. While she's conked out."

I laugh. "Let's wait until you get a little better. Besides, I've got a feeling she might be ready to help herself."

"Okay." He drinks some more juice and we watch Jaymie sleep.

I am playing $15–30 holdem, mucking a lot of so-so hands, waiting for the opportunities that will inevitably come. It's peaceful here. The rhythm of the cards is like the surf, rising and falling, always another wave. The other eight players are all regulars, guys who mostly know what they are doing. I am almost asleep, playing on automatic.

Joe Garcia opens for a raise under the gun. I fold.

"You ever gonna play a hand, Peeky?" he asks.

"Waiting on aces," I say.

Al Rafowitz throws his cards away. "She's a stone, Joe. Don't you know that?"

"What that make you?" says Ginny Chan. "Rock a Giblata?"

Joe wins the blinds. The dealer shuffles and deals us a new hand. I catch a pair of nines under the gun. Al Rafowitz looks at his cards and his posture shifts slightly. He is feigning nonchalance, but his shoulders betray him. He is going to play this hand. I muck my nines.

"Good one, Pee Kee."

I turn to find Cisco standing close behind me. It's been almost two weeks. He looks good.

"You like that muck, huh?" I say.

"I like it."

We watch the hand play out. Al Rafowitz wins a small pot with his pocket kings.

"Dodged another bullet," Cisco says.

I nod. There was never any question.

"Hey, Cisco," says Joe. "Where you been?"

"I go to poker school," Cisco says. "Work on my game."

Joe laughs.

Cisco says to me, "You got a minute?"

$A\spadesuit \quad 2\clubsuit \quad 4\clubsuit\ \clubsuit$

"You should try it sometime, Peeky. Sweat lodge make you a new woman."

"I'm afraid my makeup would run."

Cisco laughs. "Yes, it would be good for you. Make your makeup run. Find the real Peeky. We live in air-conditioning. Forget how to sweat."

"I'll let you know if I feel the need," I say. We are sitting in the cafe outside the Slot Palace, drinking coffee. I am looking at a slice of key lime pie, waiting for the perfect moment to take my first bite.

"Look at me. I go for two weeks, I sweat like a pig, I come home, my problems all solved." He really does look good. He only has a few hundred lines and wrinkles on his face now, half as many as before, and he hardly used his cane at all when we walked from the poker room to the cafe. He grins and his wrinkles rearrange into arcs. "You did good, Peeky."

"Thank you . . . but Johnson got his contract anyway."

"Even though they decided to extend the contract with Magic Hand, the council understands that this is a bad thing for us in the long run. You and Gayle showed them that. They listened to you."

"And then they decided to renew the contract with Johnson."

"They had no choice, Peeky. You left them up shit creek without a paddle. Once they saw your movie, Carlos was out of the picture. They couldn't renew Magic Hand's seven-year contract without at least one of us acting as figurehead—too proud—and they couldn't just give Johnson the heave-ho leaving no one experienced in charge. They had to make a decision. It was a political situation, Peeky. Lose-lose. Of course, none of *them* want to run the casino, so when Gayle stepped up they took her up on it."

"But they still renewed Johnson's contract."

"For one year. One year only. That was very smart of my granddaughter to insist on that. She will learn more about the casino business in one year than Carlos could have absorbed in a lifetime. And she will make sure that Santa Cruz management is solidly in place before the contract expires. Maybe this time we will find the people to take those jobs. It is more than I hoped for."

"I'm glad you're happy." I sip my coffee.

"You should be happy, too. The council gave you a reward for recovering that money. How much was it?"

"Fifty thousand, as you well know." I twist my lips into a knot. "And only eight people dead."

"It was their time to go, Peeky."

"I suppose. What's become of Carlos?"

"He has checked into Ridge Point. He'll be there for four weeks."

"And then?"

"And then we will have a sober conversation, he and I. I think maybe the casino business is not so right for him. Also, Veronica finally met Carlos's secretary. The one with the nails. We will have to see how much longer he remains my son-in-law. In any case, Gayle has his job now."

I cut the point off my slice of key lime pie and place it in my mouth. The sourness lights up the sides of my tongue and the sweetness hits me in my G-spot. At that moment I decide to replace my addiction to Ben & Jerry's ice cream with a key lime pie habit.

"You okay?" Cisco asks.

"I'm fine." I put down my fork. I lost nearly ten pounds during that week after the casino robbery. I'm trying not to gain it back.

"How is your son-in-law?"

"He's home now. He's going to be okay."

"I am sorry. We will cover his hospital expenses, of course."

"I know he'll appreciate that."

"How is your daughter doing?"

"She is with Eduardo. She says she's going to quit using, but I don't know. She's like a squirrel in a cage."

"When she's ready, we will find her a bed at Ridge Point. Maybe she and Carlos will be in a group together."

"Why didn't *you* go to Ridge Point?"

Cisco shrugs and looks away. "I am old school, Peeky. Sweat lodge is plenty good enough for me." He lifts his cup of coffee and takes a sip. "You see?"

"You look good. How is Bruce Johnson dealing with all of this?"

"He is still in charge, technically, but he will quickly find that Gayle is not so easy to manipulate. He is Gayle's boss, but he answers to the council, where Gayle now has a voice. It cannot please him, but he is a practical fellow. No doubt he will devote more of his time to filling the desert with golf balls. "

"Sounds like one big happy dysfunctional family."

Cisco laughs. "Sometimes you got to go along to get along."

"More ancient Indian wisdom?"

"More politics, Peeky. It is all about working together."

I treat myself to another bite of pie.

"Aren't you going to ask me about Buddy?"

"Why would I ask you about Buddy?"

"Isn't that why you got me involved in this mess in the first place? To get to Buddy?"

"No, Peeky. It was to get to the money. And because I like you."

"They never found him, you know."

"Yes. Dooley was alone."

I think back to my time with Dooley, sitting in his Lincoln waiting to cross the border, thinking I was the one who was going to die.

"He was really upset about those jackpots getting ripped off," I say. "That was why he had Buddy kill Tran."

"Yes. I thought that might be it."

"But at the same time he was planning to rob the casino of millions. Why should he care about somebody else stealing a few tens of thousands?"

"That was Dooley. He never cheated at cards, you know. Took a lot of pride in being a Gambler with a capital 'G.' You could trust him absolutely at the card table, but then he'd do things like walk out on a restaurant bill or steal a pack of gum from a drugstore. He was a funny guy."

"Do you think he did it for the money?"

Cisco shrugs. "I think he went on the big tilt. Started chasing a hand he could never have. He should've spent some time in a sweat lodge. Talk to his devils."

"I guess we all have our devils."

Cisco lets loose a creaky laugh. People in the next booth look over at us. I take one more bite of pie. Just one.

I ask, "Who's running the card room now? Vergie?"

"Vergie is gone."

"She quit?"

"Disappeared. Her apartment is empty. Gone. You know, I think she and Dooley had a little thing going. I do not think we will hear from her again." He lifts his chin. "As far as the card room is concerned, we need some fresh blood. Know anybody?"

"Not really."

"You sure?"

"Yes." I can see myself in Cisco's glasses. "Why?"

EPILOGUE

I HEAR THE SAME OLD PLAYER CHATTER: *Call. Raise. New deck. Chop it up. Kick it. Gotta call. I can't call. Missed again. The nuts. Drawing dead and got there. Setup! Aces up. Ship it. I got a draw. Nine outs. Nice hand. Fifteen outs. Flopped a set. Chips! You called me with* that?

I am floating, kelp in a gentle current, a spectator, watching hand after hand drift by, waiting for my share of aces. My daughter is a drug addict, my ex-boyfriend is wanted for murder, I still have no furniture, and I think I just had my first hot flash.

King-jack? I pass. The dealer folds my cards into the muck.

Gayle Vega stopped by my house yesterday to bring me a potted peyote cactus, a gift from Cisco. It came with a handwritten note:

> **The door is still open, Peeky.**
> **Happy birthday.**
> **—Hector**

I had completely forgotten that it was my birthday. Forty-five years. Half a lifetime, if I take good care of myself.

Cisco wants me to take Dooley's old job. He's given me a few days to think about it. It pays ninety grand a year, plus a tenth of a point of the gross. It's a generous offer. There was a time when that would have seemed like a lot of money to me. It still does, but I don't know—I wouldn't have much time to play cards. I'd be figuring out how to maximize profits, looking for ways to squeeze an extra buck an hour out of every poker table, dealing with tribal politics and public relations, hiring and firing staff, and God knows what else. A real job with real responsibilities and consequences.

I am thinking that I have had enough of consequences lately.

I imagine an older version of myself: menopausal, stolid and gray, wearing a plastic badge and a navy suit, looking at surveillance tapes and listening to players' complaints.

I think of the peyote cactus in its shallow handmade pot and think about Jaymie. This whole drug thing she is into, I don't understand it. Is it anything like playing poker? Maybe someday I'll drive out into the desert and eat some peyote. Maybe I will see the map of the universe and hear the singing of the moon and feel the desert wind like warm oil on my breasts.

Or maybe I'll buy that fake I.D., call myself Christine Johnson, move to Des Moines, and get a job at Wal-Mart. Buy a house in the burbs and grow myself a nice big soft comfortable butt.

Maybe Jaymie will check herself into Ridge Point and grow up to become a happy, productive member of society. I'd probably see less of her then. She and Eduardo will move to Flagstaff and open a natural foods store, tofu and trail mix for the hikey-bikey crowd. Maybe Eduardo will quit drinking. Maybe when I get old I will haunt their guest room for a few years before they put me in a rest home.

"It's on you, Peeky."

I look at my cards. Jack-six. I toss them in the muck and push my chair back and walk to the restroom to check myself out in the mirror, see if everything is holding together.

Not bad. Auburn hair, a slash of lipstick, eyes bright and just a little crazy. I laugh, seeing myself as others must: a forty-something ditz, probably doesn't know an ace from a deuce, put on this planet to bleed money and have a good time.

Time to go back to work. Maybe in some future life I'll eat peyote, run a poker room, and find true love, or change my name and move to Iowa.

But not today. Today, I'm a prop.

ACKNOWLEDGMENTS

Thank you to Lisa Cicotte, Kurt Dongoske, Jerry Fuller, Mary Logue, Jim Hautman, Jim Mitchell, Tom Murray, Alan Stesin, and Deborah Woodworth for taking the time to answer some very peculiar questions.

ABOUT THE AUTHOR

Pete Hautman is the author of the *New York Times* Notable Books *Drawing Dead* and *The Mortal Nuts*, as well as *Short Money, Ring Game, Stone Cold, Hole in the Sky, Rag Man, Mrs. Million, Mr. Was,* and *Doohickey.* In 2004, his young adult novel *Godless* won the National Book Award for Young People's Fiction. Hautman lives in Minnesota.

Visit Pete Hautman on the web at www.petehautman.com.